D0051797

HEATHER GRAHAM

THE
SEEKERS

mira

mira

ISBN-13: 978-0-7783-6879-3

Recycling programs
for this product may
not exist in your area.

The Seekers

Copyright © 2019 by Heather Graham Pozzessere

For questions and comments about the quality of this book, please contact us at CustomerService@Harlequin.com.

www.Harlequin.com

Printed in U.S.A.

For Katherine and Richard Wolniewicz,
with thanks for so much through the years.

CAST OF CHARACTERS

Joe Dunhill—
the former Savannah cop is joining the Krewe of Hunters

Keri Wolf—
the writer is used to covering historical true crime and is
shocked to get caught up in an actual murder investigation

Carl Brentwood—
the young Hollywood heartthrob bought the
Miller Inn and Tavern with plans to restore it,
but first he wants to document if it is haunted

Dallas Wicker—
FBI agent with the Krewe of Hunters showing Joe the ropes

Brad Holden—
creator and host of the *Truth Seekers* web show

Eileen Falcon, Serena Nelson and Pete Wright—
the crew of *Truth Seekers*

Mike Lerner—cameraman

Catrina Billings—
local detective with the York County Police

Spencer Atkins—
previous owner of the Miller Inn and Tavern

Rod and Milly Kendall and Stan Gleason—
caterers in York County who work with the old tavern

THE
SEEKERS

Prologue

Joe Dunhill finished his follow-up report on what the media had labeled the Forget-Me-Not murders. Why that name, he wasn't completely sure, except that the media always needed a catchy phrase, no matter what they were doing.

Night crew was coming on, and he was free to leave for the day. He was tired; it had been a challenging case. He had tracked every conceivable clue, and—until he'd called on Adam Harrison and his Krewe—Joe had been the only one convinced that the accidents had been murder, and that those "accidents" were related to disappearances—which also proved, in the end, to be murder.

Explaining his theory had been difficult, at best. He'd questioned his own sanity.

His original job had been to find a missing politician, but in searching the area of Johnson Square, a man had accosted him in the street.

He'd come out of nowhere, and said, "Detective, I don't know how or why, but they're all related. The deaths. Nothing was an accident. They were murders!

All the recent deaths in this area…not accidents!" The man shook his head with pure disgust.

"Sir…" Joe said, and his voice trailed. The man appeared to be the very missing person he was seeking, a flesh and blood version of the picture he'd stared at day after day in his search. "I swear to you, I'm following every lead. What is your name? Are you related to Mr. Drake? If you have information—"

"I just gave you my information!" the man snapped. And he started past Joe.

Naturally, Joe spun around to stop him.

But he was gone. Disappeared, vanished, into thin air.

Just like the missing politician, Simon Drake.

Joe's superiors had been supportive; he was welcome to pursue his theory. On his own time, of course. There couldn't be an official investigation regarding such an unlikely scenario.

So, Joe had contacted Adam Harrison, a man he'd read about several times, along with the various cases his unit had worked.

Adam had surreptitiously sent help, and the agents had managed to find new leads where the trail had gone cold for Joe. Their help had been invaluable in solving the case and catching a murderous pair intent on keeping the transgressions of their ancestors deeply buried.

And now, it was finally done; victims all accounted for, press conferences over, the last of the paperwork finished.

He could move on. There were other cases on his desk. But for now… Hell, he was going to get out of the office. He was going to remember he had friends, he did have a life—kind of—and he needed to get back to living it, trying to be more of a regular human being.

One thing still bugged him. One thing he couldn't shake.

Who the hell was the man who'd stopped him when he'd walked down the street by Johnson Square? He'd met most of Drake's family and close friends and associates during the initial stages of the investigation...

Joe had lived and breathed the case too long; he needed to hang with friends, play football in the park, have a beer and whine about a game on TV. Or just go home. He was drained.

As he headed out of the office, colleagues called out to him.

"Hey, man, congrats on the Drake case!" one of his fellow detectives said.

"Bravo!" someone else said.

Embarrassed, he lifted a hand. "Yeah, thanks guys, had that FBI help," he said.

Hell, help? The FBI had basically solved the damned thing, but then again, they'd been very different FBI, the kind that lived what they were doing, and who saw...

Saw what?

What was beyond the norm.

He waved a good-night and headed out. His little house was off Victory Street, and he owned it free and clear, thanks to an uncle who had sold it cheaply to him and moved to Arizona.

It was home; comfortable. He walked in, grabbed a beer from the refrigerator, sat down on the sofa and turned his television on for company. He wished he had a dog.

There were so many factors about the case still plaguing him. Things he had tried and tried to discover, and others had found, as if by instinct. As if the investigators were omniscient. The agents had come from a unit labeled the Krewe of Hunters by their co-workers in other units and divisions—and by the press. Joe had heard that they took on anything that might be considered "strange and unusual." Exactly what that meant, he wasn't sure. But it sure seemed as if they had special powers.

A life, yeah, he needed a life. He'd had one, even been very nearly engaged. But then, his girlfriend had been offered a job in Nashville, and while she was hopeful, he just couldn't leave Savannah. The fact that neither of them was willing to compromise had sealed their relationship's fate. That seemed long ago now.

He was so damned tired. He nearly dropped the bottle of beer he'd barely managed to sip. He set it down and leaned back, closed his eyes.

"Detective?"

He startled awake at the voice and started to reach for his gun and holster on the coffee table, but paused. There was no one there. Except then there was.

Just no one who would be threatened by a .45 caliber weapon.

Joe sat up straight, disbelieving. Wondering if he was still sleeping.

Bit by bit, the image of a man formed in front of him. It was a man he had seen before; the one who looked just like Simon Drake, who'd appeared to him in Johnson Square. The man who had disappeared…

"Detective, hey, don't get up. I was just trying… I'm not very good at this… I know I'm leaving… I'm ready. I just wanted to say thank you. Really, thank you. I can't thank you enough."

And then, he faded away.

Joe stared.

Maybe he did need a department shrink.

Or maybe…

He pulled out his phone and dialed a number he'd memorized over the past weeks.

Dallas Wicker, the FBI agent who'd helped Joe on the recent murder case, answered.

"I need help. I have to get out of here—I think I need to join the Krewe."

"What? Joe, I'm sure you could apply to the FBI. But you don't just join the Krewe. You're a great cop. I'd love to work with you again. But there are unique requirements for the Krewe. Agents need special abilities—"

"Well, Dallas, the ghost of Simon Drake just stopped by to say goodbye to me. How will that work for meeting any *unique* requirements?"

There was silence on the other end. And then Dallas said, "Well, hell, then, Detective. Come on up."

1

"The bodies were found in rooms throughout the inn. Four men, three women, each bludgeoned repeatedly with an ax, no fewer than ten blows on the least battered victim. Most lay sleeping in the rooms they had taken for the night. The proprietor, John Newby, was found behind the bar that served the tavern. It was also where he kept his books for his overnight guests.

"The coroner brought in several men to serve as witnesses in the subsequent inquest—Creighton Mariner, a journalist, Frank Gold, a local butcher, and local farmers Grant Fisher, Ethan Guttenberg and Bjorn Muller. Mariner wrote, 'The killings were so frenzied and brutal that blood and brain matter were found in many a room. Truly, the sight was so gruesome one could only think of the work of a demonic hellhound. Yet, none of this compared to the discoveries deep in the basement where it came to light that John Newby was ridding himself of unwanted servants and guests in the most ghastly way possible.'"

Keri Wolf, sitting at one of the hardwood tables in

the Miller Inn and Tavern of York County, Pennsylvania, watched as Brad Holden gave his dramatic intro to the camera. She'd just met the man in person, but his ghost-hunter series had apparently become one of the hottest shows being independently produced on the internet. He had started off modestly, and—whether or not any of his "discoveries" were really *true*—he had managed, with his small group of paranormal investigators, to create his immense audience on his own. He was a slim, handsome, charismatic man, and it was easy to see how his enthusiasm transferred to a large audience onscreen.

So large, in fact, he had a second special guest on this investigation besides Keri: the popular young actor Carl Brentwood, fresh off his video documentary of the McLane House in Charleston. Carl had been so successful with his shows filmed at the McLane House that, if she was correct in reading between the lines, he had purchased the old Miller Inn and Tavern where they were "investigating" reports of paranormal activity today.

She was sure Brad's charm had been convincing when he'd approached Carmen Menendez, Keri's publicity agent, about joining in on this investigation. Which basically amounted to spending the night with ghost hunters at an inn where one of the most horrific crimes of the twentieth century had taken place. The exposure of working with the Truth Seekers could bring publicity for her books that could not be purchased at any price, Brad had promised.

Keri was equally sure that Carl, the enthusiastic

young heartthrob, being involved had also swayed Carmen into thinking this was a guaranteed, *amazing* publicity opportunity, and it would be an exceptionally effective way to sell books.

And of course, it would be. Keri glanced across the table. Carl was seated with her; they were both to speak for the intro.

Also, at the table was Spencer Atkins, the man who had sold the historic inn to Carl. He had promised Carl to help him in any way, except for speaking during any project that had to do with ghosts or the paranormal. Atkins was still a nice man—Carl owned the property now and could do what he wanted, and he was welcome to lean in to the paranormal if he wanted. Atkins just wasn't going to be part of it. Atkins was simply watching the beginning of the project out of curiosity, and was due to head out at any time for an appointment in Philadelphia. He observed Brad Holden with patience and amusement.

Carl had planned this episode with a great deal of enthusiasm. He was a believer. He glanced at Keri and smiled and gave her a thumbs-up; she had to smile back. Despite his immense popularity and the fact that he certainly had the accolades that would justify him behaving like a true diva, he was simply a very nice young man.

They both glanced back at Brad as he gave the camera one of his big, we're-all-in-this-together smiles and continued, "Welcome, folks, to another fantastic voyage with the Truth Seekers. If you're joining us for the first time, I'm Brad Holden, and I and my fellow Truth

Seekers—Eileen Falcon, Mike Lerner, Serena Nelson and Pete Wright—welcome you to our online programming, offering you investigations of myth, legend, perception…and truth. We feel we'll be bringing you something extremely special with this investigation.

"We're here at the Miller Inn and Tavern, and we'll soon be settling in for the night. We're getting our cameras all set, and dark is falling. Now, the past of this inn is well documented. The building was opened to welcome weary travelers in 1770, just as the ferment of rebellion became strong in the American colonies. It's amazing just to think of those who stopped by—George Washington, Benjamin Franklin and even Patrick Henry stayed here, all enjoying the fabled hospitality of the Miller Inn and Tavern. While the inn already had a reputation for being haunted, luckily for America, those fine men survived."

Brad paused for a dramatic moment, allowing Mike Lerner, working the camera, to lower the lights. Then he continued, "It wasn't until 1926, when several gruesome murders occurred here, that the inn would be placed into the annals of the bizarre and yes, my friends, the paranormal." He turned to Keri, beckoning her before the camera.

Not sure if she should take his hand and smile or run as far as possible from him, Keri stood.

"The exceptionally lovely Keri Wolf, known for her *The Way It Happened* series, is here to join us for this investigation. Keri can tell us a little more about the history of this inn, her area of expertise, and why she found herself so fascinated by Pennsylvania Dutch hex stories—which led, we're told, to the events of 1926, and our paranormal search of this tavern tonight."

Keri still felt uncertain, but she found herself standing in the pool of light in front of the camera, taking Brad's hand.

Carmen had assured her the group really searched for the explainable—before determining if anything was paranormal.

Everyone knows Carl Brentwood! And Brad Holden is great. His video feeds of The Seekers garner millions of views. Between them, they have a huge audience. If we're lucky, we'll sell a tenth of their numbers in your books!

So, here she was.

She tried to smile as charmingly as Brad before speaking.

"We're between Harrisburg and Pittsburgh here, Brad, and as you said, there are many stories that go with the tavern, but the main story is this—on the night of June 27, 1926, a killer came in and brutally took the lives of seven people, among them Mr. Newby, the proprietor. The coroner, who was also the sheriff of the small county at the time, brought in five men to help with the inquest. In their thorough search of the premises, they discovered Newby had kept a torture chamber in his basement, along with all manner of paraphernalia dealing with witchcraft and Satanism."

"So, folks," Brad continued, "we'll be doing a thorough, room-by-room investigation. Our cameras are set to record throughout the tavern, including the infamous basement chamber, where it is estimated Newby tortured and killed at least ten young men and women, covered the remains with lime and buried them beneath the floor."

He was about to cut the introductory segment, so Keri spoke up quickly. "It's a complex and incredibly sad story, whether ghosts do or do not inhabit the tavern. It's believed Hank Bergen, the father of a young serving girl who had disappeared, lost his mind in rage and committed all the killings when he suspected Newby wasn't the respectable man he pretended to be. Bergen was caught by a lynch mob, and his guilt or innocence was never determined in a court of law.

"This story is further complicated by the fact the term Pennsylvania Dutch comes from Pennsylvania *Deutsche* and actually refers to the German population that settled this region. At the time of the incident, some locals had a strong belief that some of their neighbors were practicing witches. It was known Newby was of this creed. But until his chamber of horrors was discovered, it wasn't known that he'd also been an avid student of Aleister Crowley, the British occultist, taking to extremes the tenet *do what thou wilt.*

"As I said, the belief at the time and in the region in certain kinds of witchcraft—and the ability of one man to hex another—were broad. But the concepts espoused by Crowley and Newby's actual practice of Satanism were not in any way general. To this day, we don't know if Hank Bergen was the killer, or why he would kill the innocent guests at the tavern if he believed Newby had been the one to kill his daughter."

"And of course," Brad said, "you're researching that

crime at this moment, with us here at the tavern. The spirit of Beatrice Bergen is one that many guests at the Miller Inn and Tavern have reported seeing. A young woman in a white dress, weeping. She's trapped between worlds, seeking justice for her death. Maybe the ghosts of the dead will come out, as so many guests have believed, and help you on your quest. Thank you, thank you… And now!" Brad turned from her. "On to our man of the hour, the amazing Mr. Carl Brentwood."

Carl joined them in front of the camera. Keri was ready to slink back to her chair, but Carl grabbed her hand. "So, friends, rumor thus far, but true—I recently purchased the tavern, and that's how we've come to be here today. The historic value of this property is immense, and the possibility of it falling into disrepair was appalling to me. But since I've discovered so much lately about the paranormal, it seemed we needed to discover all the truths behind this fantastic place before doing a bit of upgrading and opening it to travelers from around the globe again.

"We won't be leaving here tonight. We'll be taking turns grabbing a few hours of sleep upstairs in room 207, where two of the victims were killed. Soon, all the rooms, including 207, will be available for those intrepid travelers who want to take a detour into a little piece of history—and mystery!"

"And that's it for our intro. We're working on our setup," Brad said. "Please join us again tonight, when we'll be showing live feed from the tavern as we turn on our screens from every room. With Keri and Carl, we'll investigate records and do our very best to discern the truth—and allow Carl to restore this place to its Colonial heritage."

"With upgrades, of course. Wi-Fi in every room, and private showers," Carl said.

"Historic and modern," Brad said. "Join us tonight!"

Mike Lerner, who had started *Truth Seekers* with Brad, knew when to cut the video. He smiled at them all. "Great, guys. I really think this will be one of our best."

"We're really thrilled you're here," Carl told Keri. He looked over at Spencer Atkins. "I mean, she is a voice of reason and history, right?"

Atkins stood. He was a dignified man of about fifty, with a lean, straight build, and a cap of snow-white hair. "She is," he agreed. "And I'm glad to see you all here and happy—even if I admit I think it's a little crazy. I'm so pleased that Carl intends to do what I just couldn't quite manage, modernize while keeping the integrity of the place as an inn. Anyway, I must go, but…" He paused and turned to Carl. "Any real questions that we might not have covered, please, call me."

They bid him goodbye. He smiled and waved, and then he was gone.

Brad turned back to Keri with an immense smile. "Seriously, so glad you're here."

"Grateful!" Carl said.

"I'm honored you asked me," Keri told him. "I'm curious, though. I don't think ghosts are going to pop up and tell us how they were killed. What are you hoping to find here?"

"Oh, Keri," Brad said. "There are so many reports of activity at this place. Lights going on and off. One lady woke up screaming. Spencer had to do some major damage control because she woke up in the middle of the night to see a man standing over her bed with an ax. She left in the middle of the night, and the closest hotel is miles and miles away. Some people began to believe that the inn was haunted—and others feared that a real killer was alive and well and 'haunting' the place with a real axe. Unfortunate circumstances."

"Sounds like she might have been the victim of a terrible nightmare or sleep paralysis," Keri said.

Carl shook his head. "Furniture moves around. Water just starts running. The ghost of Newby has been seen behind the bar. Trust me, I spent a fair amount of time talking with Spencer Atkins before I bought the place. He wouldn't sell if he didn't believe in the buyer. He loves this tavern, but he didn't have the backing he needed to restore and update. He told me about all kinds of things that supposedly happened here. There's a story of a ghost in 210, as well. A young woman who took her own life when she learned her fiancé had been killed in a duel. There was another murder out in the woods, that was about 1840, and... The inn is rich in paranormal activity, trust me."

Brad took up the story. "People have seen things... Before Spencer restored the basement, it was used for storage. Bar workers refused to go down alone or at night. They felt cold hands on them. One woman swore she was pushed down the stairs, and she was convinced only her screams brought help before the ghost could kill her."

"Keri, I have experienced things personally," Carl

said earnestly. "Honestly, what I've seen is what made me buy this place. I saw the ad for it right after I left Savannah. I saw very strange things at McLane House there, and somehow, through it all, real, contemporary murders were solved." He gave her his famous boyish smile. "And we'll have fun, too. I had caterers bring in all kinds of food. Room 207 is all set up for us to talk and rest and whatever."

She'd heard about the events at McLane House in Savannah. But she didn't know what had been the result of good detective work and what might have been imagined or embellished by the media.

It wasn't that she wasn't open to possibilities—she was. But especially in her research, she had met so many people who were out-and-out shams that she naturally entertained the concept of finding ghosts with a great deal of skepticism.

"You know how we work, right?" Brad asked her, as if reading her mind.

Carl spoke before Keri could answer. "I chose these guys very carefully."

"We always check first for what we *can* explain," Brad said. "Shorts in electricity that make lights flicker, nearby train tracks that make furniture rattle…"

"Of course," Keri said, smiling.

"We have to get going. Setting up our cameras and all that," Mike said. He smiled. "So, Keri, we'll get you into the little room off the bar there, and then, Carl, you might want to come with us. We'll be setting cameras just about everywhere and our monitors right there, at the table, where you two were sitting while Carl talked."

"Great," Keri said.

The rest of Brad's crew came into the room. She had to admit, she liked them all. Mike, of course, was the first of them she had met. He was the oldest member of their crew at forty, and resembled something of a modern-day pirate—bald with a gold hoop in one ear. Serena Nelson was in her midthirties, slim, blonde, bubbly and filled with ideas. She had worked as a production assistant for music videos before their ghost-hunting venture had started paying so well that they all worked only for *Truth Seekers*. Eileen Falcon was their steadfast rock, in her late twenties, and serious as the light of day. Pete Wright and Eileen were apparently a couple; Pete, in his early thirties, was a grounded man.

"Super intro, watched it on my cell phone," Serena said. "This is great. Carl, have we thanked you enough? Just the intro is flying off the charts. You wouldn't believe the viewers."

"Wonderful," Carl said.

"Okay, let's get to camera setups."

"I'll be here, setting the video feeds," Mike said.

"Pete and I will take the upstairs rooms," Eileen said.

"Okay, Mike, you're setting up here," Brad said. "I'll get the museum room, and Serena, if you wait, you and I will do the basement together. Carl, you've got to see it. Spencer did have a good plan for a horror house—he just didn't have the backing to get it going, but what he's done with the basement is damned eerie. There were all kinds of police photos from the day, and he's restored the basement so it looks just like it did in 1926."

"Creepy. I'm not going to be doing a horror house,"

Carl said. "I really do respect the history of this place, but I guess for the show…"

"For a paranormal investigation, a reproduction of a horror chamber is super," Serena said.

"Come on. I'll get you started in the museum," Brad told Keri.

A door behind the old wooden bar led to a room that was about twelve feet by twelve feet. The previous owner had, at the least, done his best to preserve what he had known about the property.

"The broadsides and guest books are copies, of course. The real ones are in real museums," Brad explained to her. "But the newspaper articles are real. Knock yourself out in here, okay?"

"Sure. Thank you."

Keri looked around, studying the various broadsides kept as posters on the walls; it was true the inn had a rich history.

"Hey, is that stuff true about the Pennsylvania Dutch believing in witches and witchcraft?" Brad asked her as he worked.

She nodded, admiring a poster from the 1940s, advertising a sendoff for a young man heading into the army and on to the battlefront.

"There have been a few bizarre cases. One took place not far from here, in Stewartstown in 1928. Three men murdered Nelson Rehmeyer—they were all convinced he had hexed them. They went to his home hoping to get a lock of his hair and his spell book. They wound up beating him to death, and then they tried to set him on fire, but he didn't burn.

"There were all kinds of spell books out at the time—most for ridding the harvest of rats and to bring about a mild winter. That kind of thing. One that Rehmeyer owned was a book published in 1820 by a man named John George Hohman called *Pow-Wows* or *Long Lost Friend*. And in it, there were all kinds of spells and words to the effect that the man who carried the book would be safe from his enemies, that he couldn't die or be burned up in any fire. Well, Rehmeyer did die, but he didn't burn, and the three men were tried for murder and convicted. But one man in particular was so convinced that Reymeyer had hexed him, because he'd fallen inexplicably ill—he'd gone to another witch who had told him this was so, and what to do about it—that he still believed he'd done the right thing. He was going to prison for murder, but he wasn't sick anymore.

"You must remember that wherever immigrants came from to the New World—be it Europe, Asia or Africa—we all came with superstitions and fears and beliefs. In this area—except for a few bizarre incidents, such as what happened to Rehmeyer—people were basically just hoping for better harvests, less snow and good luck."

"It's amazing to me how strongly people believed these things," Brad said.

She nodded and grimaced. "Hey, John Blymire went to another witch to get help because he was so convinced he was hexed. The witch he went to see was the one who told him to get the spell book and a lock of Rehmeyer's hair. It's a very well-known incident. Several documentaries and books have been done on the subject. The trial was an embarrassment to many people in York County, and the men who killed him did go to prison, but among many people, old superstitions die hard."

"Now, I've heard Newby called a witch, but did people really believe he was?" Brad asked her.

"From what I know, he started out adhering to a lot of the hedonistic policies of Crowley and then took them a bit further. Something of a prelude to men like Satanist Anton LaVey," Keri replied.

"I read about Newby before coming here. But I must admit, I'm originally from Manhattan. Now, Manhattan has its own weird stuff, but I thought the witchcraft thing died out with the Puritans," Brad said.

"We stopped hanging people on spectral evidence." Keri shrugged.

"Ah, yes, a ray of hope for humanity," Brad said. "Okay, well, the camera is set in here. All the cameras feed into the computer Mike has set up in the tavern area now. He'll be on guard there as soon as we have the rest of the place rigged. You'll be safe wherever because someone will always be monitoring the screens." He grinned. "In honesty, we're the only ones here. The cameras are for paranormal activity. You should be safe, no matter what. Unless the ghost of Newby is running around, or the ghost of the killer. Oh, sorry! I mean, I shouldn't joke—but I've never heard of a ghost killing someone. Although, who knows, through the years, maybe a ghost has given someone a heart attack."

With a grimace, he left her.

Keri grabbed a book from the shelves. This was an

incredible opportunity. While many of the posters, guest books and other paraphernalia in the room were copies, the newspaper articles from the time of the killings were the originals—along with magazine articles on the subject, and the several books that had been written about them. There was a bounty of resources. Keri found herself absorbed in a book written by an attorney, a man who swore that if Hank Bergen had the chance to defend himself in a court today, he would have been freed.

Keri thought she could spend days in the place, there was so much information to comb through. But as she read, she heard her stomach growl. Embarrassed, she looked around—she was alone. Hopefully, the hint she was hungry hadn't been picked up by the recorder left in the room. She'd arrived from her home in Richmond, Virginia, early in the afternoon—it was now after eight.

Brad's team was good at what they did—a catering truck had been in the drive, right in front of the massive Colonial columns that lined the front of the tavern. A delivery crew had brought in boxes of food, and Carl had seen to it that the kitchen had been inspected and cleaned. The people with the catering company—Rod and Milly Kendall, and Stan Gleason—had been enthusiastic. As they'd chatted and brought all their boxes from the van to the kitchen, they'd obviously been hoping for an invitation to stay. Carl and Brad assured them they could have a tour the following day.

There was definitely a well-stocked kitchen, and Keri was sure she could scrounge something.

She stood, leaving the book on the massive old desk

where she'd been sitting, and popped her head out to the bar area. She was sure Brad and his team were engrossed in what they were doing, but someone else had to be hungry by now.

Mike should have been watching the big bank of screens that had been set up in the tavern, but she didn't see him.

Or anyone.

She glanced at the screens. One caught her attention—it showed the infamous basement. There was a block like an altar in the center. She knew that real torture had once been practiced down there and that the previous owner had tried to come up with the resources to create a good haunted house attraction. Terror-inducing implements lined the wall.

For a split second, she thought she saw a strange shadow there. Then it was gone. She gave herself a shake—she was letting the power of suggestion get to her.

Maybe Mike had gone to the kitchen. Easy enough to find out. She walked across the bar to the door to the kitchen.

It was an immense room. At one time, great shanks of meat had roasted over an open fire on the giant hearth that stretched across the rear of the kitchen. It was fascinating to imagine that once upon a time, a meal for Washington might have roasted there.

But now, there was no fire in the hearth.

There was a giant butcher block table in the center of the kitchen. Not that long ago, the restaurant had been open. There were two freezers, three refrigerators, several ranges and three large ovens—a restaurant could easily open again. She wasn't sure which of the coffee brewers, samovars, mixers and other implements had been there, and which Carl might have just had brought in. The ceiling's wooden beams held every imaginable size bowl, pan and pot.

"Mike? Brad? Anyone?"

There was no answer. The group must have congregated in a room upstairs, perhaps filming again, chasing a gust of air—or some such other bit of "paranormal" activity.

She liked Brad, and she liked everyone working with him, and she very much liked Carl, but she had watched a video they had done. She had to admit—to herself, at least—that she'd rolled her eyes every time someone had said, "What was that?" A creak in an old floorboard turned into a footstep by a ghost.

She shrugged and looked around, nervous for the first time since coming to the inn.

She thought she heard someone whispering, so she exited the kitchen and went back into the tavern.

The great doors to the tavern had been locked; she checked them. They remained so. Otherwise, they would open out onto the large Colonial porch, where a massive curving driveway, still only composed of hard earth, swept by. Once, carriages had rounded that curve, coming off the old road that led between Harrisburg and Philadelphia.

Keri didn't tend to be frightened easily, but she was suddenly remembering bits and pieces of every slasher film she'd seen as a teenager. Not a good idea to head outside and wander around lonely woods out in the middle of nowhere. Or to open a locked door.

Of course, they weren't really in the middle of nowhere anymore. There was a large newly opened hotel just up the road about ten miles, and with it, accompanying gas stations and restaurants, all leading to the beautiful areas around Harrisburg that offered Amish country, Hersheypark, mountain hiking and so much more.

But come night, all that surrounded the Miller Tavern was heavily forested woods, haunting and deep.

No…not a good idea to open the door. At night, it was far too easy to believe someone might be lurking behind a tree.

The group was probably up in 207. It was supposedly the room where the most paranormal activity had taken place.

She started to turn to the stairs that led up, but then she thought she heard giggling and whispers. There was a door still marked Staff Only that led to the infamous basement. She opened the door and looked down; lights were low, to keep with the setting, but enough to allow for filming if a ghost were to start wandering around.

"Guys?" Keri said.

She thought she heard something of a sob, and then another whisper. Someone moaned, and it sounded to Keri as though they said, "I fell!"

If someone had gotten hurt here, they were going to have to call for help—fast. They should have been seen, of course, because there had to be a camera in every room by now. But Mike hadn't been in the tavern, watching the screens—one of them should have been there at all times. Not so much to catch ghosts, but because they were running around a historic tavern out in the middle of nowhere, and even though Carl had made sure the place had been seen by official building inspectors, the place *was* old.

She hurried down the stairs and almost tripped over something. Not something; someone.

It was Eileen. She was trying to sit up, moaning and rubbing the back of her head.

"Eileen!"

Quickly, Keri knelt by the blonde. "Hey, what happened? Are you all right?"

"Oh, thank God, thank you… Help me up, Keri, please, help me up. I came down the stairs too fast, and I guess… I felt like someone pushed me. I guess I just tripped, I don't know."

"Sit, sit, maybe you shouldn't stand yet. Eileen…"

She paused. Eileen was staring down into the room, her mouth an O of horror, her eyes transfixed. Then she screamed and grabbed Keri's shoulders, struggling to stand. "Out, out, out, we've got to get out!"

Keri turned to look.

And she froze as well, terror streaking through her like a bolt of lightning.

A dark figure stood over the "torture" table, a block placed there when the inn had been used as a Halloween attraction.

A body was chained to the table.

She didn't know if it was a man or a woman, it was

such a bloody, broken pile. Implements lay on top of and around the body, knives, pincers, mallets...

Keri screamed; she tried to tell herself it was all a show, someone had set up the basement as a prank against the team of ghost hunters, or perhaps they had all arranged it just for her.

It couldn't be real.

But Eileen's terror was. "Keri!"

Keri began to move, trying to help the wavering Eileen and get the two of them back up the stairs.

She looked back, and she saw a figure standing there, softly weeping. It was a young woman, and she was in a soft white dress, dark hair wound into a braided chignon.

The woman didn't touch the body; she just stared down at it, tears running down her face.

Transfixed, Keri stared at her, and then a sense of logic kicked in. There was no blood on the woman. None. She was pristine in her white. There was no way she could have recently beaten a body to a pulp.

"Come on, come on, we've got to get out of here!" she urged, reaching out to the woman in white.

"Yes, we have to get out of here!" Eileen said, hanging on to Keri. "Oh, my God," she moaned, "it can't be real, it can't be real. I smell it, though, something awful, blood, death. Come on!"

"She has to come, too!" Keri said.

Eileen stared at her as if she'd lost her mind. "Come with us? We can't help her, Keri. She's not injured, she—she's dead!"

"No, no, the other woman!"

"What other woman? Oh, God," Eileen moaned.

Keri looked back, and she saw that Eileen was right; there was no one else there.

No one, other than whoever lay on the block, unrecognizable.

She caught Eileen's hand and she ran. Up the stairs and out into the night, screaming for help at the top of her lungs.

2

"This is where she was found," Detective Catrina Billings said. "Blood everywhere, as you can still see. But the medical examiner says that she wasn't killed here—she was posed here. The group of 'paranormal' experts swear that they didn't let anyone else in and that the body wasn't here when they set up the cameras. I sent you emails and hard copy on the crew of the *Truth Seekers*, along with the historic true-crime writer Keri Wolf and actor Carl Brentwood."

Joe stood in the basement of the inn with Agent Dallas Wicker and the detective, intrigued. It didn't seem right. If the victim hadn't been killed there, how was there so very much blood staining the white stone altar that had held the victim?

"The killer collected the blood—and then spilled it here when he brought the remains to this site?" he asked.

Billings sighed deeply. "Yes, and all this was explained to the agents who were here earlier, as well. I thought this had been handed specifically to your unit."

"Yes, Detective," Dallas Wicker told her. "But the

victim was an agent—one of us. You know how you'd feel if a cop had been involved. You'd want all the details, even if you got taken off the case."

Joe and Dallas had tried to get as caught up as possible on the way there. Special Agent Julie Castro, out of the New York City office, was working a kidnapping. A seventeen-year-old girl named Barbara Chrome had been snatched off the street on the Upper East Side. A tip had led Castro to Pennsylvania.

"She was last seen in Philadelphia," Billings said. "So I've been informed."

"And somehow, she came from Philadelphia to the Miller Inn and Tavern," Dallas said.

"But you ought to be hunting down what happened in Philadelphia," Billings said.

Joe tried to offer her a friendly smile. "The other agents are working that angle, but you know you have to see a crime scene. Cops, agents—we're all the same."

Billings just stared at Joe.

Maybe she had a right to be skeptical. He'd never expected that he'd be out in the field at such lightning speed, even though he'd already been through a rigorous interview process with Adam Harrison and Jackson Crow. He still wasn't an FBI agent—he had to wait for the next class to begin and then graduate before he could become an agent—but he was here as a special consultant.

Adam Harrison's specific special unit was in charge; Jackson Crow and Adam Harrison maintained an excellent working relationship with the head office and with large field offices across the country. They were frequently the lead in cases that had anything to do with the so-called paranormal, strange rituals, or the like.

And an agent was dead. Special Agent Julie Castro and her partner, Ed Newel, out of the New York City office, had been investigating a kidnapping that had crossed state lines. There was no way there wouldn't be heavy FBI participation to try to solve her murder.

Carl Brentwood had called Dallas, having met him recently in Savannah. Dallas had handed the request to Jackson, who had given it to Adam. Joe didn't know what magic Adam had worked, but the Krewe was going to be heading up the investigation as part of a task force with local police and New York and Pennsylvania agents.

In this instance, Joe already had a working relationship with Carl; important, since Brentwood knew and trusted him. Carl had been a guest at a bed-and-breakfast in Savannah when a spate of mysterious disappearances had threatened the B and B's owner. He'd witnessed a dramatic showdown between a pair of killers and law enforcement, including Joe and Dallas.

Joe had become an official consultant after Carl's desperate call to Dallas. The young actor had asked for Joe specifically, convinced that between him and Dallas, they could clear him and his friends of any wrongdoing, and save the reputation of his newly purchased historic property.

Joe and Dallas would see Carl later that day, as well as those who had been at the inn when the body had been discovered. The coroner also expected them at the morgue for the autopsy later.

But first, the old inn. Catrina Billings had started

them off where the body had been found, in the basement, along with the torture implements akin to those
used by the original owner.

"We're having numerous samples of the blood tested
now," Billings told them stiffly. "We believe, as you
said, that wherever she was killed, the murderer collected her blood as she died, specifically to leave here,
where it was intended she be found."

Billings was as thin as a whippet with iron-gray hair
cut short and forming natural curls close to her head.
Her eyes were a match for her hair, and while she hadn't
been impolite, she had spoken crisply and coldly at
every turn.

Joe had the feeling that she believed they thought of
her as a country cop, not up to par with the FBI training
and technical abilities. Dallas probably hadn't made her
feel that way—he was good with people. Joe thought
that he was, too, but she evidently found him to be little
more than a nuisance.

They were still going to try for a good working rap-
port. Maybe she just needed to trust them. Then again,
maybe she was disturbed that the FBI was in on it; the
victim had been found on her turf. But the coroner's
office had made a quick match on the victim, and the
victim had been an FBI agent.

"There are only two entrances to the inn—the front
door, and the cellar, correct?" Dallas asked.

Billings waved a hand in the air. "The idiot actor
owner didn't even know about the cellar entrance. He's
really barely seen the place. When he purchased it, he
got it into his head immediately that he had to have it

explored by 'paranormal investigators' before starting his own brand of renovations and opening the place again as an inn. He's convinced that everyone here is innocent. I don't trust any of them for a minute. Of course, the paranormal crew are all certain a ghost has struck. They're convinced that their being here awakened evil. One of them is definitely guilty—oh, they're claiming that someone could have come through the cellar door, the door they didn't know about until my detectives found it.

"The coroner will determine an approximate time of the murder—how long she was dead before she was brought in here. It's late summer, but the weather has been nice, low sixties at night, seventies by day, so he's hoping to make a reasonable determination. The forensic team found blood on the cellar door—again, being tested, but we're assuming it belonged to the victim—so, the body was probably brought in that way.

"Now, of course, you're asking about planned entrances and exits. There are large windows, and a balcony out back. The right person could maybe get up or down. There are windows in the front, too, but blood evidence says the corpse was brought in through the cellar."

"May we see the rest of the inn?" Dallas asked.

"Of course," Billings said, looking doubtfully at Joe. Her eyes narrowed. "You're not one of the paranormal psychic consultants, are you? Because the dead woman is real. She's no ghost."

"I was with the Savannah police department. I left to join the FBI," Joe told her. "I recently worked a case that involved Carl Brentwood. I'm hoping my presence will help him stay calm, and I'll give him any assistance I can."

"You worked a case he was involved in?" Billings asked. "You know, those actors, thinking that they're privileged and can do what other people can't." She looked at him oddly. "Like killing people."

"Carl was innocent of any wrongdoing," Joe assured her.

She looked at Dallas for confirmation of his words. Dallas nodded gravely.

"Because we're in a bit of a strange situation right now," she went on, "I can't just arrest them all, and I can't let them all go. There's no hard evidence against any of them, just that they were all here, the only people at the crime scene. Right now, we have the group up at the new hotel. They've been asked not to leave the area. Until we get to the bottom of it, they need to be in reach."

"And they're willing to stay?" Dallas asked.

Billings rolled her eyes. "Oh, you haven't met these people. They're all claiming innocence. But they're also convinced that there's an 'entity' at the inn, and they want to get back in to keep exploring. Except for the writer, I guess. She was here for what she could gain on the old crime in the '20s. This is all in the jackets you have," she said, indicating the physical files she had handed him. "Forensic people want more time here, though, so far, they haven't found anything except for what was in the basement. Blood all over this altar or torture table or whatever it is, blood at the cellar door entry. They're almost done, though they'll be back in today and probably clear the place by tonight. If you're ready, we'll head back up. We can walk the place quickly and just get to the autopsy."

"Thank you, Detective Billings," Dallas said politely. If Billings wanted to be a little bit cold, they'd be just as warm as they possibly could. She was probably a good cop—just a little resentful of the interference.

"So, looking over the rest of the inn and then autopsy," Joe said. "And then a trip to the new hotel to meet the Truth Seekers, the writer and Carl?"

Billings nodded.

"Okay, here are the only stairs up," she said. "According to what I've learned, Keri Wolf came out of the museum—facing the inn, that's to the left of the bar—came through the tavern and looked in the kitchen. Not finding anyone, she headed back into the tavern, passed the stairs going up until she came to the basement door. The rest of the group was upstairs in 207 when Wolf came down the basement stairs and found Eileen Falcon. Falcon had fallen down the stairs and hurt herself—stunned and terrified by the sight of the corpse on the table. Wolf got her up and outside, thankfully dialing 911. Brentwood and the others upstairs heard her screaming and they went outside, too. Anyway, that's what happened here—as it was told to us."

Billings led the way back through the foyer to the tavern area. From there, they crossed to the kitchen, recently upgraded but still bearing the charm of a massive fireplace and hearth and copper cookware hanging from rafters above a workstation.

Upstairs, they visited the rooms—ten in all, with 207 being the room where the rest of the group had been gathered when Eileen and Keri had found the corpse.

According to the group, Billings had made sure to tell them.

"Why wasn't Eileen Falcon with them in 207? I understand that Keri Wolf was in the museum, deep in her research, but why wasn't Eileen with them?" Joe asked.

"And why wasn't someone where the screens were set up, watching the cameras?" Dallas asked. "It doesn't do a lot of good to have cameras everywhere if you're not watching them."

"Falcon was supposed to be taking over on the screens," Billings said. "Usually, Mike Lerner set up the cameras and manned the screens, but he went up to rest and Falcon was supposed to be covering for him. But she says some kind of a noise distracted her, and she looked in the basement. And then saw the corpse, fell, and was on the stairs when Wolf came down. That's the story as I have it."

"And there was no one else here—or anywhere near here—yesterday and last night?" Dallas asked.

Billings shrugged. "A local catering company delivered boxes of food early in the afternoon. They were here. They left."

"They have alibis?" Dallas asked. "They'd have known something about the place."

"Even the Truth Seekers say that they just came and went. Nothing about looking around the place. Maybe they wanted an invitation to stay, but they didn't get one. The guy who runs *Truth Seekers* is pretty tight on who he has in his programming."

"Did any of them say anything about the possibility of someone else being here?"

"They're paranormal kooks, you know? They believe ghosts are coming back to kill people," Billings said. "Good excuse, huh? Even the writer—a respected historian!—got involved in the idiocy of this. Miller Tavern has always had a reputation for being haunted. Very bad things happened here, homicidal crazy people… Serial killers before that was a thing. And to think they even have the writer playing into it."

"How is that?" Joe asked her.

Billings sniffed. "She said she saw another woman down there. A woman dressed in a long white gown."

"The killer could have worn a long white gown," Dallas said.

"One problem—Wolf swears there was no blood on the gown. None at all. And oddly enough, the ghost kook in with her, Falcon, didn't see the woman in white. So, you see, even the writer is seeing things here. Despite her so-called reputation…"

"Carl has owned this place just a matter of weeks, right?" Joe asked.

Billings nodded. "He bought it from Spencer Atkins, a local man. Atkins didn't have the financial backing to upgrade enough, so he told me, and he figured that a kid like Brentwood with his popularity and money might be able to keep the old place. I guess the other offers he had would have turned it into a school or a factory or something that would maintain the facade of the inn—it's on the historic register—and yet not have it be an inn anymore. Oh, Atkins was here earlier, but he had an appointment in Philadelphia and had to leave well before the body was discovered."

"Did Carl change the locks on the place yet?" Joe asked her.

"No. He had a cleaning crew in to fix it up enough for the Truth Seekers to come in for the filming. He wanted new sheets and bedding and a freshen-up so that they could film and spend a few nights here. He and Atkins became friends—I don't think Brentwood was worried about the locks." She was quiet. "Anyway, the body came in through the cellar and there wasn't a padlock. I don't think anyone ever even thought about it."

"How does Atkins feel about all this?" Dallas asked.

"He's just sick. Said he should have made sure that the place was tighter than a drum, what with the reputation. Then again, the bad stuff happened in 1926—who would figure it could start over again?" She shook her head. "Crazy people. Ghost people." She paused, shrugged and gave them a condescending smile. "Isn't your 'special unit' supposed to be a little crazy, too, Special Agent Wicker?"

Dallas could handle anything, Joe knew. He still chose to hop in with an answer, controlling his own temper and smiling as he spoke. "Crazy as loons, so I've heard. But damn, they have a solve rate that beats any jurisdiction anywhere in the country. So, let's head straight on over to autopsy, huh? And then we can go meet the loons and see if that gets us anywhere."

He looked at Dallas.

Dallas grinned, clearly amused by Joe going to bat for the Krewe.

"Perfect," he said.

"Hey, do we know where to find Atkins?" Joe asked, looking from Billings to Dallas.

"I think he's back. Like I said, he had an appointment in Philadelphia, but I don't think he was planning on staying overnight. He lives in an old wooden house between here and the new hotel, past the church and graveyard and a little forested area. He was spending most of his time here at the inn—living here, I mean—but then he moved into one of his old family places when he sold to Brentwood. You can't miss the house. You can see it right off the road, back a spell," Billings said. "Atkins is a fine man. I've known him all my life. You'll like him. Maybe you'll have a question for him that I didn't think of. And of course, you are part of a task force, so if you do get anything from him or anyone else… Remember, we are the local cops."

"We never forget," Dallas assured her.

They all left together; crime scene tape was still strapped over many areas of the inn, but across the front door, it had been pulled down.

Billings taped it back into place.

"We're really done here," she said. "Forensics spent hours and hours. Whatever happened here, though, it all happened in the cellar." She looked at Joe and Dallas. "Makes it rather a moot point, whether anyone had a key or not," she said.

"And possibly, that there hadn't been a padlock on

the door in a long while," Joe said quietly. "And lots of people had to know about the cellar."

"That's like saying you had to know that there was a property here," Billings said.

"And about all the legends that go with the property," Dallas said. "Well, we've just begun, right?"

Billings shrugged. She headed out to her unmarked car, a large blue sedan. "I'll be letting Brentwood know he can come back into the inn tomorrow," she said. "Heads up on that."

They watched her go. Joe turned to Dallas. "Have you seen the *Truth Seekers* shows?"

"No, there wasn't time to catch up on them. You've seen them?"

"A few of them. One of the cops I worked with was obsessed with the show. Enough for me to recognize the group. Of course, we both know Carl. I know nothing about the writer, though, except for what we've got in the folders." As he spoke, he flipped open the file he'd been given, looking for info on Keri Wolf.

She stared out at him from the page, an exceptionally attractive young woman, light brown hair waving around her shoulders, clear hazel eyes looking directly at the camera. It was a book-jacket photo; she wasn't smiling, nor was she frowning. She'd probably been directed to have a scholarly but pleasant look about her. She was dressed in a tailored blouse and black jacket—very businesslike. There was a very appealing look about her, as if she was someone you'd be bound to like and want to get to know. There was nothing remotely sexual about the picture, and despite it all, there seemed to be something innately sensual about her.

"A young and pretty woman," Joe murmured. "Then again, young and pretty women have certainly been guilty of crimes."

"I'm not seeing it. Not on this. She has an excellent reputation. Her work is solid," Dallas said. "She makes a clear difference between what is fact and her own theories on what might have happened."

"You've read her work?"

Dallas nodded. "I was fascinated by a man suspected of several brutal murders in Hell's Kitchen after the Civil War. She happened to have written a book on the events. She describes the New York of the time—and how the killer was able to get away with his deeds."

"We can't discount any of them," Joe said.

"No," Dallas agreed. "But I'll tell you this—Carl thinks the world of her."

Joe nodded. They needed to move. It was going to be a very long day. "Atkins, caterers and autopsy?" he asked.

"As much as we can get to. Caterers may have to wait until tomorrow. Atkins first, I think, on the way to the autopsy. So. Wooden house down the road—we see Atkins, see what he knows about the inn and the people around here, and keep moving."

"Let's do it."

"Thank you, thank you, thank you," Carl said to Keri. "I can't thank you enough. I really am so very grateful that you're staying."

Keri smiled weakly. It wasn't as if she had really been given any choice—they'd been told not to leave the area.

But while she'd been terrified, she was also angry and determined that someone find out what happened to the woman ripped to shreds on the stone slab in the cellar of the Miller Inn and Tavern.

Last night had gone from bad to worse. Or maybe not—it was hard for anything to be worse than it had been for that poor woman. The assumption seemed to be that someone staying at the tavern had killed her elsewhere, collected her blood and then brought her in through the cellar door and laid her out on the stone table so she might be found by the paranormal seekers.

Once they'd fled the basement, Keri had dialed 911 from the front lawn of the inn. She'd been terrified for herself and Eileen—the killer might have still been near, waiting and watching—but she'd also been terrified for the people still in the tavern. She'd called Carl and told him to get himself and the others the hell out.

He'd thought at first that she'd been pulling his leg.

She honestly didn't even know what he had been thinking. He'd spoken so casually, asking excitedly if she'd really encountered a ghost—and not grasping the fact that no, she'd encountered a dead woman.

And maybe a ghost. Maybe a killer...a killer in white...

But no question, definitely a dead woman. Murdered brutally, lying in an unbelievable pool of crimson blood.

Thankfully, the sound of sirens had come quickly. And though she doubted that even the victim's mother would have recognized her, it was learned within a matter of hours through fingerprints that the dead woman had been an FBI agent.

Then hours of waiting, sitting in the police station. Being questioned. Going over and over her movements the day and night before.

So, there they were, in the restaurant of the new hotel that was far closer to decent roads. A travelers' hotel rather than a destination hotel, which was what Carl had hoped Miller Tavern would become.

Keri hadn't gotten to bed until it was either very late or very early—it was already light—and to her surprise, they'd been left alone most of the day. Crawling down from her room eventually for something to eat, she'd run into Carl, and they'd ordered something of a strange very-late-lunch combo together. She had been grateful for that little bit of company. But now, finished with their food, they were just sitting there, and she was still exhausted. She wanted nothing more than to go back up to her room and try to fall asleep again.

She wasn't sure what to say to Carl. She wished she understood the law better. The way the police had suggested that they remain in the area had sounded like a threat. But if they weren't under arrest, there was really no reason that they couldn't leave.

But she didn't have to be anywhere else right now. Her schedule was her own. She was grateful that she made enough on her books to live comfortably and choose her subjects and research—even though historic crime books were not in the same popularity realm as sci-fi, fantasy or young adult fiction. She didn't knock 'em dead on the lists, but she had a steady audience that included professors and others she respected—and often relied upon for help.

Salem—her, yes, black cat—was being cared for by her next-door neighbor, a cat lover who didn't mind at all.

And Keri really liked Carl. Not in any romantic way—more like one might feel affection for a younger brother.

"Carl, I'm fine staying on here, and you're welcome," she told him. "Besides," she added with a grimace, "if I tried to leave, our dear Detective Billings might decide I need to be shackled to a chair. Or jailed for a few nights."

"She is something, huh? Hey, I know you do historic crime, but…now you're in the middle of an actual crime. Are you going to write this one up?"

"Too close to home. I like old crimes. The victims and their families long gone. No one left who could be hurt by my words. Even if there are descendants, it was so long ago they didn't know the ancestors who were involved."

"Billings is a character," Carl said. "She seems so angry—I think that her family must date back to the days when people around here believed in powwows—not like Native American powwows, but witches and healing-type powwows. Maybe she thinks that this murder brought it all back to her precious area of the country. That sounded bad, didn't it? I love the country around here. That's why I bought the tavern, but… Anyway, we won't have to worry long. The FBI is involved."

"Because an FBI agent was murdered, right?" Keri asked.

"Well, that, and… I got to be pretty good friends

with one agent. And a cop, too, in Savannah. I mean, the FBI was coming in on this no matter what, but I think Detective Billings is annoyed that I called the Feds myself—and that I know that agent well, and the ex-cop he brought with him. Consultant, whatever they're calling Joe. Man, this is sad, huh? Seems like murder is following me around. Nope, no, wait, wasn't me. All that bad stuff was in motion long before I got there. Anyway, Dallas is one cool agent, and Joe is probably the best cop I ever met—"

"A Savannah cop is coming to Pennsylvania?" she asked skeptically.

Carl sighed. "I just told you. He isn't a cop anymore. He's going into the FBI academy."

"They sent him on a job…before he graduated the academy?"

"Key word, *consultant.*"

"Oh." Keri sipped her coffee. Over the rim of her mug, she saw that Brad had come into the restaurant on the ground floor of the hotel and was hurrying over to join them.

He sat, beaming at them both. A bit of a bizarre smile, in Keri's mind, since they'd discovered a woman who had been murdered just the night before.

"My video channel is off the charts!" he said. "Our viewers didn't get much because we were interrupted, but we did manage to explain as we fled that we'd found a body…and wow. People can't wait for my next install-ment. Carl, did they tell you anything about when we might be able to get back into the inn?"

"I don't know yet. I know that the FBI is coming in

today, and that the forensic team is supposed to make a last go-through," Carl said.

"You do realize that they suspect one of us of murder," Keri put in.

Brad waved a hand in the air. "That's ridiculous. We were all together. Except for you and Eileen. And murder, seriously? They'll figure it all out. And they may think, gee, we've got suspects, but I don't think that they believe we could be guilty. They haven't got a clue, so they're focusing on us."

"But, Brad, it's still very serious," Keri said. "A woman is dead."

"We didn't do it. You and Eileen stumbled upon her. And now, to that—Keri, you're saying that there was another woman down there in the basement with you. Eileen didn't see her, but you did. Tell me more. Keri, I think you saw a spirit. All of us—well, the group of us, the Truth Seekers—we're the experienced ones. We have made recordings that have caught the voices of the dead. We know hot and cold and energy and... You really saw someone else, right? Eileen said that you did. And poor Eileen—you said you saw a woman, she didn't, and the police made that sound like she had to be guilty of something."

Keri shrugged, uncomfortable with the conversation. Brad was just too gung ho on his own agenda. And she was still horrified by the terrible death of a woman.

"I'm so sorry about Eileen. I don't know what I saw. I was in a panic. And please, Brad, I've already gone over it a dozen times with the police, and I really don't feel like talking about it anymore."

And the FBI was coming—or were already here. She'd be going through it all again.

Brad wasn't offended; he grinned. "Well, where we are, it's not like we can kill the time at the beach or anything. There's not much to do around here except go shopping to buy a few Amish quilts."

"Ah, but I can kill lots of time reading," Keri assured him. She yawned, a little too dramatically, but that was okay. "I didn't get to my room until about four in the morning, and I didn't get to sleep until hours later, and I think—"

"They'll do the autopsy today, you know," Brad said. "Not that the cops will really tell us anything, but if she's been dead for days, then we'll definitely be in the clear."

Keri had seen the remnants of the bloody corpse. She didn't know anything about an autopsy and very little about forensics, but she could swear that the woman hadn't been dead for days.

Carl's phone rang; he excused himself, rose and answered it.

"Come on. Tell me about the woman," Brad said to her, eyes wide and tone conspiratorial.

"Brad, please, everything is a haze to me. I might have been thinking of a picture, I might have been—"

Carl strode back to the table, saving her.

"Keri, I need you now. Please. Brad, forgive me, we'll be back at this soon enough. Keri?"

He reached out for her and she took his hand gratefully, rising.

He led her toward the elevators, and once there

asked, "Are you all right? I couldn't help but notice that you seemed bothered by Brad. I thought that you liked him all right."

She smiled; Carl had interrupted just because he'd noticed that she needed saving.

"I do like him. He's usually fine. I just don't... I wish I'd never spoken about what I saw. He's driving me a little crazy."

"He thinks you made contact with the dead," Carl said, looking at her with a very serious expression. He shook his head. "Keri, it is a possibility. I just came from a situation where, I swear, very strange things happened."

"I consider the murder strange and horrible enough." She yawned again, this time for real. "I'm sorry, Carl."

"I know. And you're exhausted. I thought I'd give you an escape."

"You're a wonderful mind reader."

He smiled and hit the call button for the elevator.

"I hope I can sleep," she said.

"I hope so, too," he said softly as she got on the elevator. "And tomorrow might be better."

Let's hope, she thought. But it might take way more than a night to make things better.

Far more than a night to forget the body of Julie Castro.

3

Spencer Atkins opened his door after Dallas's first knock. He was a tall man, frowning when he saw them but ready to welcome them in when Dallas showed his credentials. He quickly offered them coffee, and in the line of being casual and opening a dialogue, they accepted.

Sitting in the living room of the old wooden house, Dallas started up the conversation. "You know what happened last night?"

"Of course—and I feel responsible," Atkins said.

"You do? How's that?" Joe asked.

"I wasn't making a go of the place—it just needed too much put into it. And that Carl Brentwood, he's a good kid. A hell of a success. He could have thrown his money into drugs or wild parties, as some who get rich too quick are prone to do. No, he wanted to preserve history. And he has the money.

"But he's also a celebrity. I don't know if that young woman would have been murdered whether Carl owned the property or not, but bringing the body to the inn...

I'm afraid that it's because the inn *wasn't* on the verge of being lost to history itself. Kill an FBI agent and leave her in the old torture chamber of a sadistic killer, when the inn has internet celebrities and a bona fide movie star running around it? That's something that's not going to be left out of the news. It's my understanding that certain killers love publicity."

"Every killer, every case, is different," Joe said.

"Did anyone ever come to the inn, following you around, asking for floor plans, anything like that?" Dallas asked.

"We think the killer was familiar with the inn," Joe told Atkins, staring steadily at the man.

Atkins shook his head sadly. "There was certainly never anything that I noticed," he said. "And I believe I was a good innkeeper, but we're not talking about many guests per night."

"Did anyone creep around the basement?" Joe asked.

Atkins was a dignified man—his posture, even sitting, was straight, giving him the appearance of a man very much in charge of himself. But at that question, he slumped a little, acutely uncomfortable.

"Once I had outfitted it again as a torture chamber for tours and Halloween, I had tons of people creeping around down there."

"Guests?" Dallas asked.

"And others. I charged for the tour. Most of the time, it wasn't much of a tour, just a dramatic explanation of what we know about John Newby down in the cellar. And then, I had the bar stocked, so I'd give a talk in the tavern, too, about the days before the Revolution and on up through Newby. In October, we went the whole haunted-creepy-scary-actors thing. Schlocky, of course, but the tours helped keep me afloat."

"You just don't seem like the 'schlocky' type," Joe said.

Atkins rubbed his fingers together. "I'm not. My efforts were probably humiliating. Like I said, I was trying to stay afloat. Did I like it? No. And I wasn't all that happy when Carl told me about the paranormal investigation. He'd bought the property, and I had promised I'd help him get up and running and that he could call me anytime. I was over there yesterday, and then I had to head into Philly. I guess those paranormal types were looking for the dead—they found the dead. It was never a good idea, in my mind, to play with the past of the tavern." He was quiet a minute and gave a hard look at Joe and Dallas. "You need to investigate that crowd. They're very strange, indeed."

"But they don't come from the area," Dallas said. "What about the cellar and its entrance that apparently was never locked? Did you ever have a padlock on that door?"

"There wasn't one when I bought the place, twenty-odd years ago. No, I never put one on. And I never saw anyone going near the cellar door."

"Someone knew it was there," Dallas said.

"Mark my words, investigate that group. Carl, I believe he's just a good kid. Then again, he is an actor. Lying for a living. But still. The Truth Seekers. They were the ones in the inn. They should have seen or heard something. And what about all those cameras?"

"The camera down in the cellar had conveniently been turned off," Joe said.

Atkins lifted his hands and let them fall, shaking his head.

"You know of any practicing witches?" Joe asked him.

Atkins laughed. "Witches?"

"People believing in witchcraft. Good and bad. We are in old Pennsylvania Dutch country here. Hex country. Anyone still adhere to old beliefs?"

Atkins shook his head. "That was long ago. Sure, we're still in Amish country."

"Hardworking people with certain traditions," Joe said. "The Amish had nothing to do with this murder. This smacks of something far darker."

"Yes, darker. Now," Atkins continued, "all the old stories are just for fun, or at least contain a good moral. You must know that in the Middle Ages, every poor woman who hit on the right herb to cure a disease was persecuted as a witch. It was different here. There were no executions—just murder."

Joe glanced at Dallas. He could tell that they tacitly agreed they weren't getting anywhere. Not now. Maybe later. They'd have to wrangle trust from Atkins, if he was going to give them any deeper insights.

"Thanks," Joe told him.

"My card," Dallas said, handing one to Atkins.

"Oh, yesterday," Joe said, as if in afterthought. "You were in Philadelphia—all day?"

Atkins surveyed him and then Dallas shrewdly. "I see. I'm on the suspect list. You can exclude me quickly.

I had a meeting with my financial adviser. He can vouch for me. As can the waitress at the steak house. I was at the tavern in the afternoon—wishing Carl the best of luck. When I left, they were starting to set up, and they put a camera in the basement, so I know that the body wasn't there when I was there."

Dallas thanked him, and they started to leave.

"Autopsy today?" Atkins asked. "When a body goes in, I believe the autopsy is supposed to be done the next day. I heard the victim had coworkers in Pennsylvania. Must be hell to have to attend the autopsy of a friend."

"Yes," Dallas said simply.

"Sometimes, I wonder why it's necessary," Atkins said.

Joe was starting to think that the man was truly an ass.

Atkins added very softly, "They say she was cut to ribbons. Death by a knife, so it would seem. I'm sorry... I was just thinking for her family and friends, the nicest thing to do would be to just get her in a closed coffin."

"Well, there is the law," Joe countered.

"And we don't make the law," Dallas said. "We just try to enforce it. Thank you again. We're glad to know that you're willing to help us at any time."

"What do you think?" Dallas asked Joe when they were back in the car.

"I don't know. I wonder about his train of thought, though. He's up on the fact that in most circumstances, autopsy is the next day. And yes, we can presume she was killed with a knife. He knew she was chopped to shreds, but hell, news like that always travels quickly.

Thing is, though, you'd think he'd realize that there was so much more that an autopsy may give. Last meal, left-handed or right-handed killer—or, possibly killers. He came off like a jerk, then seemed to have some compassion later."

"He owned the place but didn't have the kind of money Carl has to keep it going. Maybe he's resentful, despite his show of courtesy."

"Right. Maybe he's just a jerk. Maybe he's so much more."

They arrived at the morgue to find that Catrina Billings was already in attendance and that the medical examiner was already at work. Dr. Gorman nodded to them politely, but continued with his measurement of the heart.

Joe had seen a lot that was horrendous and cruel. He'd still seldom seen anything quite as brutal as what had been done to Agent Julie Castro.

She didn't have much of a face left. The silver lining was that she was so cut as to make it appear that she was not real—more like a prop out of a bad slasher movie.

The bad, of course, was that she had been real, a young woman, passionate in her work, and had paid the ultimate price.

Dr. Gorman droned on with facts and figures, brain size, kidney size, and then he paused, looking at them.

"Her last meal appears to have been sushi. And here's another important factor—most of the cuts and the ripping you see were, thank the Lord above, done after her death. See the way the cuts were done to her body, and the way the skin has torn and the blood congealed? It was as if she was bathed in blood from all those cuts, but death was fast. The slice right there at her throat cut through a jugular vein, and she bled out almost instantly. The immediate hemorrhage would have been massive. But whoever killed her was prepared to catch all that blood, and then dump it over her when she had been moved to the cellar at the Miller Inn and Tavern."

"Interesting," Dallas murmured. "The mutilation wasn't done to cause pain. Rather to create a display."

"A small favor," Catrina Billings said softly.

"Detective," Joe asked, "are there any sushi restaurants near here?"

Billings shook her head. "The closest sushi restaurant is…" She paused, shaking her head, almost smiling. "Nowhere near here. Toward one of the bigger cities, either direction."

"Here's your basic—the report will be much more detailed," Dr. Gorman said. "Special Agent Castro had a meal of sushi. Tuna, salmon and sushi rice, I believe. The stomach contents will go to the lab. She was killed within an hour after that meal. She bled out tremendously and that blood was collected to be poured over her at the inn. She was not tortured, as her appearance on the altar would cause one to believe. What we've tested is her blood. Naturally, we have many more tests that will take time. My full report, as I said, will be more detailed. But that is what I can tell you at this time."

"What about defensive wounds?" Joe asked.

"None. I can only surmise that she was not expecting what happened to her. But if one of you will allow me…" He gestured for someone to come closer.

"Sure," Joe said, stepping forward.

"Actually, I need Detective Billings. You're too tall. I can show you how I believe she was killed. The assailant who delivered the fatal blow was right-handed. Detective?"

Detective Billings moved over to him unhappily.

Dr. Gorman demonstrated how the killer had come up behind Castro, caught her body to him, and made a fast, hard, fatal slash across her throat.

Billings moved away quickly.

"You know you're welcome to call at any time, if you have questions."

They all thanked the doctor, and on their way out removed the paper suits they'd been given to wear in the autopsy room.

Outside, Billings looked at them oddly. "Two of her coworkers are in the area. I'd have thought they'd be the ones attending the autopsy."

"They're in Philadelphia, following angles there. This is complicated, of course, with many leads that must be investigated," Dallas said.

"Right. Julie Castro was last seen in Philadelphia." Billings said.

"And we're here," Joe added. "Dallas is lead on the case. The other agents can read an autopsy report. I don't think it was necessary for people she knew to be here."

"I suppose you're right," Billings said. "It will be

good to tell them, though, that she didn't suffer. That it was quick."

"Yes, that will be a small blessing," Dallas agreed.

"All right then," Billings said. "I'm going to get some of my people driving out to every sushi restaurant in the surrounding area with pictures of Julie Castro. We'll keep in close contact." She hesitated, looking at them. "Between us, we'll make this right."

"Between us," Dallas agreed.

Waving, she headed to her car.

"That was…almost nice," Joe said.

Dallas laughed. "Almost."

"What now?" Joe asked.

Darkness had already fallen. Dallas looked around. "Night again. I guess we'll head back." He smiled. "You're a good cop. You're going to make a great agent. You don't seem to care much about hours. There's nothing more that we can do today, and it has been a long day. Tomorrow, we'll start out right after breakfast. I'll talk to Carl. I want to get him and Keri to come out to the inn with us—just the two of them. It's not that I don't trust the Truth Seekers, but—"

"They just might close ranks."

Dallas started for the car; Joe hesitated, thoughtful.

"What?" Dallas asked.

"Julie Castro went out for sushi. Maybe she met up with someone. Then, she drove or was driven here and killed soon after, on the same day that Carl had his paranormal group in, along with Keri. Whoever killed her walked right up behind her and sliced her throat, causing death almost instantly and managing to catch a bucket of her blood. And she was killed while those people were running around the inn, trying to communicate with the dead."

"A complicated event, yes," Dallas said. "And well planned out. What are you thinking?"

"I'm thinking that several people might have been involved. Not just two, but maybe three, four or more."

"A very good reason to start off tomorrow with just Keri and Carl," Dallas said. "But you think that the ghost-hunter group might be involved? None of them has ties to this area of Pennsylvania. Nor are they New Yorkers. Julie Castro's case started in New York City. What could they have had to do with an Upper East Side kidnapping?"

"Or how did a kidnapped New York City girl wind up in Pennsylvania? Not that we're talking huge distances, but still."

"We'll be back on it tomorrow," Dallas said. "For now, think it out, do all the armchair figuring that you want. For the moment, we need food. I do, anyway. We headed out here at the crack of dawn. Trust me, this isn't going to be any easy solve. Food, now. And rest."

Joe nodded. His stomach wasn't grumbling anymore; it was on fire. They had just left an autopsy, which seldom allowed him to think about eating. But they had been going all day.

"I wonder how the girl is involved," Joe said, thinking aloud.

"The girl?"

"The kidnapping case that Agent Castro was pursuing. Barbara Chrome."

"That's something we should investigate," Dallas said, and he started moving down the sidewalk for the car. "Let's share our info with the agents in Philadelphia. Tomorrow. For now, let's get something to eat."

Keri tried to nap, but to no avail. No matter how hard she tried, she was awake, yawning and staring at the ceiling. At some point she realized that she should just stay awake. Otherwise, she'd never sleep at night. It was already evening, but not late enough for anyone over the age of nine to go to bed without waking up in the wee hours of the morning.

For a while, she read, downloading books on Pennsylvania. She found a story about witchcraft and William Penn that made her especially happy. Penn had received the charter for the colony from Charles II in 1681. At that time, many residents of the area belonged to a Swedish colony that had settled the lower Delaware River Valley in 1654. Among them had been Margaret and Nils Mattson. By 1683, many British colonists had settled there as well, and since the colony was under a British charter, it was under British law. Margaret was accused of witchcraft for hexing a neighbor's cattle, and when she was brought to court, Penn himself was the judge.

As might have been the case in Salem, Massachusetts, whether people believed what they told themselves or not, the accusation might have had a lot to do with disputes over land and property.

Penn was not about to have a woman executed for witchcraft in his colony. While she was convicted of having the reputation of a witch, she was not convicted of doing any harm to animals. She went on to live out her years in the lower valley.

Nice! Keri approved of the judge's progressive thinking.

The area had, however, maintained a reputation for witchcraft for a long time, but a more benign concept of witchcraft was honored by most. Respecting the land and the harvest and using local herbs to heal illnesses. Not so irrational, by any means.

Hex signs had, according to her reading, only become generally popular when people started painting their barns and enjoying their artistry. Signs indicating the seasons, celestial objects, peace and more had deep roots in almost any European society. They became part of the Scandinavian/Germanic culture of the region and flourished in the twentieth century.

Nowhere could she find a history of Satanism; John Newby had stumbled upon his particular brand of worship or spiritualism on his own.

As darkness descended, she found that she was hungry again.

Keri desperately wished that there was room service at the hotel, but there was not. She could, however, phone the restaurant and place an order and then just run down and pick it up. She did so, feeling guilty. She liked Carl and the entire group from the Truth Seekers. She just felt that she needed a bit more time away from them. Especially Brad.

She had almost convinced herself that she had imagined the woman in white.

Totally imagined.

She went down to get her food.

There was a counter at the edge of the restaurant. It skirted the entrance to the dining area with the kitchen just behind it. She hurried up to the counter, afraid she had picked the exact time when everyone else was having their dinner.

To her relief, she saw none of them in the dining area.

But as she collected her to-go bag, and paid the cashier, she heard her name called softly from behind her.

Wincing, she turned.

Eileen Falcon was right behind her.

"Hey, Eileen, how are you doing? I'm so sorry. I heard that they put you through the wringer because I thought I saw someone else down there."

"Not to worry. That's the way cops work. I'm good, I'm good," the tiny, dark-haired woman told her. She grimaced. "I have Pete. We've spent most of the day in the room, trying to sleep."

"Ditto."

"Are you going to be okay…going back in there?" Eileen asked.

"Into the old Miller Inn and Tavern? I have to say, I'm not thrilled. But I care about Carl. Right now, I'm sticking here. I guess we'll all see in the days to come. The law-enforcement powers that be seem to want us to stay, so…"

"I guess I do want to get back into the inn," Eileen said. "It's fascinating. I think someone is trying to imitate what happened in the past, and they're using us. Please, Keri, we were both in absolute panic. Don't worry that you did or didn't see someone. I'm okay. They can ask me questions from now until eternity. I heard the FBI is here, too—different sets of them or something—and I'll have the same answers for them. And I'm strong. I'll be fine."

"That's good, I guess."

Eileen—always serious, so it seemed—was watching her gravely. "I wish I'd seen the woman in white."

Keri waved a hand in the air. "I was scared—no, scratch that—terrified. I have no idea what I did or didn't see."

"You saw a ghost," Eileen said. "A real ghost. Not a recording of a ghost, or a shadow on film, or a feeling, or... You saw her."

"Like I said, I don't know what I saw," Keri told her. "You all are the paranormal experts. Anyway, I'm going to run upstairs and eat this food before it's stone-cold. I'm sure we'll talk much more in the days to come."

She started to flee, ready to head upstairs, but as she reached the bank of elevators, she turned to look back toward the hotel's entrance.

There was a man standing there. He appeared to have just entered the building and was surveying the entrance, then turned toward the café and restaurant—and the bank of elevators. He was very tall, wearing a dark suit and a gray shirt, casually open at the throat. His eyes were unusual, a silver-gray that seemed to both see her and look right through her. He was in his midthirties, with a classic face—he had sculpted features, but a raw, rugged look as well. He'd have done well in a superhero movie.

He stared; she stared back.

She thought he was going to come toward her; he looked at her as if he knew her. As if he wanted to speak with her.

But the elevator door opened; she stepped in. As she turned to press the button for her floor, she looked back up at him.

He was still watching her.

She heard someone call "Joe" from the hotel entry. He inclined his head toward her and turned away, his strides long and easy.

The elevator door closed.

He stayed on her mind as she headed upstairs, set out her food and tried to eat. No more reading on witch-craft and Satanism.

She watched a Disney show, and then glancing at the bedside alarm clock, she determined that she was full, exhausted, and it finally was a normal time to go to bed.

She cleaned up her meal, decided on another hot shower, dressed in a long, soft cotton nightgown and tried to sleep.

She turned the TV back on, hoping that cartoon she-nanigans might fill her dreams, rather than the memory of the blood-covered woman atop the altar slab.

"I saw the writer," Joe told Dallas.

"Did you talk to her? Did it seem like she was going to be cooperative?" Dallas asked, paying for the bags of food they had ordered and were going to bring to their rooms.

"I have no idea. She was getting into an elevator. You called me out to grab the bags."

"Sorry. You should have gone ahead and spoken to her."

"Can't blame it on you. The elevator door closed."

"We'll find her tomorrow," Dallas said.

It had been one hell of a long day, starting with the crack-of-dawn drive from Krewe headquarters in northern Virginia out to York County, Pennsylvania. And they would be meeting at the crack of dawn again to keep going on the investigation.

"See anyone else around from the group?"

"One woman—Eileen Falcon. I saw her leaving the restaurant just as I was coming in to order. Seems like it was a brown-bag-it night all around."

They headed for the elevators, saying good-night when they reached their floor.

Joe headed for his room and started to set up his computer, but chose instead to open the folders they'd been given.

He turned straight to the information on Keri Wolf.

She was about to turn thirty, had been born in Richmond, Virginia, and still resided there. She'd written seven nonfiction books, each hailed by critics. Her major in college had been mass communication and, according to the bio taken from her books, loved travel all over the world and animals, especially her cat, Salem.

He picked up her picture again; she wasn't just attractive, she was stunning, now that he'd seen her in the flesh.

She'd mentioned something about seeing a woman

in white in the cellar—and then she'd denied her own words. Had she somehow seen the spirit of Beatrice Bergen? There had been a whole group of paranormal "experts" at the inn, but he knew the dead spoke only to whomever they chose.

He kept looking at the picture of Keri Wolf, fascinated and feeling a sort of kinship with her. But no, that couldn't be. They hadn't even met yet.

Keri researched and wrote about facts, seen and experienced by others throughout history. She didn't write about the paranormal. She'd been invited for her expertise in finding out all the little facts and figures and even the innuendos of crimes that hadn't been solved or had been only presumed solved.

He could be wrong, but he didn't think so—she had never before experienced the "unusual" herself. This would be new for her. And unsettling.

As new and unsettling as it had been for him. But he'd had help. He'd been embraced by a group of people who made what was bizarre, normal, even useful.

She was still in denial, and thus, making excuses for what she had seen. But if she did have some kind of ability, she was eventually going to have to admit it to herself.

Maybe he could help her with that. Because somewhere along the line, he was going to need her to tell the truth.

He kept going through the files. He already knew about Carl. Picked up at an early age after a talent show, he'd acted in a sitcom that had become one of the most popular on network television. He'd taken that fame on to several movies, many of which might be considered summer fluff, but he was doing extremely well for his age.

Joe liked Carl; he had liked him when he'd met him in Savannah. He knew that Carl liked and respected him as well.

Joe went on through the files. Brad Holden, communications major at Yale. He'd taken his winning personality and knowledge of film and video in his own direction. After years of working for a cable channel, he'd started his own show, concentrating first on the ghosts of his native New York. He'd gone on to involve his friends—Pete Wright and Eileen Falcon, also from New York, from his college days; Mike Lerner from his job with a cable channel, and pretty, blonde Serena Nelson after he'd met her on a haunted tour in Salem, Massachusetts. Mike was originally from Chicago, and Serena from Charleston. They had all been working together now nearly two years and had garnered a large internet audience.

His eyes were closing, he realized, as he tried to read. Dallas was right; to be useful, they had to have rest.

He closed up the folders and got into bed.

He wasn't one prone to dreams, but that night...

He was walking toward the Miller Inn and Tavern, approaching the front from the forest. The inn and forest were shrouded with mist, and the weak light from the moon and the lights within the inn served to create a macabre image stretched out before him.

He felt a sense of urgency and began to hurry. He called out as he neared the inn but couldn't hear his own words. Wrenching the door open, he entered the tavern, again calling out for anyone. Fear drove him toward the basement. He hurried down the steps.

There was a body on the altar; a woman. He had gone back in time, he thought. The body was that of Beatrice Bergen—it had to be her.

But as he started toward the altar from the cement steps, someone fell into step beside him. He turned; it was the woman in white, Beatrice Bergen.

Then the body on the altar had to be Julie Castro. But Julie had been taken to the morgue, and...

He stepped toward the altar, limbs icy, heart thundering. He was so afraid; afraid that it would be the body of Keri Wolf.

He stepped closer; he had to see, had to...

He woke up, shaking, never seeing who lay on the altar.

It was just after 5:00 a.m.

Joe was so shaken by the dream that he rose, got into the shower, and let the water run cold over him for a few minutes before he turned up the heat. He emerged and dressed for the day, picked up his files and headed downstairs.

He sat down to read and work, grateful that the restaurant would be open soon. He was going to need a hell of a lot of coffee. He turned to the files on Barbara Chrome and Special Agent Julie Castro. As he did so, he saw Dallas come off the elevator. He didn't seem surprised to see Joe.

"Well, we can definitely be off and running today," Dallas said. "You sleep at all?"

"Oh, yeah, no problem. I've always been an early riser."

"Too early for coffee, huh?" Dallas said. "I talked to our agents in Philadelphia. They'll be out here tonight or early tomorrow. So far, they haven't been able to find a soul who can explain how Julie was in Philadelphia and then dead in York County. We may have to take a trip into the city, but my money is on something happening out here."

"Hey, they opened for coffee. I'll grab it," Joe said.

He stood and hurried to the counter. The girl behind it grinned and assured him that she'd opened as quickly as possible, having seen him sitting there. He thanked her and brought two cups back to the table.

"You're my hero," Dallas told him.

Joe was thoughtful. "I hope to prove some kind of worth," he said.

"Hey, you're new. But trust me, half of our best people were new to the gift. Seriously, did you sleep?"

Joe nodded. "I don't usually remember my dreams, but…" He hesitated, then continued, "Last night, I dreamed I was back at the inn. I went to the basement, thinking I'd find Beatrice Bergen. But she was suddenly next to me. And I knew that if I looked at the altar, it wasn't going to be Barbara or even Julie Castro there."

"So, who was it?"

"I don't know. I woke up."

Dallas was quiet for a minute, and then said, "We're going to have to be careful. Very careful."

"Of course, but why would my dream add to that?"

"Hey, who can really understand what goes on, with the dead or within our own minds? But sometimes, the dead have been known to enter our dreams. Maybe because they can't reach us another way at first? I don't know for sure. But dreams… I think that they're something we need to analyze and take seriously. Just maybe, they're a warning. And because of the warning, well, we might just be able to change what is to come."

4

The woman in white was walking toward her.

Keri was back in the basement, standing at the stairs. The corners of the room were almost black, they were in such deep shadow.

At first, she thought that the woman was smiling, but bizarrely, there seemed to be an incredible fog or mist in the basement, and she couldn't really see the woman's expression. She wasn't afraid. The woman had an air about her that was gentle, as if she had been a kind person, quick to like others and to look for the best in life.

But as she neared Keri, everything about her seemed to change. The mist darkened, as if it were a forewarning of a terrible thunderstorm. In her dream, Keri caught her breath; there was an agonizing moment when she knew that everything was going to go wrong.

When she saw the young woman's face again, it was filled with dread and warning.

"Get out, get out, get out... Go!"

The dark corners of the place seemed to grow darker, and become something else, something living and breathing. It was as if the darkness joined with the mist, and skeletal hands were reaching out for her while something of a diabolical whispering laughter filled the space.

She turned to run, run as fast as she could up the stairs.

And the skeletal fingers dug into her...

Keri woke with a start, for a moment still frightened by the dream. She assured herself that she was fine, that she'd had a nightmare.

Something was digging into her shoulder. She rolled and saw that she had fallen asleep on her cell phone.

For a moment, she lay there. She had spent a great deal of the afternoon yesterday in her room. She wanted to get out, but didn't feel up to facing the others on the crew.

Still, she was hungry. Glancing at her phone, she saw that it was late—almost ten o'clock. She tended to be an early riser. Not so here, apparently. At least not today.

She dragged herself out of bed, showered and dressed, and decided that even if she was trying to avoid Brad—it just wasn't right to be so eager to continue a hunt for ghosts when a woman had just been killed—he wasn't a bad guy.

And she'd had enough of her own company.

Heading down, she saw that Carl was in the little restaurant, at a table in the center. He saw her, rose and beckoned to her.

She walked over to him but didn't quite reach him. A fawning waitress hadn't even noticed her and had walked over to see what Carl needed.

He was always courteous to others, and he was explaining that he was being joined as he pointed to Keri. The waitress moved back, smiling for Keri—still a little starry-eyed.

"Coffee, please," Keri told her.

"I've ordered an omelet. Want one? Bacon, cheese, green peppers... Sounds good."

"Sure. I'll have the same, thank you," Keri said.

When the waitress was gone, Carl studied Keri. "Don't get me wrong, you always look beautiful. But you also look a little...frazzled."

"I didn't sleep well."

"Neither did I." He sighed softly. "I spoke to Dallas Wicker and Joe Dunhill last night. They said we can get back into the inn. They also found a specialized cleaning company for me, and I have them booked for a few days from now. I guess we'll have to stay out of the basement until they come. I so hope that they find whoever did this quickly. It's horrible. And I don't know what to do anymore, really. Do I still want to open the place? The thing is, there was so much good history that came before what happened in 1926...and now. Washington really slept there. And Jefferson. It's so rich."

"I'm sure you'll decide well when the time comes," Keri said.

"Do you think he did it?" Carl asked.

"I'm sorry, do I think who did what?" she asked, pausing to thank the waitress who had brought her coffee and promised their omelets would be right up.

"Bergen—the guy who was lynched, Beatrice Bergen's dad."

"I really don't know. I thought I'd have a better shot at figuring out the truth once I'd spent more time with the letters, books and so on that are in the museum room. I can see a man becoming unhinged if he'd discovered that his daughter had been lured by an innkeeper, tortured and killed. I just don't see him going crazy enough to kill everyone else at the inn. Also, no one knew about the torture chamber until after the murders. People were going on the supposition that Hank Bergen had known—he'd been looking for his daughter for days—and that he'd killed everyone, gone back home, and just cleaned up and gone to sleep. Someone in the crowd usually has to spur the group into becoming a lynch mob, so it's possible the real killer was part of the mob and committed the murders for reasons of his own."

"Your thought process is amazing. Well, you will have more time to research, I promise," he told her. "By the way, when we go back to the inn, the FBI doesn't want the whole crew at first. Just you and me."

"I...see." Keri didn't see anything.

"They never found Beatrice Bergen's body, did they?" Carl asked.

"Nope. It is a mystery. It's presumed that Newby buried people nearby. He had a cemetery conveniently close. I do believe that Newby was a horrible human being—jovial innkeeper by day, monster by night. Several young men and women disappeared over the years that Newby owned the inn. When it came to the massacre, though, I just don't think that it was a bereaved father. The whole thing was slapdash—no real investigation was done because it was assumed that Bergen did the killings. Like I said, I have a problem believing that. He would have wanted to kill Newby, but why anyone else?"

"Witnesses?" Carl asked.

Their meals arrived, and Keri waited for the waitress to leave before speaking again. "A brokenhearted father would want revenge. I just don't think he'd care what happened to him once he'd had his revenge. He'd rather be hanged than live without his daughter, so I don't think he'd care if there were witnesses. This is just my opinion. Nothing factual."

"But I kind of agree," Carl said. "What you're saying makes sense. What happened to the lynch mob?"

Keri laughed. "The group banded together and gave one another alibis. They were all from the surrounding area. I'm sure they thought they were doing the right thing. Unless, of course, as I suggested, the killer was one of the people who roused the others and put them on a path of righteousness."

"So, the real killer was probably a local farmer. Someone living among the others. But does someone who does something like that stop killing?"

"It would depend on the real motive."

"You mean, if it was an insane ax serial killer, he'd have to keep going."

"I'm not a profiler, but as far as I've heard, killers like that keep killing. Unless they're caught and executed or locked up, or unless they move on elsewhere."

"What about the Satanism?"

"Here's the thing. If you want to worship Satan, hey,

it's your right in this country to worship as you please. When John Blymire and company killed Nelson Rehmeyer in 1928, Blymire went to prison. Not for witchcraft but for murder. Newby wouldn't have gone to prison for being either a witch or a Satanist—he was committing murder. Maybe someone else in the area was a Satanist and either wanted Newby out of the way for giving all Satanists a bad name should he be discovered or because, as a Satanist himself, he wanted to offer up a massive sacrifice. The witchcraft in the area is famous. Not Satanism."

"But—" Carl stopped, looked up and inhaled sharply.

"There you are," Brad Holden said, making his way through the tables to join them. "Carl, have you heard anything yet?"

"No, not really," Carl said. "I know there are FBI agents who have been investigating in Philadelphia, I know that Dallas and Joe are questioning people and might have some leads, but that's about it."

Brad looked at Keri. "And you. You disappeared most of yesterday."

"I was here. I guess we just kept missing each other," Keri murmured.

"Did you sleep okay?" Brad asked.

"Is any of us sleeping okay?" she asked.

"We are in a very tough situation," Brad agreed.

"And I'm so sorry," Carl said.

"Hey, not your fault," Brad assured him. He turned to Keri and plunged in with, "I'd love to either hypnotize you or do a memory session. We sit, and you close your eyes, and then go back, step by step, over everything that happened. You don't just remember what you saw—you think about textures, about smells, about everything that has to do with the senses. You might remember the woman in white."

Carl's phone started to buzz, and he excused himself, standing to walk to the front of the café to answer it.

"Brad," Keri began, "I've been over it, and I'm going to have to go over it again. We haven't even met two of the agents working the case yet. Please—"

"Keri, it's painless, I promise you. There's something there. Something in what you saw. If you'd only accept that it might be something, then we could—"

"Keri, I need you." Carl came striding back to the table, anxious. He had money out and set it on the table. "Excuse us, Brad. Please. We have to go."

He reached for Keri's hand. She rose gratefully, and yet she couldn't just walk out. "Carl, I can pay for my own food—"

"Keri, please, I work for a living. I can pay for two omelets."

"But Carl, wait… What's happening?" Brad demanded.

"We'll talk later, Brad. Keri, please, if you don't mind."

She followed him out of the café to the entrance to the hotel, thinking that he had once again come up with a ruse to rescue her.

But that wasn't it this time.

A large black SUV was waiting outside; Carl opened the back door and ushered her in.

She was glad she had come to know and trust Carl, otherwise she might have worried about simply sliding into an unknown car. Even then, if she'd just had a moment to think… But it all happened so quickly.

Carl spoke up. "Special Agent Dallas Wicker is doing the driving, and that's Joe Dunhill, ex-best-cop-ever. Joe, Dallas—Keri Wolf."

She could see that the man driving was blond; the man next to him had brown hair. Both glanced back at her in friendly but brief greeting.

She recognized the dark-haired man from the night before: Joe Dunhill.

Something about that seemed a little unnerving. He had been about to talk to her. He had apparently known who she was. And now here he was, looking at her as if he had already assessed everything about her, even her mind.

Ridiculous. She could stare back and assess them, too.

She estimated the men to be in their early thirties; good faces, with a certain look about them… She thought of it as a law enforcement look. It wasn't that they seemed hard, just…determined?

"How do you do?" Keri said.

"Hi, Keri," Dallas said, his eyes on the road.

She'd wondered if the car was going to speed off as if they were in a movie. But Dallas drove smoothly out of the circular driveway.

"Where are we going?" she asked.

"Back to the inn. The forensic team has finished there. They went over the entire place," Dallas told her.

It wasn't that she didn't want to help. Just… All she

wanted to do was roll back time, and never see the corpse of the poor, brutalized woman.

Keri glanced at Carl. "I think that Brad Holden is the one really anxious to get back in," she said.

"Yes," Dallas said. "I believe he is anxious."

"He will be soon, I suppose. You've released the inn back to Carl, so he'll be able to invite whoever he wants, right?" Keri asked, looking at Carl.

Joe turned slightly. "Yes, but he's most likely going to want to bring in a cleaning crew that specializes in crime scenes. The basement is…"

"Bloody," Keri said flatly. She was concerned and looked at Carl. "Okay, so why is it that you just have me coming back with you?"

"Because we're operating under the assumption that you're innocent," Dallas said.

She should have been relieved. She found that she was a bit resentful.

She frowned at Carl. He didn't notice.

"I'm sorry," she protested. "I just don't see what I can tell you that I haven't already told people over and over again."

Joe looked at her. "You're a historian, right?"

"I don't consider myself a historian. I look into historical crimes, but that doesn't mean that I know anything beyond what I'm doing my research on. I mean, a bit of context of the era is necessary…"

Joe smiled grimly. "You were researching the Miller Inn and Tavern, right?"

"Well, yes, of course—"

"You're what we need then," Joe said.

"You just said I'm presumed innocent," Keri snapped. "But am I under arrest here or something?" She was tired. She'd slept, but she'd had that dream... That nightmare.

Dallas glanced at her through the rearview mirror. "We're asking for your help," he said.

"Please," Carl added softly.

She fell silent and soon they rolled up into the driveway at the Miller Inn and Tavern. She was out of the car before anyone could open the door for her. Joe stood by the rear passenger door; he'd been going to open it, she knew.

She looked up at him.

He was tall. He had broad shoulders and a smooth lean build that, she imagined, could be deceptive. She had a feeling he was pure muscle. His hair was brown, the cut just a little long, but his eyes were what impressed her most—they were a clear, cool, unusual silvery gray. The way he looked at her was not appreciative of her manner.

She was resentful, she realized, because she was afraid.

She wished that she hadn't barked at him so sharply. She almost apologized, but he turned away from her silently.

She followed him up the few steps to the broad Colonial front porch. She almost jumped when Carl set an arm on her shoulders. It was just a comforting arm, and Carl was truly a decent young man. She just wished he hadn't chosen her to come along for this first trip back.

He stepped ahead of her to open the door and they all

walked into the tavern. The bar area stretched to their left. Ahead and to the right were the stairs that led up to the rooms—and the door that led down to the basement.

"So, I'm going to need a specialized cleaning crew now that they're done in the basement," Carl said. "I mean, I've already seen an architect about maintaining the integrity of the place while doing some updating... and the basement was last, anyway, but of course, the blood... There's a lot of it, right?"

Keri remembered that Carl had never been in the basement; he and the others had realized that they had to get the hell out.

She didn't have to answer. Joe said bluntly, "There's a lot of blood."

"That's so confusing," Carl said.

They all looked at him.

"I mean, I am just an actor, and what I know about any of this is from crime shows. But if the victim was killed before she was brought in, wouldn't the blood be at the crime site?"

"We believe," Dallas said, "that when she was killed, the murderer collected her blood and distributed it here."

"No one knows where she was killed?" Carl asked.

"Not yet," Dallas said. "But we will find the place."

Keri leaned against one of the tavern tables. She noticed that the monitors remained, but that Mike's computer that received the camera feeds had been taken away.

"There's a secondary crime scene somewhere," Joe said.

Keri frowned. "Wouldn't that be the first crime scene? Where she was killed?" she added.

"Goes by what is discovered first," Joe explained.

"Keri, could you describe for us what happened when you went down to the basement?" Dallas asked gently.

Again. She'd gone through this at the police station.

"Please," Joe said. "Starting from earlier in the day."

"Okay," Keri said. She took a deep breath.

"I arrived early afternoon. Brad wanted to start right off with a live internet feed, so we did. He talked first, then I talked about the history—"

"And then I talked about why I bought the place," Carl said, nodding his head.

"After that, everyone did different things. The crew was going to set up cameras, and Mike was supposed to be watching the screens. I went into the little museum room—there—and I admit to becoming immersed in all the resources available there."

"And where were you?" Dallas asked Carl.

"I went upstairs with Brad to room 207. It's one of the most haunted rooms—a couple was murdered there. Everyone in the inn was murdered that night but reports of the paranormal are heaviest from room 207. That was the room we chose for the crew's general meeting place... We had cameras in there, too."

"Brad was with you the entire time?" Joe asked him.

"Yes—no. I was watching one of their thingamajigs," Carl said. "Some kind of a sensor. It's important not to keep it by a phone or an electrical outlet, because that will cause it to react when there is nothing there. So, I had it on the table there when Brad went out to see that the others had the cameras all set up. A little bit later, we were all up in the room, talking about what

Keri might be able to discover when she went through all the research."

"Okay," Joe said. "But, Carl, there was a time when you were all alone up in room 207."

"Yes, but—I don't know how anyone in the inn could have left, killed a woman and dragged her into the basement. There were cameras everywhere."

"There are a lot of blanks—places where the cameras apparently stopped working and just showed gray static. Police techs have been going through it all night," Dallas said. "Of course, I know that the police have been hard on Mike Lerner—he oversaw the cameras. But he swears he didn't turn off the basement camera or mess with the others. The camera in the basement went out soon after it was turned on. Footage from other places in the inn have skips in them. Mike swears up and down that he wasn't responsible."

"You're certain you were alone in the inn?" Joe asked. He looked from Carl to Keri. They looked at one another.

"We did lock the front door," Carl said.

"But you haven't had the locks changed since you officially took possession of the inn," Joe said.

"No. I wanted to let the Truth Seekers have a chance to come in before I started with renovations and stuff," Carl said.

"Have you spoken with Mike since the night at the police station?" Joe asked.

Again, Carl and Keri looked at one another, frowning.

"I've only seen Brad and Eileen," Keri said. "Brad

just wants to get back here and keep working, and Eileen still seems a little scared."

"I've seen Mike. He's pretty bummed. Said the police grilled him really hard," Carl said. "He's upset and confused. He is the camera guy, but the cameras are simple—I figure anyone could turn them on and off. You'd think someone would be seen in the video, though. I've seen everyone since that night—Brad, Mike, Pete, Serena and Eileen. They're all nervous and anxious, and we want to be at the inn, but we're a little afraid of it. They love ghosts. They're not so good with living killers. Then again, who isn't scared of a living killer?"

Keri took his hand and squeezed it.

Joe turned to look at Keri. "You were downstairs the entire time. You didn't see anyone else—anyone come and go?"

"I was in the museum. No one came to see me, and I didn't hear anyone, not even a door open. When I realized that I was hungry, I came back out to the bar area, but Mike wasn't in front of the screens."

"I think he was upstairs then," Carl said.

"You were looking for the others, but you wound up in the basement?" Joe asked Keri.

She took a deep breath. Those silvery eyes of his made him look like a werewolf. She was supposedly presumed innocent. If so, why was he looking at her that way?

"I was going to head up the stairs," she said. "But I heard something—a sound—as if someone was distressed, and it was coming from the basement."

"You heard something weird in the basement, and you just went down?" Joe Dunhill asked.

"It sounded as if someone was in trouble or pain—and yes, I went to see if they needed help," Keri said.

"You weren't afraid?" Joe asked.

"It didn't occur to me at the time that I needed to be afraid," she said, her aggravation with him growing.

He seemed oblivious to her tone. "And then?"

She realized that this was an important point to them, and she felt again as if she was being accused of something, even though they'd said she was presumed innocent.

"Then, I went down the stairs—not all the way. I found Eileen on the steps, and she was hurt. Then I noticed the corpse, and we ran back up and out."

"You said there was a woman in the basement. Eileen didn't see her, but you thought you saw another woman down there," Carl added in a helpful tone.

She inhaled sharply, wishing that she had never spoken, that she had grabbed Eileen and run out as quickly as possible.

But she had seen her, the woman in the long white dress, and she had seen the sadness, the tragedy in her eyes, and she hadn't wanted to leave her.

And now she was dreaming about her.

"You know what, guys?" she said. Screw titles for the lawmen, special agents, or whatever title they might bear, "I was terrified. Absolutely terrified. I don't remember. All I remember is that I wanted to get out. I wanted to help Eileen, get out, reach the cops and the others. I'm sorry. I can't tell you anything else."

Despite the fact that they had seemed to expect something more of her, Keri was still stunned when Joe asked his next question.

"Why are you lying?"

Fury ripped through her.

"I am not lying!" she told him adamantly. "That's what happened. What is the matter with you people? I know that the woman killed was an FBI agent. They have it all over the news. Why aren't you out there looking for the truth? Carl has been used, this place has been used, all of us have been used! Dammit, ease up on us and start looking for the real criminal out there, whoever it is who wanted to get rid of an FBI agent!"

5

"Well, that didn't go so well," Dallas told Joe dryly. He raised a brow as if to question Joe's manner with their witness.

"Sorry. Miss Wolf is lying," Joe said, shrugging.

He could see Keri Wolf as he spoke; she was standing at the back window of the Miller Inn and Tavern, watching as Joe and Dallas explored the land that stretched behind the structure. To the left of the back of the inn, there was a rolling expanse of overgrown lawn, and in the distance, the remnants of a small church and the burial ground surrounding it. To the right, nothing but a bit of meadow and then forest.

Dallas didn't believe that the killer had simply driven up to the inn with the corpse in his trunk, which was the theory Catrina Billings seemed to embrace.

Joe didn't believe that the body had been driven to the inn at all. It seemed unlikely that no one would have seen or heard an unfamiliar vehicle arriving. He believed that Julie Castro had been killed in the surrounding area and then transported into the cellar.

It was too bad that the crew hadn't set up any video cameras on the exterior of the property.

Keri stood at the window alone; Carl had remained inside, on the phone with someone.

Joe studied her with interest. She was a very attractive young woman. He hadn't realized it at first, but he did recognize her name, and then seeing her, he'd recognized her face. She appeared on crime documentaries and news programs now and then, when the focus of a show was a long-ago crime she had researched and written about.

Her face was slim, cheekbones high, eyes large, a bright green that enhanced the darkness of her hair, cut in a feathery style with layers that seemed to sweep around her face in casual abandon that was incredibly natural—and sensual.

"Beautiful woman," he said. "Too bad she's such a…witch."

"You were a cop a long time. You just about skyrocketed your way through the ranks," Dallas told him, looking back at Keri as well. "In all that time, you never learned the art of finesse?"

Dallas wasn't angry. His question was just dry. Almost amused. Joe wasn't sure why his friend was taking his mistake so well. He hadn't intended to, but Joe had pretty much shut down the one person who might give them a bit of a deeper insight into Julie's murder.

"She's lying," Joe repeated.

"Yes, but we need to coax whatever it is out of her. In time."

"Time, my friend, is always of the essence," Joe said.

"The first twenty-four hours mean so much. So, who was the woman in white? The woman Keri told Eileen about and even admitted she *thought* she saw while talking to the police?" he asked, shaking his head. "Now she's denying she saw anyone else down there."

Dallas shrugged. "Keri did have a point. We have to find out just what Julie Castro was working on. Jackson should have a more detailed report soon. What we do know is that Castro was from the New York City office, and she and her partner, Ed Newel, were on the case of a kidnap victim, a young woman named Barbara Chrome. You read the files, right? Barbara Chrome went to a private school in the Upper East Side—her father is a venture capitalist and the family is very wealthy. Friends saw a rusty old van go by, the sliding door opened, and Barbara was whisked into the van.

"The friends couldn't say if she'd been kidnapped or if she'd gone willingly. The family waited for a ransom demand and none came. There was one mysterious call to the Chrome household from a landline—an independent clothing store in the heart of the city. Someone whispered something about Barbara still being alive, and so Julie and Ed came down to Philly. Ed was hit by a car when he was chasing after Julie, who thought she saw a girl who looked like Barbara. Ed is still in the hospital. Julie was with him at first, but then she got a phone call and told him that she'd be back—and then all contact was broken. New York and Philadelphia agents are trying to find out what happened after that."

Joe hunkered down, inspecting a fleck of color on a blade of grass. "I read the file. Julie's cell phone hasn't been found, but techs are tracing her last calls," he said. "But while we may not know yet where she ran off to, we do know where she ended."

"Two agents from the New York City office, Jared Cabot and Dot Harrington, are down here working with the locals," Dallas said. "As Detective Billings told us so nicely, they were out at the Miller Inn and Tavern earlier. They're supposed to be reporting to me, and I don't think they like it, either. I understand. Julie Castro was a New York City agent, and this is brutal to her coworkers. Cabot and Harrington came out here earlier, while we were still being briefed, and they've gone back to Philadelphia to work on the phone call angle and try to find out where Julie went when she left the hospital."

"So, NYC agents already came down to the cellar and inspected the inn," Joe mused. "But they haven't spoken with the Truth Seekers or Carl or Keri?"

Dallas nodded. He glanced at Joe. "They came out and searched the inn along with the police once they learned that the victim was one of their own. They only beat us out here by a matter of hours, but the group from the inn had already been sent to the new hotel after a whole night of questioning. Maybe that's why Detective Billings was so...uncordial? Is that a word? Anyway, I don't think that Detective Billings and the first group got along so well, but it doesn't really matter. She's the local lead on the case, and she'll work with us."

"Dallas," Joe said.

"Yeah?"

"There's blood here, on a blade of grass."

Dallas hunkered down by him, pulling an evidence

bag from the pocket of his jacket. He looked to the back of the inn—and the hatch door that led to the cellar. He scanned the tiny church and graveyard and then the forest.

"In there... Somewhere in the trees?" he asked.

"Or by the chapel?" Joe asked.

"I'll head for the trees, you take the graveyard," Dallas said.

"I'm willing to bet we'll find that a tomb slab made for a butcher block," Joe said.

He started for the graveyard with its broken stones and lichen-covered tombs while Dallas headed off in the other direction. No wall surrounded the old burial ground anymore. What had once been a stone enclosure was now spotty and low in places at best.

As he walked, Joe studied the ground. He hunkered down again, certain that he saw another spot of blood.

Yes.

A drop of blood.

It seemed odd, almost unlikely, that these tiny drops had fallen when there had been so much blood. The victim had been already dead, possibly wrapped in a tarp or something that would have kept her from dripping from her many wounds, but these droplets may well have snuck out while the body was being moved. Or the killer might have cut himself in his savage attack. It might be his blood.

Joe dug in his pocket for an evidence bag. They might get incredibly lucky. He doubted it, but—

"Mr. Dunhill!"

He turned. Keri was running toward him, soft wings of hair sweeping around her face.

He rose, waiting. She slowed to a stop a foot from him. Her cheeks were flushed, and she suddenly appeared to be awkward.

"Um, what are you doing? Agent Wicker has disappeared into the woods, and…"

She hadn't wanted to stay where she was in the back of the inn, alone, he realized. He couldn't lie to her.

"Looking for the place where Julie Castro was killed," he said softly.

"But I thought… I mean, it seemed that the police thought…that she was killed somewhere away from here and then brought to the cellar."

He nodded. "She was brought to the cellar. We just think that the place she was killed was near. It's not so easy to transport a body, and no one has reported hearing or seeing any extra vehicles near the inn."

"Oh." She looked back toward the inn.

"Maybe you should go back inside with Carl," he suggested.

"I'm all right here," she said.

Great. It was fine for her to be with him—as long as he was a barrier between her and a possible killer lurking in the woods.

"I don't know what I'm going to find," he told her, hoping she understood that he might find something she didn't want to see.

"I already saw that poor woman's brutalized body," she said. "I'm sure I'm all right with—with whatever you find."

"All right," he told her. "If I tell you to stop, stop. If I tell you not to walk somewhere, don't walk there. You understand."

"Perfectly," she told him.

He felt her as she trailed along behind him, silent, cautious.

He stepped over a piece of the old, broken stone wall, entering the burial grounds.

"Careful," he told her.

"Thank you. I see the stones."

The church and the burial grounds were sad and desolate. There were no windows in the church anymore. They'd been broken years ago, he imagined, and time and nature had taken their toll. Vines crawled up around the broken windows. Aboveground tombs were interspersed with broken headstones and the occasional angel—one missing a head, another with broken wings.

Day was turning to dusk, and a soft crimson color was spreading through the sky. It didn't seem to add eeriness to the area so much as sadness.

The Miller Inn and Tavern stood far from the highway; once, Joe thought, there had been farms all around the area, and the little church had beckoned to the population. Now, the large churches in the towns and cities of York welcomed Sunday worshippers.

And it seemed the long dead who rested in the graveyard had been as forgotten as the church.

"Pity," she murmured behind him.

"What's that?" he asked, pausing.

"Look at that broken stone. You can still just read the date of death—1822. And see that big insignia left there? He was a Patriot—a Revolutionary soldier. I hope that someone designates this soon as a place that should be on a historic register. Our Patriots should be remembered," she said.

"Maybe talk to your friend Carl. He could probably do something," Joe told her.

"Maybe he could."

She seemed to forget that they were tracing clues to a murder and stepped ahead of him, walking toward the abandoned church.

"The building looks as if it is actually sound. I imagine that the church was deconsecrated long ago, but as a museum, it could be restored."

"I imagine so," he agreed, drawing out his flashlight to better search the gravelly earth, tufted here and there with weeds.

She stepped into the church. He followed with his light.

The pews were gone. Plaques on the walls honored those buried beneath the old stone floor. He shined his light down the length of what would have been the aisle. The altar remained.

Keri gasped.

Joe saw the dried red-brown spray on the altar, and he knew that they had found their secondary crime scene.

Julie Castro had been killed there. Not far from the Miller Inn and Tavern.

Not far at all.

Keri sat in one of the old, heavy wooden chairs in the tavern of the old inn, across the table from Carl.

Joe, Dallas, Detective Billings, more police and more agents were working with a forensic team again out at the old church and graveyard.

Keri didn't know why she was still there. She wanted to go back to the new hotel where everything was shiny and there was even a placard—meant to be amusing, in an area that bordered upon Pennsylvania Dutch land—that no ghosts of any kind lurked in the halls or rooms.

She was convinced now that she hadn't seen a ghost; she'd experienced a terror so real that it had caused a hallucination. These people seemed to want to make her talk about her imagination in the midst of a horrendous murder investigation.

She was not going to do it.

"I'm an actor. I *should* know," Carl said suddenly. "But I don't. Plethora—a plethora of law enforcement is just feet away. Just how is that said properly? Plee-thora? Or pleth-ora?"

"I believe it's pleth-ora. The English language adapted it from the Greek back in the 1500s, if I remember correctly. It means abundance, excess, or I think it can also signify a physical condition with an excess of blood causing a florid complexion."

"An excess of blood," Carl said, shaking his head. "I accidentally nailed it on that one." He looked at her with wide eyes and said, "You're really being a good friend. I mean, you're doing all this for me and, well, I was kind of a jerk when we met."

"You were?"

He laughed. "I thought we'd have an affair. I mean,

usually, women kind of fall for me. I just assumed… But you didn't even realize I was giving you lines."

She smiled at him across the table. "I guess I was oblivious. This whole thing seemed a little crazy to me. But hey, I sell books for a living, in a weird niche market. Still, you seemed like an honestly nice guy—"

"I am," he assured her. "But you don't want to date me."

She didn't answer that, but went on with, "The Truth Seekers looked pretty legit, too. Anyway, now here we are—waiting for your agent friends to finish with the *plethora* of law enforcement going over a crime scene." She hesitated and said, "I guess I'm kind of surprised that we're back here already."

He shrugged. "There was a shoot-out in an LA bank once. They had it opened again for business the next morning. Cops and forensics get what they want and leave the cleanup to the owners. Other places, maybe they close for a day or two, depending on the crime, but if you're a business, I guess people try to move on as quickly as possible. Anyway, I don't even know how I feel. I do want to let the Truth Seekers back in here, and…" He hesitated again, then leaned toward her, hands folded. "I'd still like you to see if you can find anything that might lead to the real killer from 1926."

"How will that help now?" she asked softly. "We know that someone came in and killed the guests in their beds and John Newby behind the bar. It was assumed that Hank Bergen did it. He was seen near the property that night. He might have done it."

"I don't believe it and you don't believe it," Carl said. "And…"

"And what?"

"It just might matter." He took a deep breath. "I'm sure you had to have seen something about the case in Savannah. Here's why I wanted Dallas and Joe involved so badly—Joe was one hell of a detective. All these things were happening…accidents or maybe suicide. Joe knew that wasn't right, but that's how it was going down officially. He wouldn't accept it. He went to the head of Dallas's specialized unit. And they found the truth and saved some lives, and in a bizarre way, it all related back to something that happened over a hundred years ago. They're the best, Keri. I mean, the FBI would have come in on it anyway, but I can't tell you how good it is that Dallas's unit is involved. They're who we need on this. Both of them are great people."

"I'm sure," she said.

"Okay, okay. I just think it's more important than ever that we solve the mystery of the past and now the present. I'm not as shallow as most people seem to think you have to be if you're a young blond man gifted with decent looks and the ability to read a script."

"Carl," Keri said, feeling that she had to interrupt there. "You're a very good actor, and honestly, I don't think people just assume that you're shallow."

"I've been lucky," he said. "But the public can be fickle, which is why it's important to stay in the public eye. I really did fall in love with this inn. The building is protected, but it might not have been maintained as an incredible piece of Americana for the public to visit unless someone dedicated to preservation bought it. It was important to me. I was inspired by the old bed-and-breakfast where my interest in the paranormal began with a séance. And I love Americana, and this was real for me. I wanted to make a go of it."

"You don't want to do that anymore?"

"I do. I do. That's the point. When I started this whole thing, I wanted to know the truth about the past. Now, I can't go any further until we know what happened here."

"I understand."

Carl's phone rang. It seemed like it was always going off. He excused himself and rose and answered it. Keri stood and stretched and then moved behind the bar.

That was where John Newby had been axed down by his attacker. A man who had, perhaps, deserved what had happened to him, considering the deaths he had brought about in his torture chamber.

But what of the others—his innocent guests?

What if they hadn't been so innocent?

"I'm so sorry," Carl said. "My people. They're very hands-on, which has been great for my career, but right now, I need to be away from them." He grinned. "I had to talk all night to assure my parents that I was doing all right, and they didn't need to come out."

They both sat again.

"How old are you?" Keri asked. She winced slightly. "I know I should have read it on a magazine cover, but…"

He laughed. "Don't worry. A good majority of the world has no idea of who I am or what I do."

"I'm sure I have a much larger percentage of the world on that," Keri told him.

"Twenty-three. And you?"

"Twenty-nine. I talked to my mom last night, too. I played it all down and made it seem like our poor victim had been taken for being FBI—which is probably the case—and that I was surrounded by cops. Which, at this moment, is pretty true."

"Parents never stop being parents. That's a cool thing. You're twenty-nine. And you've done so much."

She shook her head. "I got lucky. History fascinates me, and I hate books where authors are sure they've found an answer when there's still no solid proof. You can put a theory out there and support it, but sometimes, you just can't prove what happened years and years ago."

The front door to the tavern suddenly swung open. Keri couldn't help it; she jumped.

She and Carl both looked up.

Joe Dunhill was back. For a moment, he stood as a silhouette, tall and imposing there in the doorway. She realized that it was night; the world outside had gone dark again.

Joe walked in and took a seat at the table, looking at them both, and they both waited for him to speak.

"Well, it appears that Julie Castro was killed in the abandoned and deconsecrated church. Now, the trick will be finding out how and when she got there, and why the killers wanted her to be found down in the cellar."

"Killers?" Carl said.

Joe nodded gravely, silver eyes catching the lights

of the tavern, probing as he looked at the two of them. "That leaves several questions. Why did the killers want her found here? To ruin your reputation, Carl, or ruin the possibility of you making this a popular destination for history-seeking tourists? Or is there some significance to the church and to the cellar here?"

"You think that a cult may be at work?" Keri asked. "Like Newby's in the past?"

"At the moment, it's too early to think anything. But the history of a place can inform its present. While you have a local population of good, hardworking people, you also have the story of John Newby. A person suspected by his neighbors of being a witch but not known to have been a practicing Satanist as well."

"Do you know anything about that old church, Keri?" Carl asked.

"No. But I'm assuming there are records regarding it and that they can be found. I think that the church and graveyard were abandoned a long time ago— before the twentieth century," Keri said. She realized that Joe Dunhill was staring at her. "I did a lot of research on the tavern before coming here for Carl's event, but I have to admit, I didn't know anything about the church. This area was remote for a very long time. Most people—farmers out here—would have traveled on Sunday to get to church. Pastors and priests have to live—a community has to be able to support their wages. When this little spot could no longer support a leader and a congregation, it must have been deconsecrated. I can find out, of course."

"That's what we're hoping," Joe told her.

She quickly glanced over at Carl.

"Keri?" Carl asked softly.

"I already told you that I'd stay," Keri said.

"And the Truth Seekers?" Joe asked Carl.

"They want to be involved more than ever now," Carl said.

Joe was thoughtful for a minute, his fingers drumming on the table where they sat. "Carl, what if they are involved?"

Carl frowned. "You don't think that they conspired to murder this woman—Julie Castro? I don't see how. I was with them most of the time..."

His voice trailed. The church wasn't that far from the inn. It wouldn't have taken much time for someone to have slipped out and brought a body back, coming down to the basement through the cellar entrance.

"I will be open to all possibilities," Joe said. "And you," he went on, staring at Keri. "You need to be honest."

She was instantly defensive. "I have been honest."

"Not entirely. You told other people that you saw a woman in the basement. You refused to mention her to Dallas and me."

She shook her head. "Because, obviously, I didn't really see anyone. I saw what remained of Julie Castro, and... I'd just been in the museum, reading that the room had been Newby's torture chamber... Please remember, I write about very old crimes. I'm not a cop, and what I saw terrified me to no end. I might have seen anything then. Rays of light, buckets of blood. I'm not lying. I don't know what I saw."

"A woman in white," Joe said.

Keri shrugged, acutely uncomfortable. She wished that she hadn't promised Carl that she would stay. There was something about Joe Dunhill. She had just met him; she wanted to get away from him.

Yet she found herself watching him, fascinated. His eyes were such an unusual color, and his hands drew her attention as he drummed his fingers on the table. Long fingers, clean-cut nails and large hands. He was very tall.

And she didn't know why she was thinking about his anatomy in any way.

"Honestly, and I swear this to be true," she said. "I don't know what I saw."

He studied her for a long moment. "Okay," he said at last, and then he leaned toward her. "But anything you see, or think you see, may be important in the future."

"Do you think that there *was* someone down there?" she asked curiously. "Okay, when I thought I saw a woman, she wasn't covered in blood. She was…pristine. You say *killers*—do you think that she was part of a group?"

"At this moment, anything is possible," Joe said.

"I just can't believe that. I mean, the Truth Seekers?" Carl shook his head. "They can't be involved. I mean, we were all here. Yes, we were in various places, but still, I can't believe it. Not Brad, surely. He's so passionate about ghosts. If he were a killer, wouldn't he be afraid that a ghost might come back and kill him?"

"I have no idea what goes on in Brad's mind. We'll be questioning everyone who had anything to do with any of this, one by one. Anyway, Carl, I'd like to get us all back to the hotel for tonight, and then possibly come back here to stay tomorrow," Joe said.

"Stay overnight you mean?" Carl asked.

"Exactly," Joe told him. "Dallas and I will want to start staying out here, anyway. To be honest, I'd be happier knowing that you two were safe."

"Wouldn't that mean staying at a nice new hotel with really good locks and cameras in the lobby and elevators?" Keri asked dryly.

"You'll be welcome to do so," Joe told her. "But, I seriously believe that we'll find some answers here and that you're safest with Dallas and me. We might have a few more Krewe members come up, depending on how the investigation goes. For tonight, if you're ready, we'll head back."

"More than ready," Keri said. But as she stood, ready to head out, she couldn't help but turn to Carl. "May I take a book out of the little museum room?"

"Of course," he told her. He smiled. "You can do anything you want, you know that."

She realized the way that he spoke, he made it unintentionally sound as if they were a couple. She let it go.

"There's a book in there that was published right after the Civil War. It's about the area and the people, and I think I can find mention of the church in it."

"Finding out about the church might be important," Joe said. He paused a moment, looking at her. "Thank you," he added.

She nodded and hurried back into the museum room. She found the book in the low bookshelves beneath several pictures hung on the walls. As she picked up the book, she found herself studying a picture with a caption that read, *The Front of the Miller Inn and Tavern, circa 1918, Fourth of July Celebration.*

The inn hadn't changed at all. Same tall Colonial columns and little step-up porch to the front door. Move aside the people in their period dress, and the picture might have been taken today.

The people drew her attention. She'd seen a few pictures of John Newby and recognized him right away. There were at least twenty people in the picture, men in handsome, tailored vests and jackets, several in pinstriped suits. The women were in short dresses and long dresses, in snug little hats, and…

She paused, feeling as if an icicle had broken off from somewhere and slithered down her throat and right into her stomach.

There she was.

The woman in white. A soft white summer dress, capped sleeves and a high-waisted bodice. She was arm in arm with an older, bearded man.

Her father?

Keri recognized him, too. The lynched killer, Hank Bergen. Which, of course, made the woman in white Beatrice Bergen, tortured and killed in the cellar beneath Keri's feet…

Couldn't be. The killers were playing tricks. They were part of some sick group, and part of their game was to have someone who looked like a long-ago victim stand next to Julie's body when she was discovered.

Maybe it was even meant to say, *Look, it's all happening again*.

"Keri?"

Carl was calling her. She took a second to breathe. Then, she grabbed up the book, wondering if she should mention the photo, or...

Honesty. She had promised honesty.

She'd known, really. She'd known all along she'd seen Beatrice. Or she'd suspected at the very least. Her dreams had been honest, even if she didn't want to admit the truth herself.

Well, she would give them all honesty now. As soon as she convinced herself she hadn't completely lost her mind.

6

"We were horrified, of course. I mean, anyone would be horrified, right? To hear what had happened, and we'd been there—there at the tavern!—just hours before!"

Milly Kendall, caterer, was about five-five, with red hair wound into a bun and covered with a hairnet. Her husband, Rod, was a medium-sized man with red hair as well. He was freckled and a little bit portly—maybe a living, breathing advertisement for the taste of their food. He stood at his wife's back, hands on her shoulders, at the butcher block in the middle of their kitchen. Their business was in their home, and the kitchen had been nicely revamped to allow for the business.

Joe and Dallas had dropped Keri and Carl at the hotel before heading out to meet with Milly and Rod Kendall and their partner, Stan Gleason. They'd called ahead and arranged the meeting.

"We heard she was an FBI agent," Stan Gleason said. He, too, was behind the butcher-block table, facing Dallas and Joe across it.

They'd been working on fruit-filled pastries, but Milly had assured them that they were all right to speak for a few minutes.

Dallas nodded. "Yes, she was an agent." He produced a picture of Julie Castro from a file he was carrying. "Did you ever see her in the area?" he asked.

The three of them studied the picture and then looked up and shook their heads with grave expressions.

"This area is so small. If she'd been around, we should have run into her," Stan said.

"Maybe not," Rod argued. "There's the highway. People are on and off that highway by the new hotel all the time."

"Is that how you sustain your business?" Joe asked. "Sorry, not inferring anything, but in an area this small, how do you make any money? The new hotel has a restaurant, and right off the highway there are several restaurants and gas stations."

"We do all right. We work through the new hotel sometimes," Milly said.

"And we do one of those prepare-your-own meals kind of things—Make It Easy on Yourself," Stan said. "We deliver ingredients to put together meals that take less than twenty minutes. They're big these days, you know. People tired after work, don't want to have to shop and then cook, but then, they're really too tired to go out at night, so…it's a good business."

"You also catered to the Miller Inn and Tavern for Carl Brentwood," Dallas said.

Milly nodded.

"We went over, set up the food in the kitchen—" Stan began.

"We didn't cook anything," Milly said, interrupting. "We just delivered. All kinds of casual stuff. Peanut butter and bread, eggs, bacon—"

"Turkey and salami for sandwiches, and some premade pasta dishes. Casual things that they could nuke in a minute or two, or just throw together," Rod told them. He was still holding his wife's shoulders, looking shell-shocked.

"Did you see anyone else in the vicinity when you were there? Cars, people at the abandoned church, tourists in the graveyard?" Joe asked.

The three of them shook their heads.

"No, it was just dead out there," Rod said, and then winced. "I'm sorry. Wow. That sounded terrible, under the circumstances. But no. We were talking about the fact that there is so little there. I mean, once, the inn was the only place to stay for a weary traveler. People had food and spent the night and went on. I just wonder how well it will go when Carl Brentwood tries to make a go of it. You have to leave the highway and come some ways out. And then, you have to be in love with the inn and the graveyard to stay."

"You could do day trips out to a lot of places," Milly suggested.

"You head to Gettysburg, you're going to want to stay out there," Rod said.

"Philadelphia, you'd stay in Philadelphia," Stan put in.

"But you can drive through beautiful country here," Milly argued. She winced then, realizing they were getting off subject. "I'm so sorry," she told them. "I didn't see anyone, any cars. Anything."

"Thank you. And what did you think of the group at the inn?" Joe asked them casually.

"Well, that Carl Brentwood—heartthrob!" Milly said. "Sweet little cutie. Such a young one."

"Did you find that the rest of the group was behaving oddly in any way?" Dallas asked.

Milly touched her chin thoughtfully, dusting it with flour. "Oddly... Now, there's a question. They are odd. They think they see ghosts. They were walking around with all kinds of equipment. There were recorders and cameras and... What did they call them, ETPs?"

"EVPs," Rod said. "Electronic something-or-others. Were they weird, yes, weird as hell. But of course, they were very nice, and they seemed to be fascinated by what they did. Oh, and that other woman, the crime writer—she was supersweet. Such a hottie. She looked really good with Carl Brentwood. A gorgeous couple when they were setting up."

Dallas produced a card and handed it to Rod, who had no flour on his hands. "If you think of anything, let me know. And thank you for your time."

"You bet," Milly said, wide-eyed.

"We're sorry for that poor woman," Rod said.

"And glad we were long gone," Stan said, and then looked guilty. "I'm sorry—I mean, it's pretty frightening, too. A thing like that to happen..."

"I'm making Rod double-check locks and stay in the bedroom with his shotgun when I take a shower," Milly said.

"Never hurts to be too careful," Joe said.

They thanked them again and were out the door.

"What do you think?" Dallas asked, setting the key in the ignition.

"They look like an unlikely trio," Joe said.

"But they didn't see anyone? Not another car anywhere near, nothing?"

"I said unlikely. But then again, I've seen a lot of unlikely turn out to be likely, so…"

"I'll get the head office researching the caterers," Dallas said. "Still seems odd to me. Why would you become a caterer in an area like this?"

"Maybe, just maybe, to get into peoples' property," Joe said. "A good way to get the lay of the land, so to say."

"And then again, maybe they are just unlikely."

It was late when they pulled into the hotel.

"Dinner?" Dallas asked.

"An excellent plan. I need a minute to clean up," Joe said. "I still feel like I have blood on my hands."

Keri had escaped to her room the minute Joe and Dallas had dropped off her and Carl. It was late enough to grab dinner before running up, but she had a book to read, she was tired, and she didn't particularly want to be with other people for a while.

So, she read the book, thinking that a key of some kind might lie with the old graveyard and the church. According to the book, it had been called The Church of the Little Flower, a Protestant church, and served a group that had been largely Lutheran. By the 1870s, the dwindling congregation joined with a brand-new church that had been built in the city, about twenty miles away. The Church of the Little Flower was deconsecrated in May of 1880 and abandoned.

For many years after, relatives of those buried there brought flowers and kept up the wall and the little graveyard. Then even those loved ones passed on. Every few years, it was brought up by local government that the burial grounds and church should be restored as a tourist venue, but nothing ever happened. Like all other such venues, it quickly became a place for teens to bring their dates, to scare them perhaps, to tell tall tales and get close, which meant it was also a venue for drinking, smoking pot and indulging in other drugs.

Like many a spooky graveyard, there were tales that had arisen from it. Stealing from Washington Irving, one tale centered around a headless soldier. He didn't ride around the community lopping off heads, he just tripped people and breathed a ghostly breath upon them—difficult with no head, Keri thought.

There were also tales of witches, but then again, this was an area where many people had believed in forms of witchcraft for years, usually the kind that had to do with healing and thinking hard on what you wanted to make it so. Of course, it was also hex country, so not all witches were good. It seemed likely that, through the years, many a coven might have met in the old graveyard, perhaps carried out rites and more.

The abandoned church wasn't far from Rehmeyer's Hollow, the area where the murder of Nelson Rehmeyer took place in 1928.

She set the book down and stared at the TV, which she had put on for company. At first, there had been a silly sitcom, but now the news was on.

An attractive young anchor came on and spoke seriously, a photo of a smiling Julie Castro up on the screen.

"No arrests yet in the murder of FBI Agent Julie Castro. The FBI and local police, however, are both involved, and while Detective Catrina Billings has informed us that she cannot comment on an active investigation, she says that law enforcement—federal and local—is following several leads, and that no stone will be unturned. If you have any information that might lead to an arrest, including suspicious activity, you can call the police hotline."

The picture of Julie showed a pretty young woman in a blue pantsuit, smiling for the photographer.

Keri felt an incredible sadness and a mixture of fear and anger. Julie Castro had been a trained agent. How had she been taken? And why had she been so brutally murdered?

The anchor went on with the news, talking about Julie's dedication to the job and how she had traveled from New York to Pennsylvania in search of a kidnapped teen, Barbara Chrome. She had been with her partner, Ed Newel, who had been injured on the job and remained in a Philadelphia hospital. Any news regarding Barbara Chrome should also be reported to the hotline.

Keri found herself curious as to why Julie Castro and her partner had headed to Pennsylvania; they must have had a clue that led them there.

The anchor did not say, but a picture of Barbara

Chrome flashed on to the screen. She was in a prep uniform, looked young, sweet, blonde and innocent. Just seventeen. An impressionable age. Some worried about their futures, about colleges, about the military. Some were in love, some dreamed of marriage, and almost all yearned to be adults and rule their own lives.

Keri reached for the remote and turned off the television. She glanced at her watch, felt her stomach rumble and remembered that there was no room service.

She was still tired, and she didn't want to see people, but she had no choice if she wanted something to eat.

She headed down to hopefully find a quiet table in a corner all alone.

There wasn't much in the immediate vicinity of the Miller Inn and Tavern except for the new hotel, where Joe and Dallas would be staying one more night. But just up or down the highway, Pennsylvania offered all kinds of incredible delights: all manner of patriotic tourism, beautiful Amish country or the fun of Hersheypark.

Joe guessed they could find something for dinner at a chain restaurant down the highway, or maybe a bar. But it had been a hell of a long day that included updating Billings about the blood at the old church and getting a forensic team out again, so Joe and Dallas opted for the restaurant at their own hotel. The food was quite good after all.

They happened to head down to dinner at the same time as Carl and Keri.

It seemed that Carl and Keri were a couple, although

to Joe's understanding, they had just met when they were scheduled to do the paranormal investigation at Miller Inn and Tavern. He knew through their files that Carl was just twenty-three and Keri was twenty-nine, an age difference that probably didn't mean much of anything, except that Keri seemed far more mature. Carl certainly behaved very much like an adult—and not a spoiled one, at that—but still, he was a heartthrob.

Of course, Keri was extremely attractive herself. She had a way about her, casual, down to earth and somehow incredibly sensual, as well. Just as she appeared in her picture in the police file. Maybe it was just the fall of her hair. Or the way she moved or walked, or the light scent of her perfume.

Maybe he was becoming a bit too enchanted...

No matter his thoughts on her—and the odd kinship he felt—she was lying. Perhaps she couldn't quite admit the truth.

Joe and Dallas ran into Carl and Keri in line to be seated; the restaurant was rather busy.

"Hey, cool, we'll probably get seated more quickly as a foursome," Carl said, seeing them. "Unless, of course, you need to talk business or, I'm sorry, if you just don't want to eat with us. Of course, we will not be offended."

Neither Joe nor Dallas had a chance to answer. The young hostess hurried up to Carl, stars in her eyes, and said, "Please, sir, bring your party and we'll seat you immediately, away from people."

"Sounds good to me," Dallas said to Joe. Joe shrugged and looked at Keri. Her face was impassive.

They followed along. The hostess was busy telling

Carl how much she had loved his last movie and how shocked and horrified everyone had been to hear that a murder victim had been found at the Miller Inn and Tavern. Carl was very polite to her in turn; she thanked him, telling him how wonderful that he had come to her little area of the world.

She turned to look at Joe and Dallas, smiling and stepping back as if she appreciated height in a man. Then she glanced at Keri and let out a sigh, as if envying a woman at a table with three men.

Keri smiled, apparently amused, and thanked the hostess for seating them. Joe liked that about her; she had her own brand of confidence and was simply comfortable with herself. Of course, she should be, since male heads seemed to turn when she walked into a room.

The hostess had found them a table in a little alcove with windows that looked out to the road and a carved wooden divider between them and a row of booths. All three men waited for Keri to slide in first. To Joe's surprise, Carl was the first to take the opposite side and Dallas took the seat next to him.

Joe found himself next to Keri, startled again by the strange instinctive pleasure being so close to her awoke in him. He reminded himself that she was with Carl, whether it was a casual or deep relationship.

"We didn't actually mean to horn in on you," Joe said apologetically.

"But it's been a long day, and so we're just grateful," Dallas said.

"I didn't mean to hang on to Carl's star, either, but

I'm grateful to do so as well," Keri said, picking up her menu. "Long day, I agree."

Their waitress came to the table, harried that night but sweet and quick to point out a few specials. She recommended the Feel-Good Meatloaf, and everyone ordered it, clearly too tired to think harder.

Their food arrived quickly, and they all tucked in immediately, quiet for a while as they ate in semi-comfortable silence.

"Did you get any sleep last night, given the night before?" Joe asked.

"Some." Then she paused. Listening.

"Ditto," Carl said softly and paused, too.

They could all hear a woman speaking—loudly—at a table just beyond the divider.

"It's those people—the ghost hunters. That dead woman. She was a sacrifice, I bet," the woman said with assurance.

"You're wrong, and I will be proved right," the man with her said. "It's all because she's an FBI agent. She went after a girl, and the girl is probably a...a runaway, conspiring with drug runners, in love with a kingpin, and ready to kill anyone trying to take her home."

"I guess everyone has a theory," Dallas admitted. "But at this moment, who would we be to say that either one of them is wrong?"

Joe turned to Keri. "Are any of your people in here?" he asked.

"My people?" she asked him, wariness in her eyes.

"Sorry. I meant, the paranormal group. We have yet to meet them."

"And we all have yet to meet the New York City agents." Dallas glanced at his phone. "They're still in Philadelphia." He looked up. "We'll be wanting to talk with your group tomorrow when the agents arrive. I'm sorry. I know it's difficult to repeat your stories over and over, but sometimes, it helps. You remember something you didn't know you knew."

"I'm not an expert on current investigation in any way," Keri said, looking from Joe to Dallas, almost as if she expected one of them to tell her not to offer any suggestions.

"But do you have any ideas?" Joe asked her.

"I brought back a book from the inn about the church. Through the years, it seems, young people did there what they usually do in abandoned places. They went to drink, tell tales, boys liked to scare girls... and it was suspected that witchcraft took place there. I couldn't help but wonder... I mean, just what went on there exactly isn't in the book. But we know that Newby considered himself to be a witch and a Satanist. Or maybe he was a Satanist masquerading as a witch. People trying to coerce others will try anything to get them to obey or be part of something. I can't help but think that just maybe there is a new group believing that they're witches or Satanists...and that Julie was murdered in the graveyard for a reason."

"Wow," Carl murmured.

Keri looked at Joe and then Dallas again. "Do you know why Julie thought she could find Barbara Chrome in Pennsylvania?"

"I'm expecting to hear from our agents who have

been in Philadelphia some time tonight," Dallas said. "Julie's partner has been in and out of consciousness, and the doctors allowed Dot and Jared to see him for just a few minutes tonight. They'll give a full report when they get here."

"Maybe the girl's kidnappers planned on using her for something," Keri said. "And Julie was in the wrong place at the wrong time and became the sacrifice instead. Maybe that poor girl is still in danger, being held somewhere. I know that you're the investigators, but, well, that's a theory. And a fear."

"It's a good theory," Dallas assured her.

"Given the way Julie was killed, yes. It has something to do with ritual. Or it was a cover-up for the real reason she was killed," Joe said. "Either way, I think you're right. The history of the church and graveyard play into it. And adds to the idea that someone local or at least very familiar with the legends of the church and the tavern had to be involved."

Keri was listening to him but looking toward the door. "There's Brad," she said. "And troop."

A strange hush had fallen over the dining area. Joe looked to the entry to the café, following Keri's line of vision. People apparently knew Brad Holden by sight—he was a star in his own right, thanks to the internet and a general pursuit of the paranormal and all things creepy and scary.

The hostess was happy to see him as well and gushed a bit. Not quite as much as she had gushed for Carl.

As Keri had noted, Brad had come in with his group of "experts." Joe tried to identify everyone in the group from their pictures in his files. Serena Nelson, small and blonde, had her arm locked through Brad's. Eileen Falcon, medium in height and build with brown hair pulled back in a bun, was with the man in her life, Pete Wright, who was just about six feet tall, with close-cropped, sandy hair. The group was rounded out by Mike Lerner, the oldest in the crowd and with the look of an artist, his head shaved clean, his build stockier, his stance—tired.

"I think I'll introduce myself," Joe said. "Excuse me."

He set his napkin on the table and rose, waiting for the hostess to seat the new crowd. They were at a booth by the window, too, but down a few tables from the couple who had been solving the murder so loudly with their opinions.

Joe stopped at the table as the Truth Seekers were just opening their menus.

"Hello, sorry to interrupt. I just wanted to introduce myself—Joe Dunhill, special consultant with the FBI. I'm here with Special Agent Dallas Wicker, and we'll be joined by other members of the FBI soon. I'm sorry for the continued questioning, but this is a murder investigation being handled by a joint task force between the FBI and police. We spent the afternoon with Carl and Keri over at the Miller Inn and Tavern, and tomorrow, we'd appreciate some time with each of you."

"Of course," Brad said immediately, rising to shake Joe's hand. "I'm Brad—I guess you know that. Mike there, Pete and Eileen and Serena."

Everyone murmured a greeting.

"Anything, anything at all, we're happy to do anything that we can," Brad assured him.

Pete and Mike rose as well and shook hands with Joe.

Eileen smiled cheerfully. "Glad to have you working this. Hopefully, you're all a bit...friendlier than the cops. Detective Billings could convince a pope he was a horrible sinner."

Serena stared at Joe, frowning. "I don't think we need to be all warm and cozy. I just heard the word *appreciate*, but I think that meant we'll talk to the FBI tomorrow whether we like it or not. The same questions we went through for hours at the police station. And there just isn't that much for us to say. Eileen and Keri just...found her down there. I never even saw... Keri was screaming, telling us to get out, and we ran, and then there were sirens... We got the hell out. I'm just not sure what more we can say."

"I'm sorry," Joe said. "I know this is an inconvenience for you, but a woman is dead. She was brutally murdered. Yes, it's a lot of questioning. But now, you've had some time. We won't talk until tomorrow, and by then, you may remember little things. Noises, smells, you just never know."

"Serena is just tired," Eileen said, setting an arm around her friend and coworker.

"And scared," Serena said. "What if whoever did that to her is...is still around?"

"All the more reason to help us find whoever did this as quickly as possible," Joe said quietly.

"I just don't think we can help," Serena said. "I'm sorry. I must sound terrible. And ridiculous. We prowl around old abandoned places and graveyards and we look for the dead. But the dead are long gone, and whoever did this—"

"It's okay, Serena," Brad said. "I won't leave you. There are two patrol cars outside the hotel, and they'll be staying there." He looked at Joe. "And this guy seems pretty competent. You're a consultant?"

"Savannah police almost a decade, military before, and now into the academy," Joe said. "I'm with an experienced FBI agent, and two more FBI agents will be back here by late tonight. Detective Billings has ordered protection for the hotel. We are watching," he told Serena.

"Watching? Or keeping us here?" Serena asked.

"I like to think my first line of duty is always to protect and serve, under any title," Joe told her.

"We'll do anything to help," Pete said. He looked at Serena. "All of us. We'll be happy to go over it all again."

"Thank you," Joe told him. "I'm sorry. I'll let you have your meal now, and we'll call you in the morning and arrange a time to talk. We'll get it together so that we don't make it too painful, going over it all again."

"We're all suspects, you know," Serena mumbled.

"Obviously. We were investigating at the inn," Pete told her. "Another reason we need to help."

Brad ignored them both and spoke anxiously to Joe. "You said that you were back at the Miller Inn and Tavern with Carl and Keri. Does that mean we can get back in?"

"The forensic teams have finished. Carl has access.

He needs to have a specialized cleaning crew come out, and then… Are you hoping to finish what you started?" Joe asked curiously.

"We were looking for the past, but maybe what we discover could be of help. Lots of people are skeptical, but you know—and Carl certainly knows!—that the dead can be contacted and that they can help."

"I'll keep that in mind," Joe promised. He was sure that although Brad did believe in ghosts, he really had no idea how right he was about the dead helping the living. Brad didn't have the proof that Joe had.

He felt Dallas come up beside him, and the introductions went around again.

"FBI," Serena muttered. "Cops and FBI."

"Serena is scared," Eileen explained, her tone defensive.

"I'm sorry," Serena said suddenly. "Of course, we'll go through it all again. And again, if you all ask. I just…" She let her voice trail and then sighed, hugging Eileen. Tears glazed her eyes. "Eileen is the one who found the body, and I'm falling apart…and Keri, she's been so great, so strong. Screaming her head off and getting us out and the police there, immediately, barely batting an eye. I'm sorry. I'll tell you all anything that I can." She looked at Dallas and Joe, brown eyes hopeful.

"We appreciate it," Dallas told her.

Joe turned to see that Carl and Keri had grown weary of sitting alone at the table. They joined them by the Truth Seekers.

"Keri," Eileen said, standing and hugging her. "You're doing okay? We didn't see you today."

"I'm all right," Keri told her.

"I'll never forget what we saw," Eileen whispered.
Keri nodded.

"We're being questioned again tomorrow. Unless you
were already questioned. There will be more agents,
too," Eileen said.

"I know," Keri said.

"Carl, you're back at the inn?" Brad asked.

"Almost," Carl told him, glancing at Dallas. He
smiled grimly. "Let's just get through tomorrow, huh?"

Keri seemed to realize that Carl was uncomfortable
and not sure what to say or do at this point. She let out
a sigh and said, "I have to call it quits for tonight and
try to get some sleep. I'll see you all in the morning."

"I'll head up with Keri and see everyone in the morning, too," Carl said.

"That's it for me, too. Very, very long day," Dallas
said. "Enjoy your dinners."

"Good night," Joe said, and started after Dallas. He
paused, seeing their waitress. "I'll just see to the check,"
he said. But when he spoke to the waitress, he found
that Carl had already paid. Of course.

He was aware of the paranormal investigators at their
table, watching him and Dallas and speaking softly
among themselves. Was one of them a cold-blooded
killer? Or worse…were they all cold-blooded killers?
And what was the Philadelphia connection? Just how
had Julie Castro come out to York County when she had
last been seen in the heart of the Big City?

As he and Dallas headed to the elevators, he said,

"Have we learned anything more about the kidnapping victim Julie Castro was trying to find?"

"We'll find out more from the agents tomorrow," Dallas said.

They reached their floor and headed out of the elevator. "See you around seven downstairs in the restaurant, I guess. Seems to be the place," Dallas said.

Joe nodded. "I'll be packed up and ready to stay at the inn."

They parted ways. A door opened in the hallway as Joe headed to his room. Instinctively, he swung around.

Keri Wolf was setting a Do Not Disturb sign on the door. He noted that she was already in what must have been her bed clothing, a long soft T-shirt in a misty gray that fell gently over her body. It was bizarrely provocative, just like the featherlike layers of hair that framed her face and fell around her shoulders.

She was surprised to see him, or probably anyone, in the hall, and she flushed and smiled awkwardly.

"Hey. You and Dallas are on this floor?"

He nodded. "Are you all right? You're alone?"

"Yes, yes, I'm fine, thank you. And yes," she added irritably. "Yes, I'm alone. I'm also a little unnerved. Terribly sorry for that poor dead woman, but... Anyway, I'm glad to know the law is near."

He pointed to his own door just across the hall from hers.

"A loud scream—even a semi-loud scream—and I'm here," he promised.

She nodded. "Thanks."

"Good night, then."

"Good night."

He headed into his own room. He didn't bother with a Do Not Disturb sign; he'd be awake and ready to start the day long before a housekeeper arrived.

He locked the door and sat on the foot of the bed, his mind racing with what they did and didn't know. In his mind, it had to be connected.

A kidnapping in New York City, leading to a murder in York County.

A historic inn, an abandoned church, a paranormal investigation group...

And just what else?

Keri had looked into the church. It had been used by teens trying to get lucky, drink beer and smoke pot. It was also suspected that people had used it in their practices for witchcraft and perhaps Satanism.

John Newby had been a Satanist, evidenced by the insignias he had left in his basement, discovered after the mass murder at the inn.

It was all connected.

But how? Or was it all just being used as a cover-up for a different motive for murder?

He really did need sleep; it was important to keep a clear head. The questions would be there in the morning.

Keri was proving to have a sharp mind. Of course. She wrote books. On old murders, and yes, things had changed through the years. There was so much more technology available now. But human nature remained the same.

As he lay down to sleep, he found that he did clear his head. Of the questions that were arising, at least.

He hadn't cleared his head of Keri Wolf. He wondered if he should challenge her outright—tell her the truth about himself.

The truth? What if he'd been wrong himself? What if he'd imagined the man in the park, the victim who had stopped by to thank him?

Keri wasn't terribly fond of him, he knew.

He closed his eyes and realized that he was almost smiling, rather ridiculously glad that he had found her getting ready for bed alone.

Whether she was fond of him or not.

7

Keri woke feeling almost as exhausted as she had been when she went to sleep.

And yet again, her night had been filled with dreams and nightmares, only snatches of which she remembered when she was fully awake. There was no way out of what she had seen—the woman laid out on the stone altar in the basement, torn and ragged and covered in blood.

The woman in white, standing by her side, watching Keri.

It was all so explainable. She'd spent the day in the museum room, and she had seen the picture, and she'd just moved the woman from the picture into the basement, standing there, over the body of Julie Castro. She'd probably already made the connection somewhere in her subconscious that the woman in white was Beatrice Bergen, the local girl who had most likely been kidnapped, tortured and killed by John Newby in his secret chamber below the tavern.

That's why she had imagined she had seen her.

Her phone rang at 8:00 a.m. It was Joe Dunhill. She

was disturbed by her reaction to his voice; she had decided yesterday that she didn't like the man, but there was something about him that was both compelling and frightening. He reminded her of something out of the movies, hammering away at her, demanding to know what she just wasn't going to say.

Those silver-gray eyes of his, so intense. So probing. And yet…

She'd been glad to know that he was just right across the hall. Despite the fact that he could be so annoying, she had felt an odd attraction sitting next to him at dinner, and a definite relief in the fact that he was so near. She'd been tempted to scream when she'd awakened with a start from one of her odd snatches of nightmare, intrigued to see if he would come running from across the hall.

She pushed the thought aside. He was annoying, hard, pedantic. She would bet he'd assumed she was sleeping with Carl. Just another woman taken in by the Hollywood glamour. He didn't seem to have much patience for her.

"The other agents are here," Joe said over the phone. "There's a small conference room on the ground floor that the hotel has let us take over. They'd like to meet you."

"Meet me or grill me?" she asked.

"Both," he said flatly. There was silence for a few seconds. "Would you like me to come up and escort you down?"

"No, thank you. I have to get ready, and I'll pick up

a cup of coffee before being skewered again," she said sweetly.

"As you wish." He hung up. Keri set the phone down hard and cursed at it.

Jerk.

She showered, and it helped her to feel more awake. She dressed quickly and then hesitated, packing all her toiletries back into her bag.

Did she really want to go back and stay overnight at the Miller Inn and Tavern? Carl had just about begged her to do so. And even when Joe was being a jerk, he did seem to think that her expertise with research could help.

She thought of the murdered woman, Special Agent Julie Castro. Keri hadn't known her, had never met her.

Did that matter? Julie had lived and breathed, and she'd known that she risked her life to be an agent and do fieldwork. She might have fought for her life while trying to save another. She was part of humanity, or had been, with a family somewhere, and people who had loved her. She deserved justice. Keri couldn't help but remember the picture of Julie in her blue suit, smiling.

Of course, what had happened to Julie could happen again.

Keri could just go home to Virginia, far from here…

Far enough? She was so obviously a part of this now.

At that moment, she could have doused her publicist in a trough full of icy water. Publicity! Just wonderful. Whoever had killed Julie now knew Keri, who she was, and everyone else who had been at the inn at the time. Were they all possibly in danger now, no matter where they went? Julie had been from New York; she'd traveled to Philadelphia, and she'd died here.

Still, a killer would have to follow Keri to Virginia. Maybe it would be crazy to think that anyone here really cared that much about her. She wasn't an FBI agent, she wasn't on to anything—she was a writer. The crimes she covered were so old that few people involved with them were still alive.

With her bag ready if they were to leave the hotel, she headed downstairs. The front counter was open in the restaurant, and she went up and ordered a cup of coffee.

The conference room was on the ground floor somewhere. She headed down the hall and discovered Brad coming toward her.

"Your turn for another round?" he asked her. He looked tired but he also looked strangely exhilarated.

"My turn, I guess. The conference room is over there?" she asked, pointing toward the door just down from the way he had come.

He nodded grimly, and then said, "Keri, you have a lot of sway with Carl."

"I do?" she asked.

"He really respects you. I'd love to get back into that inn. I swear, if we'd had a chance, we might have even gotten some voice recordings. That place is haunted."

"Brad, a woman was killed," she said.

"Right, and if we can get back in, maybe we can find out what happened to her."

"You...think she might have been murdered by a ghost?" Keri asked carefully.

"No, no. I mean, I've heard of poltergeist activity or

maybe even a push down the stairs. Eileen believes she was pushed. But I've never heard of a ghost ripping a person to shreds. But there may be clues all over that, well, cops wouldn't see. Or even agents. Hey, by the way, Dallas and Joe are nicer than these guys. But if you have any sway with Carl, do you think you could get him to let us back into the inn? I mean, if we have to stay here and the forensic team has cleared the inn—"

"I'll, um, do what I can," Keri said. "Excuse me for now, though, I've got to get in there."

She hurried past him, finding it ironic that she was looking forward to an interrogation by the FBI, as long as it got her away from Brad for a few minutes.

Keri entered the room, smelling subtly of a compelling soap or perfume. She managed to dress in a mode that was both casual and dignified—dark jeans, a tailored shirt, vest and long jacket. She was grave when Joe and Dallas greeted her and introduced her to Dot Harrington and Jared Cabot.

Joe and Dallas had already spent time with the two New York agents; they were both decent, level and apparently competent. They knew how to follow a trail.

Dot was in her midforties, with curly red-blond hair, a thin pale face and a strong handshake. Jared Cabot was younger, maybe late thirties, tall and fit, dark-skinned, with a serious expression. Because the murder might be directly linked with a New York case, the agents—who had been working with Ed Newel and Julie Castro—had received permission to follow the clues where the clues might lead, reporting to the Philadelphia office as well as to Dallas and drawing upon local expertise when needed.

"I also worked in the Philadelphia office until recently," Jared had told them. "My transfer was less than a year ago when I moved out of organized crime and into Julie's squad."

He was, in essence, one of the locals. He had grown up in Hershey, Pennsylvania, and had traveled between his home and Philadelphia more times than he could remember. He knew York County well.

"You know all the stories, right. History of the area?" Dallas had asked.

"Of course," Jared had said. "What do kids tell at campfires by night? Myth and history always blend, though."

The hotel had allotted them a small room with a round table, allowing everyone to be easily in on the conversation and creating something more casual than a real interrogation room.

"You're a historian, Miss Wolf?" Jared asked, indicating that Keri should take a seat.

"No," she told him, taking her chair. "I can't really say that. I love history and weird bits of history, and of course, I love studying old crimes."

"And you were studying the massacre at the tavern?"

She took a deep breath, not because she was nervous, but rather, it seemed, because she had told her story one time too many already.

"Carl Brentwood read some of my books. He contacted my publicist after he'd bought the inn and been in touch with the Truth Seekers. My publicist thought that appearing in a video with Brad Holden and his group would mean more publicity than I or my publishing house could afford. I looked into all the research I could find on the area, and I find it a fascinating mystery."

"You think?" Jared asked her. "I was always taught that Bergen did it. Though, I believe he would have been found temporarily insane, at the least, in a court today."

"Good lawyers do wonders," Dot said.

"He never had his day in court," Keri said. "He was lynched. I can easily believe he might have killed John Newby, if he knew what Newby had done to his daughter in the basement. But from everything I found out about the man, there was no reason for him to have killed all the people in the tavern."

"And you were researching. That's why you weren't upstairs with the others. That's how you found the body?" Jared asked.

"I wasn't the first down in the cellar," Keri said. "I was about to head upstairs. I heard a cry of distress. I went to the basement door and found Eileen Falcon on the steps. She'd fallen and was hurt, and terrified, of course. She saw the body first."

"And then you got her out, warned the others and dialed 911," Dot said.

Keri nodded.

Dot leaned forward. "You were the only one alone at the tavern for a great length of time."

"I suppose I was," Keri said, unruffled. "I am also new to this area. Whoever did this had to get the body down to the basement after carrying out the murder in the graveyard and collecting Julie's blood. That requires understanding of the area. I met Carl Brentwood over the phone and didn't meet the others until an hour or so before we started filming. I think you know that I didn't have anything to do with this, so, I'm not sure where you're going with this."

Dot continued to stare hard at Keri. "Do you believe in ghosts, Miss Wolf?"

Keri still didn't miss a beat. "I suppose I do. I grew up in a Catholic and Anglican household. We say the Nicene Creed, which includes the words, *I believe in the Holy Ghost.* But do I think the spirits of the departed stick around and haunt inns? No. I don't disbelieve—but I am a skeptic."

"What about your woman in white?" Dot demanded.

Keri sighed deeply. "I don't know what I saw. I was terrified. I had just come from the museum, where I was reading and looking at all kinds of pictures from the past. The cellar was not well lit. Most of the light was coming from the entry above. I think that there was a very poor bulb burning from what had once been a candle sconce. I don't even know. I don't know what I saw except for Julie's body. I was scared out of my wits, thinking of nothing else but getting out of there."

Dot sat back at last, looking frustrated. "But there might have been someone down there."

"Might there have been someone down there? Please, we need help," Jared said.

Keri shrugged. "I just don't know. Yes, there was a moment when I thought I saw a woman. I wanted to get her out, but then, she wasn't there. Honestly? The corners of the cellars were all dark. I remember stark raving fear. Could there have been someone there? Yes. Would I ever be able to tell you who? No. Maybe the killer was even near, anxious to watch what happened. You didn't get any video?" she asked. "They had cameras down there."

"Blank," Dot said.

"Someone messed with the cameras," Jared muttered.

"Then you are looking at someone who knew the Truth Seekers and how they operated. However, that wouldn't be difficult. They have an incredibly popular show, and it's watched by hundreds of thousands of people. Their audience might be up to a million or more, really. Each show, you can clearly see that they set cameras and recorders in every room. I admit, I don't know a lot about videography—and that's not to make myself appear innocent, I just know how to shoot a pic on my cell phone—but I think that a lot of the world is savvy."

Keri leaned forward again. "So, in my mind, you're looking for a local connection. Anyone could know about the inn and the legends and take the time to study what the Truth Seekers do. But to know about that cellar door and the graveyard, the actual layout of everything, you have to have a local connection."

"Perhaps you should stick to your historic crime, Miss Wolf," Dot said.

"I'm quite happy to do so," Keri assured her pleasantly.

"Special Agent Harrington," Joe said, keeping his voice as smooth as possible, "it sounds to me as if Miss Wolf is right on. I would even push that theory. Whoever kidnapped the girl in New York apparently brought her to Philadelphia, which suggests that they might be very familiar with Pennsylvania in general, and Philadelphia specifically. Possibly even this area."

"We certainly follow all leads," Jared said. Joe thought that he might have kicked Dot's leg under the table. He did seem to be the more reasonable of the two, with a kinder, gentler nature.

Then again, who was Joe to judge? Who knew where Dot's career had taken her?

Keri took a sip of her coffee. She had to be annoyed, but she didn't betray her emotion. Joe wondered if she even cared that he'd been offended on her behalf, that he'd been compelled to come to her defense.

"Anything else?" Dallas asked.

"I think we've covered what we needed to cover," Jared said.

"For now," Dot said.

Joe stood. "Keri is going to be staying in the area. She's a special guest of Mr. Brentwood, who has kindly allowed us to explore all possibilities near the Miller Inn and Tavern. Since Julie was killed in the neighboring church, we're taking him up on his invitation."

"We'll have you reporting to us there," Dallas said.

Dot looked grim; it was obvious that she wasn't pleased with the fact that Dallas had been given lead on the case.

Joe didn't think of himself as a bitter or malicious person; the fact that Dallas was in charge still made him smile.

"Keri," Dallas said, "we'll be here a little longer.

Checkout isn't for a while, so if you don't mind waiting for us, we can all head out to the inn together."

She lowered her eyes, probably hiding the fact that she had many questions herself.

She rose, pausing in front of Dot. Her words were sincere, heartfelt. "I'm so very sorry about Ms. Castro. I'm sure she was a wonderful agent and a wonderful woman. If there's anything that I know that can help you in any way, I swear I will tell you. If in some small way I'm able to help, I'll be grateful to do so."

Dot stared back at her. She nodded slowly, eyes lowered. Then she said, "Thank you."

Keri didn't speak to Joe, but told Dallas, "I'll be in my room. Just let me know when we're about to leave. Thank you."

She left the room, and they all stared after her.

To Joe's surprise, Dot said softly, "I am a dick."

"It's all right," he was even more surprised to hear himself say. "Julie was someone you knew. Your coworker. Your friend."

"Our assistant director almost took me off the case," Dot said. "Told me I shouldn't be working this. But we were on the kidnapping along with Julie and Ed, and I said that I would be entirely professional." She gave herself a shake and looked at Joe and Dallas. "All right, we're heading back into the city."

Dot began to speak earnestly. "Barbara's parents have offered a million-dollar reward for the safe return of their daughter. We got lots of calls on the hotline, and most of them were just hopefuls, claiming they'd seen Julie. She was everywhere from a block away to Timbuktu. But the tip that brought Julie and Ed out here, the call from the clothing store, was different. This person could describe a tattoo on Barbara Chrome's thigh. The call made her mother hysterical— Barbara had promised she wouldn't get a tattoo until she was eighteen, but then she jumped into the pool during a family vacation and her mom saw it.

"Anyway, we all believed that the caller really had seen Barbara, and that honestly she had to be one of the kidnappers. Ready to sell out on her group to collect the reward. Whoever this person was—they used a voice changer, but our experts say it was a woman— swore that she'd contact Julie once she and Ed were in Philadelphia.

"Julie and Ed went to the store, and the manager was irate. All the employees were questioned, and between the Philadelphia bureau people and Julie and Ed, they determined that the caller wasn't a shop employee. But the phone is in an alcove behind the counter, and the manager believes that only a regular standing in that area wouldn't have been noticed by one of the employees. Jared and I went back to the store yesterday. We spent some of our time waiting and watching, and we went through every employee again."

"You think whoever made the call would go back to the shop?" Dallas asked.

Dot gave him a dry smile. "You and Joe and Detective Billings can cover this end. Most probably someone local is involved. But there has to be some kind of connection between the city and what happened out here. Naturally, we have our computer whizzes going through records to come up with connections between store employees and the area out here, and we're looking into the angle that the hit-and-run that nearly killed Ed wasn't an accident at all. It might have been a way of getting one agent down so that they could get to the other one."

"If that's the case," Joe said quietly, "someone knew that one of their number had called the FBI about Barbara Chrome. If a traitor is suspected, we might find that another sacrifice is being planned."

"Possibly," Dot acknowledged.

"I'm curious," Joe said. "What do we know about Barbara from her family and friends? From what you've said, she could be rebellious. All young people can be—but was she more so than average? Prone to follow down a dark path if a charismatic person led her that way?"

"Yes, I guess. But youth is always capable of foolishness." She shrugged. "Was she the kind who never did anything wrong and walked the line for her folks? No. Did all her friends have only good things to say? Not really. Teen girls can be self-centered."

Dot took a deep breath and looked at Dallas. "I know that you've been given lead on this, but I think that it's important that Jared and I remain in Philadelphia. Ed has been in and out of consciousness, but all we learned from him so far was that Julie got a phone call, kissed his forehead and promised she'd be back, and then she was gone. Her cell phone disappeared with her. The records showed only that she received a call from a disposable phone that couldn't be traced. So, she was lured to wherever she went."

"And she had sushi, according to the medical examiner," Joe recalled. "Detective Billings has her people heading out to every sushi restaurant within a hundred miles, showing them Julie's picture. We can hope someone might remember her and who she was with." He hesitated just slightly. "You've read his report, right?"

"Yes. We're grateful to know that she died quickly," Dot said. "But still…"

"She's gone," Dallas said quietly. "So, where we are now. If the murder is connected to the kidnapping, more than one person had to be involved. We need to find the connection. There's been no sign of Barbara Chrome. Her picture has been blasted all over national news, but she might have gone a long way to change her appearance, or her kidnappers might have changed it for her."

"You really think she might have been in on her own kidnapping?" Dot asked.

"It's just a possibility," Joe said. "You interviewed her friends and parents. Did it seem that she might be rebellious? That growing up rich might have made her a candidate for persuasion from a cult leader?"

Dot and Jared looked at one another. "One girl did report what happened almost immediately. The rest of her friends pretty much pointed to the van whisking away and said, 'Oh, look, there goes Barbara.' Nothing stood out until she didn't come home that night. No one was able to get a license plate or anything on the vehicle that we were able to trace."

"No one suggested that she might have friends outside their ranks?" Dallas asked.

"No, and we asked if she'd been seeing anyone lately

that no one knows well. We followed through on her friends' friends, too," Jared said.

"Let's still consider the fact that she might have been a willing participant. Will you send us everything that you have on the kidnapping?" Joe asked.

"Of course," Dot said. "I'm curious, though. I've never worked with anyone before who hadn't made his way through the academy. You're going to the academy next class, but you're a consultant? Dallas, I don't understand this."

Joe didn't want Dallas on the spot, so he answered quickly. "I'm kind of on a ride-along here, possibly joining the unit, and I've dealt with a few cults and murders with twisted motivation that were difficult to fathom. I just recently left the Savannah police department."

"Ah, that's how you found the secondary site in the church," Jared said.

"Actually, we just determined that she had to have been killed somewhere near," Joe pointed out.

"Anyway, I think it's a sound plan for you and Jared to keep following the Philadelphia angle and watching over Ed," Dallas said. "We can hope that he'll be able to tell us more when he is solidly conscious."

"If he's solidly conscious again," Dot said. "We have police and local agents watching over him. If he was hit on purpose, whoever tried to kill him might try again."

"And you'll keep these people here, right? I have a bad time with so-called paranormal experts," Jared said.

"We'll keep an eye on them, and yes, we believe that one of them might be guilty, too," Dallas assured him.

"And Carl Brentwood and that writer—having fame

and critical success does not make a person innocent," Dot said.

"How will you keep them here? No one is under arrest. Not enough evidence," Jared said.

Dallas glanced over at Joe. "Oh, I don't think we'll have a problem keeping them," he said.

"How's that?" Dot asked.

"I think that eventually our problem will be getting them to leave," Joe said. "They can't wait to get back into the inn. We'll be bringing them back in tomorrow. That may go a long way in proving if any of them are involved."

It was noon when Joe called Keri's room to tell her that they were ready to go. He offered to help with her luggage; she told him that she had only a rolling bag and she was fine.

Carl was downstairs waiting, as were Joe and Dallas.

"Let's move. I don't want to be explaining why it's just us today," Dallas said.

When they were in the car, Keri asked, "Sorry, but why is it just us today?"

Joe was driving, so Dallas turned around to explain.

"We have copies of the video from the police station that we want to go through without the Truth Seekers present and we need to go through a few things with just the two of you before we bring in the crowd," Dallas explained.

"Keri, we're going to have you spend the day in the museum and see what you can find out about any kind of devil worship or cult activity," Joe said, glancing at her through the rearview mirror. "You've touched upon it. One of the biggest questions facing us is was it a cult killing or was it meant to look like one?"

"But Julie was an FBI agent," Keri said. "Wouldn't that make it more likely that she was killed for what she was on to and someone made it look like devil worshippers were busy at sacrifice to throw off the authorities?"

"Maybe. We don't know yet," Dallas said.

"I thought it was going to take days to get the specialized crime scene cleanup crew in, but I got a call last night. They're coming today. One of you greased some squeaky wheels," Carl said.

"Believe it or not," Dallas said, "Detective Billings greased those wheels. I think she's really okay."

"And Special Agent Dot Harrington," Joe added. "She was sorry for being so harsh on you, Keri." He turned to look at her and grinned. "She actually called herself a 'dick.'"

Carl laughed, delighted. "Well, she can be a dick," he said, smiling as well as he looked at Keri. "When she was talking to me, she made it sound like I had plotted the whole thing out long ago, arranged the kidnapping of Barbara Chrome, the purchase of the inn and the murder of Special Agent Castro."

"That's a questioning technique?" Keri asked.

"It's one technique," Dallas said.

Keri was barely listening. They were driving up to the inn and she was surprised to see that there were two patrol cars sitting in front of it along with a large, beige-colored van with large letters proclaiming Purity Cleaners.

"They're here already!" Carl said with pleasure, hurriedly stepping out of the car.

He was instantly approached by a police officer who left his car. Dallas hurried out as well, drawing his credentials from his pocket to show the officer. Keri saw the officer nod, and Dallas and Carl went to the inn.

"They don't need me back in the basement, do they?" Keri asked Joe as they walked up to the building.

Joe turned to look at her, and his silver eyes were soft for once. "No. We figured you'd want to start back in the museum after we settle into rooms."

"Are we choosing who stays in what room in any peculiar way?" she asked.

He nodded. "Our rooms connect. Dallas is going to take 207, Carl 206. You'll be 205, and I'll be 204. We'll be bookending you, and a police car will be out here for the next week, at least. If we need to bring in more agents, we will. I hope you're all right with this."

"The rooms all connect?"

"Yes. Is that a problem for you?" he asked.

She still wasn't sure what she felt about him—did she like him not at all, or too much?—but he was tall, muscled as tightly as piano wire, and while he might not be much protection against her nightmares, she was pretty sure he was damned good against a living threat.

"Hell no," she said. "Should we get our things inside?"

"I'll handle the luggage," he told her.

"I can roll a bag," she said, but she didn't need to. One of the officers was heading toward them, ready to give a hand. Joe greeted him pleasantly, introducing the two of them and starting to show his credentials, but Officer Jordy was quick to say that they'd been expected and he'd be watching the inn once they were safely inside.

"I guess everyone is taking this to heart," Keri murmured to Joe.

"No law enforcement officer anywhere is unaffected when something happens to one of their own. I guess Detective Billings was a bit put out when the Bureau came in—this is her territory—but she understands. And she wants the murder solved and the killers caught."

They entered the inn right behind Officer Jordy, and for a moment, Keri paused. Light streamed in from the front doors. To her left, the tavern tables sat just as they had. The bar was behind them, and to the right of the bar was the museum. By the bar, the entrance to the giant kitchen, and to her right...

The stairs down to the basement.

Jordy and Joe headed on up the stairs.

"I'll drop these and be right back," Joe said, referring to the bags he carried.

She could hear people talking in the basement, and then Carl came rushing up the stairs. "Keri, you good with everything? They're almost done down there. I'm thinking we'll put Dallas in 207, and us between him and Joe. That okay?"

"I'm fine, Carl," she assured him.

She wasn't fine. She wasn't sure she should be there at all. She kept thinking of one of her dreams; a mist had swept eerily into the basement, creating shadows and creatures in the corners.

As promised, Joe came hurrying back down the stairs. She wanted to run to him, she realized, and let him hold her. Protect her from the shadows and the mist and the uneasiness sweeping through her.

And then, quite suddenly, she was angry with herself. Police were staying outside the inn, taking shifts, watching over them all. Joe and Dallas would be watching from the inside. She lowered her head, smiling slightly at the way they told her that Dot Harrington had called herself a dick.

Well, now Keri needed to grow some balls herself.

"Thank you," she told Joe. "I'm going to head straight into the museum, if that's all right with you all. The collection is really rich, and hopefully, I can find something that might give us more on whether a cult might have been operating over the years, or if someone is simply trying to repeat something that happened long ago."

"Keri, I love you," Carl said, giving her a big hug.

She smiled. "Thanks, Carl." She escaped his embrace to look around at them all. Officer Jordy, Dallas, Carl and Joe were silent, watching her. She made eye contact with Joe. His silver eyes gave nothing away.

She gave a wave and walked into the museum, blushing furiously.

8

Joe watched Keri go, proud of her. Certain that she'd been afraid, but more determined than afraid. *Way to go, girl*, he thought.

Still, he worried for a moment. Julie's murder had been premeditated, lightning fast and brutal. Could they really protect anyone here? Would anyone be safe if they didn't find the killers?

"We're here," Dallas said quietly, as if reading his mind.

"Yeah, yeah, I know," Joe said.

As he spoke, two men and one woman in white coveralls, black rubber gloves and protective eye gear came up from the basement. "All done here. Take a look, Mr. Brentwood," one of the men said, but looked around for approval from all. "You had one hell of a mess down there."

"Thank you for cleaning it up," Carl said.

"I'll get back out to the patrol car," Jordy told them. He looked from Joe to Dallas, not sure who he was reporting to. "We have two cars, four officers. We switch out every eight hours, and we'll be on this for the following week. After that…budgets, you know?"

"We do. With any prayer, that will be sufficient," Dallas said.

"Wow. You guys are good. We've had murder cases on the books for years. Oh, not so much out here in York County, but…"

"We have to stop these killers now," Dallas went on quietly. "If not… Well, we have to catch them. And we will. Your department is on it, we have agents all over working it."

"Well, for now, I want you to know that I'm out there," Jordy said, and then he headed on out.

Dallas looked at Joe, offered him a half smile, and told Carl, "Let's go on down and check the work in the basement so that we can let the cleaner and his people go, eh?"

Carl headed down, followed by Dallas. Joe remained in the tavern with the cleaning crew until Carl came up and handed over his credit card, thanking them again.

"Want to show me what was going on upstairs and tell me what you know about the rooms?" Dallas asked Carl when the cleaners left.

"Sure. The place is so cool. Room 207 is the one that's supposed to have the most paranormal activity, but they think that Washington slept in what's now 204," Carl said.

"Lucky me," Joe said.

"Are you coming?" Dallas asked him.

Joe shook his head. "Think I'll hang here, just in case."

"Watch closely over Keri," Carl said with approval.

Joe nodded, and Carl and Dallas headed up the stairs.

Joe found a place to sit at the rear of the tavern, in the shadows. He sat still, waiting. He thought that the quiet might do something. Bring something out. But nothing moved, appeared or happened.

He was growing restless, ready to head on into the museum and at least find reading material when Keri suddenly emerged. She didn't see him sitting in the rear of the tavern.

She headed for the front door. He stood quietly and followed her. As she went on out on the porch, she called to the patrolmen.

"I'm just walking over to the cemetery. I'll be fine. I'll stay in your line of sight."

"Thanks, Keri!" Jordy called out.

Joe followed her silently, lifting a hand to the patrolmen. They waved back, and he kept walking, keeping his distance from Keri. She didn't turn around and seemed unaware that he followed.

She walked around the side of the inn, footsteps sure and long, until she came to a portion of the broken wall around the old church. She paused there, looking out at the cemetery, and he moved closer.

He heard her when she asked, "Are you here? Are you real? I'm so afraid, but I have to sleep, so if I did see you… Beatrice, please, if you need to be seen, or heard…let me see you."

He thought that she had finally heard him or sensed his presence, but she didn't turn around. She inhaled a hard gasp, and he looked along her line of vision.

And he saw what Keri saw.

She was there, Keri's woman in white. At first, he saw the broken stones and the cherub and angel statues of the graveyard through her; he could even see a portion of the little church. Then the apparition seemed to grow more solid, and still, she just stood in her white dress. Her hair tumbled around her shoulders, and it moved as if caught in the breeze.

"You're real. You can't be real," Keri whispered.

Joe walked up behind Keri, setting his hands gently on her shoulders, hoping not to startle her. She jumped nonetheless, and he whispered, "Please, don't scream. She seems to be a very shy ghost."

"You see her," Keri said.

"Clearly, and she is gaining strength as we stand here."

She was. The ghost of Beatrice Bergen moved toward them, trying to speak. At first, her lips moved, and nothing came from them.

Joe reached out a hand. "Beatrice, it's all right."

The ghost stood still and smiled slowly. "You see me."

"We see you, and now we hear you," he said.

Her voice was weak. A bare whisper, like the movement of the air through leaves or a recording, distant and faded.

"It's happening again," she whispered. "My father didn't do it... I must prove that he didn't do it, I can't bear that he be blamed."

"I never believed that he did it," Keri said. "I'm looking for who might have done this thing. Beatrice, your father didn't slaughter people, but did Newby... Did Newby kill you?"

The ghost lowered her head, nodding sorrowfully. She raised her head and looked at them with pride and strength.

"It is happening again," she said, and then, as if she had spent what talent she had for appearing as she had in life, she began to fade.

And then she was gone.

Joe felt Keri shaking beneath him.

"You did see her. You saw her, when you found Julie."

"I thought I was just seeing her in my mind. There's a picture of her in the museum, so I thought I'd just put her image in the basement, because I'd known she'd been there at one time... And then today, I wanted to work in the museum, but she's haunted my dreams... and I need to sleep, really sleep. I thought that if I came out here... She's buried in here somewhere. Newby just brought his corpses out of the basement and buried them right in this graveyard. The basement must have been... horrible. But people never knew... They never knew..."

She was still shaking; she didn't try to throw off his touch. "You—you saw her, too," she said.

"She's trying to help."

She swung around to stare at him, repeating, "You saw her."

He nodded and suggested, "Let's get back to the inn. We can talk."

He thought that she would protest, and for a moment,

she just stared out at the overgrown, sad little grave-yard and the church.

Then, she started walking, and he followed. He waved to the cops watching over the place as they headed back in. Sitting her in the tavern, he asked, "Water, coffee, a soft drink?"

"A big shot of whiskey," she said.

"Okay. Let's see what they've got behind the bar—"

"I'm kidding, I'm kidding," she said, waving a hand in the air. "Right now, I certainly don't want to be im-paired in any way."

"Okay."

She stood, telling him, "I'm half asleep all the time now. Let's brew some coffee."

She walked past the bar and into the kitchen. He fol-lowed her, watching as she searched the cabinets for cof-fee. The pot was a one-cup instant maker and she drew down the collection of coffee, saying, "I'm going for a Hawaiian brew. Would you like Hawaiian, light, decaf, Brazilian, Sumatran, or let me see, there's also—"

He walked over to her, setting his hand on hers where she was rifling through the little pods. "Sumatran is great. I'll get some water for the pot."

She nodded, lowering her head. He filled cups with water.

"Cream, sugar?" she asked.

"Black for me."

"Do all cops drink black coffee?" she asked him.

"One of the guys I worked with in Savannah loved flavored creamers. He said that all cops made bad cof-fee and the creamers made it drinkable."

She smiled at last, stepping back while the first cup brewed, looking at him.

"Have you seen dead people before?"

He nodded slowly. "I've been waiting for you to admit that you saw the dead. But this is new for me, too. I believe you heard about the case in Savannah. A politician was involved, and a house with incredible historic significance, and it was all over the news."

"Yes, I heard about Savannah. That's why Carl wanted you and Dallas on this so badly, but he didn't say anything about ghosts."

He took the first cup out of the little machine and put in the second.

"People don't usually announce to the world that they see ghosts. But what I've been learning, working with the Krewe of Hunters and getting ready to go into the academy, is that it may well be like inheriting a rare trait from someone in your family history. It's rare and yet a percentage of people have it, and sometimes it lies dormant until an occasion when the dead see it in someone they might need or like or see as a kindred spirit. I don't think we're so different when we're dead than we are when we're alive. No matter what it is we're seeking, our triumphs and failures, ecstasies and tragedies, are all important because of the people in our lives. Parents, siblings, lovers, friends, children. Our relationships are often what's most beautiful about us as human beings.

"I'm not that experienced myself, but I know that lives were saved in Savannah, and the truth was known because a ghost came to me. Dallas did the heavy work, but if it hadn't been for a ghost—who I didn't accept as a ghost at first, mind you—a number of other people might have died. Frankly? I was just about worthless myself, but because of that ghost, I called the Krewe for help."

She watched him in silence. The second cup of coffee finished brewing; he handed one cup to her and kept one himself.

He smiled. "I'm trying to read your expression. I think you might have decided that I might be decent and almost likable?"

She took another little pause to answer, and then she shrugged. "Oh, I wouldn't go that far. Almost okay and not entirely despicable," she told him, but she had a half smile on her lips, and he couldn't help but smile in return.

"Good," he told her. "Because I don't like leaving you alone. I was lurking in the corner when you left for the graveyard. Now, I'd like to help you with what you're doing in the museum. I'm pretty good at reading."

"Okay," she said.

She stayed still, looking at him. "I've heard of…feelings. Like when you live in a house where a loved one died, and you kind of feel them at certain times. I've heard of people seeing soldiers marching at Gettysburg when the fog rolls in, but that's so suggestive, of course you see soldiers. But she looked so real. As if she was standing right there."

"She believes in you, I think."

"That's crazy. I'm the last person she should believe in."

"Maybe she was there, all the while, watching. And

she knows what you do, and believes that you can help her."

"She also said, 'It's happening again.' I—I don't know how I can help her."

"Maybe what you discover about the past will help with the present."

"I really wish I could help. I saw Julie on that altar. I didn't know her, but I know that the other two agents down here did, and she was very real, and what was done to her was so terrible and so very wrong. Are the answers in Philadelphia? Have they murdered the girl who was kidnapped?"

"Maybe we'll go into Philadelphia ourselves at some point. Right now, Dallas and I believe that there's a connection between everything. If we can find out what went on here, it could lead us all the way back to the kidnapping in New York."

He followed her back to the museum. Keri took a seat behind the desk. Going through the drawers, she took out a set of old manila files and immediately began reading.

Joe took a minute to walk around the room. Most of the pictures on the walls had little signs beneath them, naming the people in them. Many of them were from around the Civil War.

"No picture of Washington up here—wait, sorry, found a sketch," he said.

She ignored him. He winced. She was working; he was talking and being a distraction.

There were images of Newby. He looked so damned normal, but then, most of the time, the most dangerous men and women did. People were far more easily taken in by someone who was charming.

Newby didn't appear to have been particularly charming. Just very normal.

On the other hand...

Joe studied a picture that included Beatrice Bergen. And her father, Hank.

Hank had been a tall and distinguished-looking man, beard and mustache nicely clipped, dark hair wavy and swept back from his head. His suit was probably not at all a good one; Hank had been a farmer.

The salt of ye olde earth.

"What about the rest of the Bergen family?" he asked, and then quickly added, "Sorry to interrupt."

"It's okay. I was ready to get into the next file," Keri said. "What I've found in local records is that Beatrice's mother died when she was four. Her father raised her. No siblings. With Beatrice nearly grown, Hank had started courting a widow down the road, Maya Bentley. I haven't found anything more on that relationship. Obviously he didn't marry again."

"Thanks." He'd seen the pictures; gotten what he'd asked. Except for...

"Sorry, quick interruption, and then no more. What about Newby?"

She gave him a grim smile. "Mildred Newby supposedly went to see relatives out west. She left one day and never came back. Newby would inform those who asked that she'd left him. She'd lied to him and gone off with a man and was living somewhere out west."

"So, in other words, she might have been his first

victim and might lie in an unmarked grave out by the church."

"Quite possibly."

He sat down quickly and pulled out his phone; Keri seemed to have some kind of method with what she was doing here. Grateful that Carl had seen to setting up the Wi-Fi—only way to get the video stream from the Truth Seekers out—Joe logged on to a bookseller account and downloaded something he found on the history of Satanism.

Of course, he knew what people in general knew—Satan, or Lucifer, was a fallen angel. While pagan religions flourished in early societies, Satan became a frightening entity as Christianity began its spread across Europe. Therefore, it was easy for settlers in areas of heavily forested, dark and mysterious New England to believe in the devil, especially beneath a religion as restricting as Puritanism. In the darkness of the forests and the dreariness of winter, it was easy to see how the imaginations of young people were stirred—and how easily their beliefs might be swayed to encompass the feelings, wants and needs of their elders.

The first witch, or devil worshipper, to be executed in the American colonies was Alse or Alice Young of Windsor, Connecticut, and she went to the gallows in Hartford in 1647. Many more were accused, tried and hanged throughout New England, but it was the infamous Salem Witch Trials that turned neighbor against neighbor in a frenzy during which nineteen were hanged and one pressed to death.

Much of the persecution of witchcraft in the American colonies had to do with the dogged determination of James I of England, who studied Satan and witchcraft and was convinced that it was all real; he believed that a witch had caused the storm that upset the ship bringing Anne of Denmark, his future wife, to his side, though she did survive to marry him and bear three children. Toward the end of his life, James determined that there were many counterfeit accusations, but a desperate fear of witchcraft and Satanism had been set in motion, along with the idea that Satan could provide a life filled with dancing, lewdness, drink, sex and more, without consequence.

Witchcraft was listed as a crime in the American colonies in 1715, but by 1750, it was no longer mentioned as anything illegal or legal. In the creation of the United States, the founding fathers, familiar with religious persecution, set forth an absolute separation of church and state. Of course, it was illegal to kill, if a religion called for killing, but otherwise, religious practices were not illegal.

The contemporary religious practice of Satanism officially began in 1966 when Anton LaVey founded the Church of Satan.

But many had been accused of being Satanists long before, back as far as the Middle Ages. The Knights Templar had been accused of Satanic practices, but that had most likely been a greedy king trying to get his hands on coveted Templar riches.

Aleister Crowley had been seen by many as a Satanist, but his mantra, *do what thou wilt*, was part of his own religion, Thelema. The religion was based on practices he had studied throughout his life, as a magician and a poet. He embraced the old gods of the Egyptians, as well as others during his travels in the Middle East, Asia and Africa. Because of his drug use, bisexuality and hedonism, he'd often been thought of as a Satanist.

"Hungry?"

He looked up, startled that Keri was standing there in front of him, bending over with a smile, her hair almost touching him.

So much for being aware at the drop of a pin.

"Sure."

"Do you cook as well as you make coffee?" she asked.

"Coffee is my forte," he assured her. "Hey, I spent over a decade as a cop. I'm a wonderful stereotype, except I don't like donuts. Can you cook?"

"Depending on what they have in there. What were you reading? Anything that was any help?"

"Not yet. A lot of history of witchcraft and Satanism, but I've not really gotten anything on the Pennsylvania Dutch beliefs yet or the possible practice of Satanism here."

"Ah, but an understanding of the present often comes from an understanding of the past," she said, walking away. "I'll be in the kitchen. Maybe I should run up and get Carl and Dallas. They must be getting hungry now, too."

He wasn't sure why—some bodyguard; she'd been in front of him and startled him—but he didn't want her away from him. "I'll just give Dallas a buzz," he told her.

She paused, looking back, and said, "I'm coming to

terms with it, but do you think we could not mention the…ghost…we saw to anyone else yet? Carl believes in séances and such, from what he's told me. I don't really adhere to the belief that you can summon someone's dead grandmother but—"

"Dallas is far more experienced than I am. You could ask him questions," Joe suggested.

"What?"

"Dallas sees the dead. When they choose to be seen, of course. And when—when they have remained, for whatever reason."

"Dallas…sees…"

"Yes. The whole Krewe, in fact. You should hear some of his stories."

She took a deep breath. "Not yet, please. I'm not ready for that yet. Since we've been back… I've begun to wonder again. Maybe we're sharing a hallucination."

"We're not, but we'll move along as you wish."

She went to the kitchen; he dialed Dallas as he followed her. Dallas said that he and Carl would come right down.

Joe didn't know why he was worried about the safety of the inn. There were patrol cars outside, each bearing two officers, and the officers seemed competent. One of the four at the very least should have noticed if anyone had approached the inn. He was equally certain that Dallas would have checked out every room upstairs before settling down anywhere, just as he and Carl had gone down to see the basement after the cleaning crew had gone through.

Joe still felt that he needed to keep an eye on Keri.

Maybe it was this rather bizarre kinship—the way they were both new to seeing ghosts.

In the kitchen, they both dug through the cabinets and refrigerator, keeping up a running dialogue about the various supplies they found. There was a beef stew and macaroni casserole, and they decided to put that in the oven and make a salad while they waited.

As they worked, Carl and Dallas came down to the kitchen. "Anything interesting up there?" Joe asked.

"We went through every room. Almost all of the Truth Seekers equipment is still here. I guess you all had to rush out, and then the police were here, right?" Dallas asked Keri.

"They didn't let us back into the house. They went and got handbags for the women, and of course, checked them before they allowed us to have them back. Someone went back in for our luggage when we were sent to stay at the new hotel. I suppose Detective Billings ordered them to get what we might need, but nothing else. No wonder Brad wants back in so badly. I hadn't realized that all his equipment was still here." She hesitated. "So, were you playing with it?"

"Those EVP things seems to record all the time in this place," Carl said. "EVP...means what?"

"Electronic voice phenomenon, or something like that," Dallas said. "Carl thinks we heard a whisper. I'm pretty sure we heard an air-conditioner kicking on."

"Skeptic," Carl said.

Dallas smiled. "Smells good, whatever it was that the caterers left," he said. "Salad looks great, too. Good call on dinner. I realized we hadn't eaten as soon as you called."

"We're looking at five more minutes," Keri said. She'd been chopping cucumbers and carrots; Joe had been slicing tomatoes. The scene was oddly domestic.

Joe found plates in a cupboard and set them around the table while Carl searched for flatware and napkins. The caterers had supplied beer and wine, but none of them wanted anything that dulled the senses, so bottles of ice tea were found and passed around the table.

For the first few minutes, they all just ate, noting that the caterers were very good.

"Wow, love this stew," Carl said. "I felt badly… I know the caterers wanted to hang out. You know, to be invited to be a part of the investigation. But Brad is exacting on how he likes things done. He thinks that people who don't understand his work method and are just in it for the thrills mess up a real investigation…" His voice trailed. "I guess it's a good thing they didn't stay, with what happened and all. They're nice people. If we do get through this and I do keep the tavern… Well, I'll have to reopen the restaurant and the bar, but you never know when you're going to need a good caterer."

"We met them," Joe said.

"You did?" Carl asked, surprised.

"Of course," Keri said. "The caterers were here that day, too. Naturally they were questioned as well. And I assume, you also went to see Spencer Atkins. He was here as well."

Carl looked from Dallas to Joe, and they both nodded. "Silly me. I've played in a few films about murders, but the real thing…" He paused, shaking his head. "Anyway, what are we going to do for the rest of the evening?"

"Keep a watch on the inn, the graveyard and the little church," Dallas told him. "Joe and the cops will watch out front, we'll be watching out back. The backside of the inn has that balcony."

"Oh!" Keri said suddenly. "The hatch door to the cellar… It never had a lock. I don't think we should sleep here with that open. And, Carl, you have to change the locks."

"We're doing that tomorrow," he said, "but there's a lock on the cellar door now. Only way through it is with a hatchet."

"I'm glad you thought of that," Keri said.

"I didn't. Dallas brought the padlock."

Keri laughed softly. It was nice to hear her laugh.

"What did you think of Milly, by the way? And Rod and their partner, Stan?" Dallas asked them.

"They were…nice," Keri said.

"Really intrigued about what we were doing," Carl said.

"And good at what they did. They had boxes and boxes in here quickly and all set up for us," Keri said.

"Did it seem to you that they knew the inn well?" Joe asked.

"Well, they had to know it, but I don't know how well," Carl said. "They've worked here before. Spencer Atkins told me to call them, so I'm assuming he used them at some time."

"I'm assuming that anyone from the area knows the

inn," Keri added. "It's the only real historic thing standing, besides the church and the graveyard, for a number of miles. I think the new hotel has only been open about five years or so, and before that, there weren't all the fast-food places around the highway. While Spencer had the inn, this would have been the only real restaurant around here."

"All the new places opening probably caused Spencer to sell to me," Carl said. "He owned it twenty years or so."

Keri was frowning. She jumped up suddenly, half of her food still on her plate. "I have to go look at something," she said.

"What?" Joe asked, standing as well. Carl and Dallas followed suit.

"I just flipped through some of those files today... I don't know if it's important or not, but Spencer kept information on the different people who worked for the place. Sometimes his notations were just 'in for the day.' And he used just first names a lot, with a mark that he'd paid them in cash."

Everyone followed her out of the kitchen and behind the bar across to the museum.

In the museum, she sat at the desk and dug into the manila folders, flipping quickly through them.

"Here... This was just four years ago. 'Milly.' He paid someone named Milly a hundred dollars for two days 'stand-in' work." She set the file down. "I guess that doesn't mean anything, except that he tried to help her make some money while she and Rod got their business going."

She looked at them all for a minute.

"That doesn't mean anything, does it? This place is small. I guess everyone knows everyone."

"It may mean something, and it may not, but it's good information," Dallas assured her. "We know now that they know each other well."

"But I guess they would have known one another well enough whether she'd ever worked for him or not," Keri said.

"It may also mean that Milly Kendall knows the place better than she might have implied when trying to get Brad to let her stay for the ghost investigation," Joe said.

"But what does that mean?" Carl asked, confused.

"No idea," Dallas told him. "But it's something we need to find out about."

"And why is that?" Carl asked.

"Because," Joe explained, "this whole thing could be a conspiracy. Perhaps we're dealing with a coven or cult of some kind. What I'm afraid of is this—it's possible that one of the kidnappers decided that the million-dollar reward Barbara's parents were offering was worth a lot more than loyalty to the group. Now, if someone did betray a group, and they were found out, that person is in serious danger. If we can figure out who it is—"

"Before they're killed," Dallas put in.

"Then we might find out exactly what happened here," Joe said.

9

"There's an Amish community about fifty miles from here," Keri noted, looking up from the ledger she'd been reading.

They were gathered upstairs in room 207; Joe and Dallas were seated in a pair of armchairs by a small side table, and Keri had plunked herself on the foot of the bed. Carl leaned against a dresser. It was growing late.

"This is York County," Dallas said, frowning. "There are a number of Amish and Mennonite communities near us, although I believe most of them are actually in Lancaster County. Which is a different jurisdiction, but we could still drive there quickly."

Keri spoke up. "But there's a notation about this one in particular that was made by John Newby, about three months before the massacre took place. 'No longer attempt purchase from Matthew Graber. Will not supply.' I'm just curious as to why they couldn't purchase from the man anymore. I came through here on a road trip with my parents once, and we stopped and bought all kinds of food and other things at a stand. I'm sure that over the years, the owners here at the tavern did a lot of their shopping out at the Amish markets. They have wonderful, fresh produce. I might be grasping at straws here, but if farmers were unwilling to sell to Newby, they might have known or suspected something about him."

"We can drive out tomorrow," Joe said. He turned to Dallas. "I can take Keri, and you and Carl can hold down the fort here. When are you thinking of bringing the rest of the Truth Seekers back in?"

"A couple of days," Dallas told him. "Drive out tomorrow and see what you can learn."

"I'm confused," Carl said. "You think that seeing an Amish farmer—or the descendant of an Amish farmer—can help solve Julie's murder?"

Joe looked at Keri before answering, understanding her train of thought.

"Julie was killed in a ritualistic manner. Or, at least, displayed so. If there's a conspiracy going on, it could help if we find out there's been some kind of secret society meeting out here for years. It may be a stretch, but Julie's death was carefully planned. The killer needed help to get her body into the house. If Barbara Chrome met someone recruiting somewhere in New York and came out here willingly, she might have spurred the group into killing Julie."

"Dumb way to get the FBI off her trail," Carl noted.

"Yes—unless the killers believe that we know nothing about them at all, because we'll be looking for someone who killed her in the inn to discredit you or the Truth Seekers," Dallas explained.

"Why would anyone want to discredit me?" Carl asked.

"Possibly because you're rich and famous and could buy and refurbish this place," Joe told him.

"Am I really that famous?" he asked Keri.

She laughed softly. "Getting there," she told him.

Carl stood, looking at Dallas. "If Joe and Keri leave tomorrow, we've still got the cops out there, right?"

"Thanks for the vote of confidence," Dallas said, grinning. "But yes, the cops will still be out there tomorrow. We have them several more days. And if we need to, we can call on our local federal office as well."

"Okay. Great. And Dallas, I have complete confidence in you. I only play tough guys onscreen. Basically, I don't want to die, so all protection is welcome. And you, my friend, do you know where to go to get to this Amish community?" he asked Keri.

She lifted the old ledger she'd been reading. "Newby drew a little map," she told him. "Times have changed, but the landscape, not so much."

"We'll find it," Joe said.

"Probably a waste of time," Carl warned her. "You could be bonding over creepy stuff with me and Dallas and looking for clues out in the graveyard."

Keri took his words seriously and looked from Joe to Dallas and back again.

"I don't ever mean to waste your time," Keri said, "but we're here because we think something has been going on around the inn, and it may have to do with Julie's kidnapping. Many people may be involved. I still think it's a good idea to try to become friends with someone out in the community—I believe they would help us."

"I think it's a good call," Dallas said.

"And I think I'm going to bed. I'm going to leave the doors open," Carl said. "Do you mind, Keri? I am definitely creeped out. You know, my publicist and my agent wanted to be with me on this, and I said no. I wanted to do this all on my own. I think I'm still glad that they're not here, but I'd have them in blow-up beds in my room, if they were."

"One of us will be on guard through the night at all times, so you really can try to sleep," Dallas assured him. He glanced at Joe.

"I'll take first shift. I'm going to keep reading," Joe said. He waved his phone in the air and grinned. "Glad I got the larger size."

Keri unwound from her spot on the bed; it seemed that those who were going to sleep this shift were supposed to try, which meant she needed to be out of Dallas's room.

"All right, then. Good night," she said.

"And all doors wide open," Carl added. "You know, it may not be so creepy, once we have the Truth Seekers back in. Safety in numbers, and all that."

No one replied.

Carl groaned. "You still think one of them is involved."

"We don't know who is involved," Joe said quietly. "But tonight, Dallas and I are here and four cops are just outside. The tavern door is locked, as is the cellar door. No one here to worry about."

"Except for the dead. Ghosts," Carl said. He grimaced and started through the open door connecting to his own room.

Keri followed him, wishing he hadn't said that.

Joe was behind her. Carl threw himself facedown on his bed. Keri went into her own room, and Joe stopped at the connecting door to his room, turning to her.

"I'm up for first shift. Don't hesitate to call, scream, yelp, anything, if you need me."

She smiled. She was tempted to ask him if he could just sit in her room and watch her sleep. Or hop on the bed beside her.

She'd keep him awake.

Her own idea made her wince inwardly. But when he wasn't being a jerk—which he didn't seem to be anymore—he was a very attractive man with all the right stuff. Those eyes of his, stormy gray sometimes, silver sometimes. And his height which hid the wire-muscled appeal of his build.

"Thanks," she told him.

Like Carl, she decided she would just lie down. She shed her jacket and decided that sleeping in her shirt and jeans would do her well. She'd be prepared if she had to jump and run.

She pulled back the blankets on the queen bed and crawled beneath the sheets, plumping her pillow. A small light burned on the dressing table, and dimmer light streamed in through Carl's room from Dallas's.

Joe's light was also on.

She was glad.

She lay there, wide awake, staring at the ceiling.

"You okay?" Joe asked. "I can sit in a chair right here, by the door. Unless that keeps you awake?"

She sat up and looked at him and smiled. "I think it would be great if you sat in a chair right by the door."

He grinned and gave her a thumbs-up, taking a seat in a chair he brought over from the dressing table in his room. He had his phone out, and seemed to be quickly absorbed in whatever he was reading.

She still didn't think that she'd sleep.

She did.

That night, she dreamed of being in the forest. Mist fell, but she wasn't afraid. She was laughing and running around with friends. She was in a dressing gown, something long and white.

The dream was strangely enjoyable at first. The earth was soft, with rich grass growing thickly on the ground. Her feet were bare, and she thought that she and her friends might be playing a game of hide-and-seek. It occurred to her that she had never played hide-and-seek in a forest with friends, but she mentally shrugged it off as a dream.

The light, silvery mist began to darken. She thought she heard someone chanting, but she couldn't make out the words. She couldn't even be sure that words were being said, that what she was hearing came from people—it might have just been the sound of the breeze rustling through branches, cool and pleasant.

The darkness continued to creep in. The trees began to sway as if the breeze had become a violent wind.

She knew she needed to wake up. She tried to force herself to do so. When she opened her eyes, she was lying in her bed, but she was staring at a man in his late forties, with a lean face and a neatly trimmed mustache and beard.

She was awake, she realized. The room was hardly dark or shadowy. But she found she couldn't move her arms or legs, couldn't even turn her head to look away from the man looming over her.

"Please, I did not do this thing," he said.

Keri meant to scream. The sound came out as garbled, pathetic little gasp—and the man disappeared.

It didn't matter; as he had promised, Joe was quickly up and at her side, kneeling by the bed.

"Keri, what happened? You're all right, I'm here."

Yes, she knew now that the woman in white was real. Or as real as a ghost could be. She saw the dead; others saw the dead.

But this ghost had really shaken her...

She threw her arms around Joe. He accepted her wild hold, his arms coming around her close. His fingers stroked gently over her hair.

"It's all right. It's all right. If you can tell me what happened, or what you saw, it might help."

She held tight to him for a long moment, glad of his arms around her, of the heat streaming from him and into her. She hadn't even realized until he touched her that her limbs were as heavy and cold as ice.

He kept soothing her. She didn't want to pull away. She knew she had to.

"I'm sorry," she murmured, gaining control.

"You never need to be sorry," he assured her, his silver eyes soft. "I know how startling it is, I know just how frightening it can be. Hey, I once nearly drew my Glock on a ghost, okay? It's tough, it's scary. Until you get used to it."

She managed something of a smile. He was still so close to her. In her current state of heightened senses, she felt that he all but reeked of masculinity and sexuality.

"I was just dreaming," she admitted. "And the dream was okay... I was running in the forest and playing hide-and-seek. There was a light mist, and then it began to turn dark. I thought that people were chanting. Maybe not, because it got windy. Windy and ominous. I knew I had to wake up. I thought that I woke up, and then there was a man, bending over me. He said something like, 'I didn't do this thing.' And then he was gone."

"I see." His words weren't skeptical or condescending.

"I saw him, really. Maybe I was still dreaming, and I woke myself up when I screamed."

Joe smiled. "That didn't really qualify as a scream."

"Choked, garbled...whatever."

"Do you know who he was?"

Keri inhaled deeply, lowering her head and wincing. "We spent so much time in that museum, and we saw all those pictures on the wall. We're in a supposedly haunted inn, where terrible things happened. I believe we are sadly impressionable as human beings, so—"

"Keri, do you know who he was?"

She nodded. "The man I saw was...Hank Bergen."

"If he's trying to tell you he didn't do it, maybe he just needs help. Beatrice's ghost said that her father didn't do it, and now it seems you've seen his ghost as well. They need you," Joe told her.

As he spoke, they both turned, hearing footsteps on the hardwood floor. Dallas was there, at the connecting door from Carl's room.

"Hey," he said, his tone curious.

Joe explained.

Dallas looked at Keri and nodded slowly. "You seem to be the conduit."

"I am not any kind of a medium," Keri protested. "I scream every time a ghost shows up. Shouldn't they be looking for one of you?"

"Hopefully, soon enough," Dallas said. "Anyway, Joe, you can sleep if you want. I had a pretty decent half a night." He smiled.

Keri swallowed. She didn't want Joe to leave her. He started to rise; she almost begged him to stay. She didn't have to.

"Move over," he told her. "I'll be right here, on the edge. I will try to sleep, and not to worry—Dallas will be right there, between Carl's room and yours." He hesitated. "Did you—want Carl in here?"

She frowned, confused. "What? Carl? Why?"

"Aren't you two...together?"

"No!" Her word was emphatic, and she shook her head. "No—I like Carl. He seems to be a nice and bright and even giving person. But—no! There's nothing going on between us."

"Okay, then...you're all right with me being here?"

"Yes, thank you." She shifted far over.

The bed was certainly big enough. He stayed on

his side, not touching her, sleeping on his back, hands folded over his chest.

Curled to her own side, well aware he was there and tempted to curl up right next to him, Keri forced herself to close her eyes.

Exhaustion was a good thing. She slept.

This time, no dreams plagued her. However, when she awoke, she was curled up beside Joe, and he was lying on his back, one arm around her as her head rested on his chest.

And of course, he was awake...

She flushed and sat up. He smiled and asked, "Were you able to sleep at all?"

"Yes, thank you," she told him, and she quickly rose, mumbling something about a shower. She hurried toward the door, then had to hurry back, since she had forgotten to get fresh clothing and her toiletries.

It just wasn't going to be an easy day.

Inside the closest shower, she closed and locked the door and set her things down. She whispered softly aloud, "Please. Whoever you may all be, do not scare me to death in here and make me go running out dripping wet and naked into the hallway."

No one answered her. She winced, gritted her teeth and turned on the water.

Ghosts or not, she had to have a shower.

"Modern Satanism, from what I've managed to find, began with men like Anton LaVey," Joe said as he drove. The scenery they passed was exquisite. Rolling land so green it looked like velvet beneath the sun. Occasionally an old barn with pastureland surrounding it. Hills that rose to be captured by rich trees, their leaves as saturated as the grass.

"But the original Hebrew word for *Satan* came from a word that meant *opposed*. Really, some form of Satanism has been practiced all around throughout history. As time went on, pagan religions became mixed up with Christianity, and witchcraft—pagan healing and appreciation of nature, to modern wiccans—became just as mixed up with Satanism. Since those medieval times—say, in the eighteenth and nineteenth centuries, societies against the rigor of religion began to form, such as the Hellfire Club."

She glanced over at him. "Those were widespread," she agreed, "but the name often refers to Sir Francis Dashwood's Order of the Friars of Sir Francis of Wycombe. It was set up for elite members of society who loved to take part in the most immoral acts. It was also believed to be related to a secret society known as the Order of the Second Circle."

"You read what I read," Joe said.

"I've read a lot through the years. Let's see, the first official Hellfire Club was in London, founded by Philip, Duke of Wharton, and then others were set up around England and Ireland. According to sources I read, while the devil was the president of the Wharton's club, the members weren't really devil worshippers—just impious rakes. They accepted women, and since women weren't allowed in taverns at the time, they met in houses. Anyway, Wharton's club was disbanded in 1721 when

George I put out a bill against 'impieties.' It was really a bill to get rid of the Hellfire Club."

"Ah, but rich boys will be rich and elite boys," Joe said, "and they still cropped up. Such as Dashwood's club, which became so infamous. And when they kind of fell out, clubs still existed over in Ireland."

Keri, smiling, nodded. "Thanks to Dashwood's nephew, the Phoenix Society rose. You can actually visit the Hellfire Caves in Wycombe where Dashwood's group met. There are still rumors of such clubs all over the place, but in most, the image of Satan is used to show disregard for the teachings of religion, rather than as something truly worshipped. Ben Franklin was a member, by the way. At that time, Dashwood's club was called the Monks of Medmenham Abbey."

"Franklin was a rascal, all right," Joe said, "and yet, the only man to sign the Declaration of Independence, the Treaty of Paris and the United States Constitution. I'll bet you knew that," he added, glancing over at her.

"I didn't, but I did know that he was an incredibly free thinker, that he believed adamantly in the rights of men, and that he was a terrible womanizer and even an adulterer—but the way I see it, that was between him and his wife. Though, poor thing, come to think of it, at the time who knows what she could have done about any of it?"

"Okay, so a rock band has the name," Joe said.

"And there are many social media pages," Keri said. "I do think it's quite possible that someone out here started their own Hellfire-type club—really worship-ping Satan, maybe, just as Newby might have. Maybe they made Julie their first sacrifice. Because she got too close to them?"

Joe shook his head thoughtfully. "I don't know how that could relate to an Amish farmer. Pennsylvania Dutch came from Pennsylvania Deutsch—or Germans. But didn't the Amish religion develop in Switzerland?"

"It did. Remember, Pennsylvania offered religious freedom, so it was a place many people fled to when they were being persecuted. There was a schism between the Swiss and Alsatian Anabaptists in 1693 led by a man named Jakob Ammann. Originally, the term *Amish* was derogatory, indicating those who followed him. Naturally, people came and went over the borders between Germany, Switzerland and Alsace-Lorraine, and thus the creation of different sects within a belief."

Joe looked over at her, shaking his head and grinning. "You're like a walking encyclopedia. Or a walking hit on Google, these days."

She flushed. "I've been looking all this up. Anyway, the farm we're looking for is traditionally Amish, but I don't know how well we'd do just knocking on a door. The family sells produce at a market just off the highway. Maybe they'll talk to us there. And we can bring back some fresh veggies, too."

"Do you think it's possible that anyone there today will know about something that happened in 1926?" Joe asked.

"The oral tradition is strong. These people aren't watching television or playing the latest video games," Keri reminded him.

"True."

They were both silent for a minute, and then Keri asked, "Dallas just…expects to see ghosts?"

Joe sighed, trying to figure out how to explain the Krewe of Hunters—and Dallas. "Okay, so, there is a man named Adam Harrison. His son was ill, and he probably wouldn't have lasted long, but he died in a car accident, in the arms of one of his closest friends. She found that she had a gift, and could see Adam's son, and other ghosts, and she helped solve a particular crime and… I don't know the specifics, but she helped solve the crime thanks to ghosts. Because Adam Harrison has always been a supporter of law enforcement, a major philanthropist, and a man befriended by all kinds of people, he knew others around the country who had… gifts. He'd have them help out with seemingly unsolvable mysteries, and then, one day, he had the idea to form the Krewe. He started with Jackson Crow and the woman who is now his wife, Angela Hawkins, and a few others, and over the years, the Krewe grew and grew."

"There are that many ghosts wondering around?"

"It's a very big country," Joe told her softly. "Anyway, when I went to Adam Harrison and Jackson Crow about the case I was working in Savannah, they sent me Dallas. I couldn't officially ask the FBI in, so he did it quietly for me. After that, I figured out that it was a dead man who first came to me. And I guess it was time to move on. I love Savannah—I'm from Savannah. I'll go back, and it will always be home, but I love working with the Krewe of Hunters. I do still have to make it through the academy, though."

She glanced out the window as they drove.

"Have you worked with Dallas frequently?" she asked him.

He laughed. "I haven't worked with anyone frequently," he told her. "I've only known any of them a few months. But Dallas is amazing. I like to think that I at least helped him solve the whole Savannah thing—and Kristin, too, of course." He kept his eyes on the road, remembering. "She spent half her life growing up in a haunted bed-and-breakfast. Like you, she only saw the dead when it became important for her to see them. She just moved up to be with Dallas, and of course, Krewe headquarters is not that far from Savannah. The bed-and-breakfast has been in her family forever, but she has great people running it for her, and she can do her graphics work from anywhere—and we wind up just about anywhere. You'd like her very much." He shrugged. "Maybe she'll come up this way before it's all over. She was finishing a job, but—"

"That's nice," Keri said. "You just picked up and moved."

He nodded. "I have great friends in Savannah, but it was time for something new. You're from Richmond, huh? Do you like it?"

"I love all of Virginia, and a lot of places," she told him. "We have a beautiful country. Wonderful things and places everywhere." She hesitated, smiling. "I'm an only child. My parents are on a trip in the Amazon, and I'm glad. They haven't heard about the murder here, and I don't have to try to explain why I'm still here."

He pointed ahead. "I think that's what we want, right?"

A large covered stand was ahead of them; several

Amish buggies were parked alongside the stand as well as a multitude of cars.

Joe pulled off and parked.

The people working the stand were all Amish—men dressed in trousers with buttons, plain cotton shirts, some in suspenders, and some with vests and jackets; women in simple dark dresses and white caps and collars. People in all manner of apparel were shopping, though many of the shoppers were Amish, as well.

"Who do you want to try to speak with?" Joe asked Keri.

"Let's shop, and see who we see. An elder, I'm assuming."

They shopped, finding woven baskets to use for their purchases. Keri found rows of tomatoes, and then hit upon blackberries with pleasure, showing him how fine and fresh they were. He found green beans and melons, fresh vegetables straight from summer harvests.

As they shopped, both of them watched the workers. One of the men, with a long, gray beard, was telling a tale to a girl standing with him where he was taking payment—cash only, no credit cards.

"He's in excellent shape, but I'd bet he's close to eighty," Keri murmured.

"We'll have to pay him. Maybe we can get close then. It looks like he's friendly to everyone, whether they're Amish or not," Joe said quietly.

A woman standing behind them at the melon stand obviously overheard. "Mr. Graber is a wonderful man," she said. "And not to worry—he knows what his own beliefs are, and he wants them respected, but he's fine with other people believing as they wish, too. That's his precious little granddaughter at his side, in her plain dress."

She smiled broadly and nudged Keri. "The women, my dear, own just four dresses. One for wash, and one for wear, one for dress, and one for spare."

"Actually, that's very practical," Keri said, smiling back.

The woman had only a few things in her arms, and she was the only person behind them in line. "Please," Keri said, "go ahead of us. We have a bundle here, and you have just that."

"Oh no, I couldn't, really—"

"Please," Keri insisted.

"Well, thank you, dear, that's very sweet of you."

She went ahead of them and smiled and laughed with Mr. Graber as she made her purchase.

Joe and Keri stepped up. Joe was surprised when Keri started right in. "Mr. Graber, please forgive me, but this is very important. I know you don't know me. We're here because a friend just purchased the Miller Inn and Tavern, and I found a mention of a Matthew Graber—"

"Excuse me, I apologize for interrupting," the old man said. "I'm glad to be of assistance, but did you really wish to purchase the items I'm counting up?"

"Oh yes, please." She paused and then dove in again. "You might have heard that a woman was murdered, and we believe that bad things have been happening at the inn for a long time, and we have to…to stop bad things happening."

He kept counting for a moment without answering, and then looked up at her. "We've heard, of course. And a murder brings great sorrow. I can tell you what my grandfather told me—my grandfather was Matthew Graber. He said that he would not sell to Mr. Newby or his friends. We know that we are the minority, miss. But our beliefs hurt no one." He paused, looking at her curiously. "You're not from here, nor are you, young man."

"No, sir," Joe answered honestly. "I'm here as a consultant with the federal government."

Graber surveyed him a moment and nodded. "Times have changed. The highway came through. There are many fine people in the county. But I never sold to anyone from the Miller Inn and Tavern before. My grandfather said that there was something evil going on out there, more than the evil with Newby. He gave me no names, but..."

"We're afraid that a cult might be at work. And no, sir, we're not thinking it's an offshoot of your beliefs. We believe that this is a group of people enjoying rites that may well hurt others. We appreciate your help."

Graber nodded again. "Rumor has not died," he said. "I can tell you that, and no more, really. But you might well look to the past. Many have been here as long as we have had our homes here. Now, sir, there is a gentleman behind you, if you don't mind paying..."

Joe quickly paid him. Keri thanked Graber, and they hurried on.

"I'm sorry," Keri said as they walked back to the car. "I thought maybe we'd get a name, something that pointed more specifically to someone."

"We did get something," he assured her.

"You mean something that we can give Detective Billings so the local police can start searching?"

"No, something we can give to Angela back at the Krewe headquarters. We need to find out about everyone involved with this—Truth Seekers, caterers, cops, everyone. We'll find out who just may have had an ancestor back in Newby's day, and then find out who might be carrying on a tradition—like a truly warped Hellfire Club—into today."

10

That night, the officers assigned to watch over the Miller Inn and Tavern were Milo Roser, Belinda Emory, Jamie Brubaker and Henry Schultz.

Keri certainly didn't consider herself to be much of a cook, but whether they had gained any information from Mr. Graber or not, they had procured some wonderful fruits and vegetables. While Joe sat in the kitchen reading—and hopping up now and then to ask if he could help—she put together a chicken stew over brown rice, cooking up some of the vegetables, and making a raw platter out of the rest, and creating another attractive tray with the fruit.

She did have Joe prepare the green beans. Preparing them was time-consuming and after all, he'd been the one to find them.

It was fun being in the kitchen with him, except that more and more, each time she brushed by him, she noticed that she was finding reasons to stand close.

Little sparks flew when their fingers touched accidentally, and she realized—sometime between the

chopping of the tomatoes and slicing of the peppers—
that she was seriously, sexually attracted to him. When
their eyes met and she felt the silver sizzle of his, the little sparks became laps of flame, and she had to quickly
move on to some other task a good distance from him.

She learned that Carl had spent time that day reading
two new scripts that had been sent to him while Dallas had spent time with the video feeds around the inn.
Whatever his findings had been, he didn't talk about
them at dinner. They'd invited the cops in, two by two,
and they were all pleasant and grateful for the meal, not
minding their patrol duty at all that night.

"We want to know what's going on, too," Belinda
assured them.

Belinda's partner, Jamie Brubaker, a tall, young fellow, probably in his early thirties, offered to help clean
up after the meal. Keri assured them that she was fine,
and that Joe, Dallas and Carl would help.

Belinda waved a hand in the air. "I'm all for equal-
ity of the sexes, but honestly, if you let me help out, I'll
have everything whipped into shape in a matter of minutes." She made a face. "Macho cop dad meant that we
girls cleaned up. Boy, was he in for a surprise when his
daughter became a cop and his sons went into finance."

"I'll head back out, then," Jamie said, grinning. "As
you can see, the lovely Belinda seems to wear the pants
in this relationship."

"Never," Belinda protested, teasing. "Back to work,
young'un, I'll handle this from here."

She made everyone smile. Belinda was maybe five
feet six inches and maybe a hundred and thirty pounds,

but Keri had the feeling she was very efficient. She had a great smile, gray-peppered brown hair and dark eyes that seemed to dance with humor.

Joe wanted to talk to Dallas in the library; Carl stood to go with him. He was still going through the screenplays he had received, trying to decide which offer he wanted to accept. "The one is a lead role, but the part... ho-hum. The other is not the lead, but man, what a character to sink into," he told Joe.

Joe looked uncertain as he followed, pausing to tell them, "I'll be checking back in on you every few minutes. Make sure it's all going smoothly."

Belinda laughed at that. "Hey, we've only got some rinsing and storage to do. We should be okay."

"Never hurts to check on people," Joe told her.

Belinda patted the holster she wore on her belt. "You can never have too much protection, but I'm pretty good with this thing. But of course..."

Her voice trailed. Julie had been a trained agent. Julie was dead.

Keri thought that Joe surveyed Belinda before making up his mind to actually follow Dallas and Carl to the museum. He had been a cop himself a long time. Maybe he felt he had some kind of radar that judged a person.

Maybe he did.

Belinda stood at the sink, rinsing dishes. As Keri collected more plates, Belinda told her, "I guess I should tell you, I'm a fan."

"How sweet of you. Thank you."

"And you're here to work on the old case. That's why they brought you in, right?"

"Yes. I think it's fascinating."

Belinda set a plate in the dishwasher. "Well, I'm awfully glad, and awfully glad that you're staying on to see it through. I always thought it was a bunch of malarkey."

"Are you from the area? Did you grow up with the stories?" Keri asked her.

"No, I'm from New York City. Manhattan, no accent," Belinda told her. "My husband is from Lancaster, though. He works for the highway department, but he was born Amish. His community of Amish have something called Rumspringa—a coming-of-age kind of thing where they're released from their commitments to the church and community and find out how others live. Then they make the choice whether to be baptized into the church or not. He went to NYC, we met at a museum, fell in love and he left the church. We were young. Everyone around us wondered if it wasn't a huge mistake, but we're going on three kids and almost twenty very happy years."

"Congratulations," Keri said. "Did your husband's family wind up hating him, or you, or anything like that?"

"Oh no. That's the point—a person makes his own choice. We are what they call 'outsiders' now, but his folks know that we're teaching our children about the Amish faith. While it's not easy, they can join the church if they choose to."

"That's nice."

"The Amish don't mingle with outsiders often because they're afraid it will taint their faith, but they're not mean or hateful. Naturally, they are human beings, some better than others. But as a whole, the communities are very fine."

"That's great to hear. So, what does your husband think about the Miller Inn and Tavern?"

Keri laughed softly. "Ethan thinks it's a beacon for pure evil. I've tried to tell him that buildings really can't be evil—they are made of concrete, wood, stone. He actually knows I'm right, but he still believes that this area is evil and has been for a very long time."

"People can be evil," Keri told her.

"Oh yes. There have always been rumors about something going on out here. Many like to believe that it's some kind of a sect broken off from an Amish community, but that's because they don't know anything about the Amish. From what I understand, the young people from Ethan's old community avoid this place like the plague, even when they head out for Rumspringa. There are rumors that the devil lives in the woods, or one of his minions, at least. There are rumors of people just disappearing out here. Tales by teenagers drinking beer in the graveyard? Who knows. I couldn't have said anything that was fact. Until now. But if the powers that be know if Special Agent Julie Castro was killed in a rite or killed for being too close on a case, it's not filtering down the ranks."

Keri shook her head. "If anyone knows anything, they haven't told me, either."

As promised, Belinda was very good at cleaning up. They quickly had the kitchen tidy.

"Well, I need to get back to my post," she said.

"If you want me to send you some books, I can," Keri promised.

"I'd love to read your work! Now, let me walk you to the museum and deliver you safely to Mr. Joe Dunhill. He's popped his head in here a few times."

"Really?" Keri said. "I didn't even see him."

"He's looking out for you, big-time. I don't blame him. Safety in numbers here. And, if you don't mind my saying, he's a good-looking dude. Hot. Those eyes of his. You two dating?"

"Um, no. We just met."

"Hey, hey, hey, sometimes that's the best way, to just sleep with someone, huh? Oh, wow, sorry, too much, way too soon. Um, please, don't report me to the battleship."

Keri laughed. "I wouldn't report you... The battleship?"

"Detective Catrina Billings. Hell on wheels."

"I promise, I won't report you. I like you far too much."

She wasn't all that surprised when Belinda gave her a warm hug. "Let me get you back to your boys and get me back to work."

Back in the museum room with the "boys," Keri sat down at the desk. The three men looked at her.

"What?" she asked.

"Curious as to why she wanted to be alone with you," Joe said. "Did she have some kind of astounding revelation to make?"

"No, not at all," Keri said. "She was nice. And as efficient as promised. She rather affirmed a concept we're working on, though. Her husband was Amish, grew up in Lancaster, but left the church after his Rumspringa."

"His rumspring?" Carl asked. "They…drink a lot of rum?"

"*Rumspringa.* It's a period of freedom from obligation," Joe said. "Amish young people get to make the choice to stay with the church or not."

"Oh, that's a very good thing then. Choice is always good," Carl said. He looked at Keri. "And by the way, I actually am quite good at cleaning a kitchen, too. Okay, so if I happen to be alone, I usually eat on a paper plate. But my mom made me clean. I'm okay at it. I like doing dishes, in a way."

"We all do dishes," Dallas said, grinning. "Self-sufficient."

"You like doing dishes, too?" Keri asked Joe, amused.

"I do them well. Do I like doing them? Not particularly, but they're there. You do them. Back to concepts—what else did Belinda say?"

"Oh, her husband, Ethan, believes that the inn itself is evil, which she tells me he knows isn't true, but there's a long-standing rumor that the devil himself lives in the woods. And we agreed that it's people, not buildings, who can be evil."

"Definitely true." Joe taped a sheet to one wall.

She saw that they had made a display, removing the pictures that had been there, and putting up specific likenesses and sheets of paper as well. A time line depicted the past and the present. Newby was there, and Hank Bergen, along with a picture of Beatrice, and sketches and photos of those who had been murdered the night Newby had been hewn down. In place of a crime scene photo, there was a sheet of the words that had been written by the journalist Creighton Mariner, describing the scene at the inn when he had been called in with other men by the coroner:

The killings were so frenzied and brutal that blood and brain matter were found in many a room. Truly, the sight was so ghoulish and gruesome one could only think of the work of a demonic hellhound. Yet, none of this compared to the discoveries deep in the basement where it came to light that Mr. John Newby was ridding himself of unwanted servants and guests, in the most ghastly way possible.

Next, there were pictures of Julie Castro, kidnap victim Barbara Chrome, Spencer Atkins, Milly and Rod Kendall and Stan Gleason, and each member of the Truth Seekers.

And Carl. And her.

"Nice. You're going to have that up when you bring the Truth Seekers back in here?" Keri asked.

"Not sure yet," Dallas said. "I have you and Carl up there. Doesn't say that you're suspects—just that you're the folks who were here when Julie Castro was found. And here," he added, pointing to Spencer and the caterers, "are people who were in the house on the day the body was found."

She noticed as well that there were notations beneath each picture. The old pictures listed date of birth and death, and the contemporary pictures noted date and place of birth. Carl Brentwood from L.A., Brad Holden, Pete Wright and Eileen Falcon were all from New York, Mike Lerner was from Chicago, and Serena Nelson was from Charleston. Rod and Milly Kendall were from York County, as was their partner, Stan Gleason, and Spencer Atkins.

"I think we'll leave them up. Make people question just what we're doing," Dallas said. "There are two theories we're working on and they might go together. The first is that there's a cult at work here. The second is that both someone local and someone not local may be involved."

"And there may well be a New York connection," Joe said.

"Because Brad is from New York?" Keri asked skeptically.

"Because Barbara Chrome was abducted in New York," Dallas said. His phone rang, and he excused himself to answer it but didn't leave the room.

"It's Angela," he told Joe.

"Angela Hawkins, back at headquarters," Joe told Keri and Carl.

Dallas listened a few minutes and glanced over at Joe. He thanked Angela and rang off.

"She checked back over the last two decades for me, looking at missing-person reports. There are dozens that center around Philadelphia. And literally thousands in New York… Well, the police always have a tough time when young adults go missing because some are almost grown-up runaways, some go underground because of drugs or criminal activity, some are really in trouble and some are never seen again. There is no direct tie-in, as in people disappearing straight from the Miller Inn and Tavern, but Angela did find three women who stayed here, showed up in Philadelphia and then disappeared—one a year ago, one five years ago and one eight years ago."

"Three," Keri repeated. "That would mean that they're possibly luring people out here and then killing them every few years?"

Dallas and Joe looked at one another. "Yes," Dallas said quietly. "But the end game is out here. Maybe most of the time in the church, but since we know about the site now, they may have to have a change of venue, or maybe the church wasn't their usual venue. The thing is, we think that these three might be just a few of the people taken."

"Oh, my God. You mean, they might have been killing for years and years, and no one has had any idea?" Carl asked with a choking sound.

"Yes, and it's really gone far enough. You two should just get out of here. Honestly, Carl, if you could just close the place, you might be way better off," Joe told him, waving a hand toward the screenplay Carl was holding. "Shoot your movie."

"I'd sure love to. Sadly, I'm a coward at heart. I have a beautiful life, and I want to keep leading it. I can't go now. Neither can Keri," Carl said.

"What?" Dallas asked.

"We're trying to let you off the hook," Joe said.

"We're in charge. Unless you have a traffic violation

or something else she could use against you, Detective Billings can't keep you here," Dallas told them.

"You don't understand," Keri said. "We can't move on."

"We're scared. We'd never know who to trust again. These people have kidnapped and killed—I'm in New York a lot. We have to stay with you until you catch these people."

Joe and Dallas looked at one another again. Keri knew they were thinking that even if law enforcement was incredibly good, killers weren't always caught.

"Here's what I don't get," Keri said, bringing the conversation back to point. "Why kill an FBI agent and put her in the Miller Inn and Tavern in the middle of a paranormal investigation? They've been killing so quietly. Why would they do something like that?"

"That is a good question. They had to know what they were doing. The only thing I can think is that whoever is leading them had it all happen as a way to keep control," Dallas said.

"Control... When the murder went all over the news everywhere?" Keri said.

"The 'if I go down, you go down' mentality," Joe told her.

"This is a federal crime," Dallas said. "The murder of a law enforcement officer, a federal agent. There's a moratorium on the death penalty in Pennsylvania, but when you've got a dead FBI agent and you're in federal court..." He let his voice trail, lifting his hands.

"So, we think that there's a cult or sect or something like that," Keri said, "and they've made use of the reputation of this place, and Julie was killed on purpose so that people would be too terrified to talk?"

"We're still on working theories," Dallas said.

His phone rang again. He answered it and listened, thanked the caller and hung up. "Detective Billings," he said. "They've been questioning people at sushi restaurants all over the area and they haven't come up with anyone who saw Julie Castro. Of course, they'll keep going. She said that she'd been doing a lot of the questioning herself."

"That's good. Anything new from Special Agent Dot Harrington and her partner?" Joe asked.

"She called earlier. The doctor thinks that Ed Newel will be cognizant enough for a real conversation tomorrow. Dot thought one of us might want to be out there," Dallas said.

"I'll head in," Joe said.

There was a knock at the wooden door to the tavern. Keri jumped.

"Hey," Joe said softly. "Someone knocked. That's a good sign." He smiled at her.

She flushed and nodded, following him to the door. Dallas was there already, opening it to see Belinda with a small group of people.

The Truth Seekers.

Dallas appeared aggravated, but he was controlled when he spoke. "Brad, I told you Carl would be in contact with you when it was time to come back in."

"I know, I know," Brad said, waving at Carl and Keri, standing a few feet behind Dallas and Joe.

"So?" Dallas asked.

"We just thought it would be okay to come in for a minute. We hadn't heard from Carl, and you've been gone a bit, and frankly," Brad said, "we were worried."

"We're fine, just waiting for real clearance," Carl said.

"We're not ready for everyone to come back in yet to stay," Joe said, "but I think we have some great pastries that need to get eaten. Dallas, they're here now. Let's talk for a minute in the tavern."

"Sure," Dallas said.

Brad entered first, Serena behind him, then Mike and then Pete and Eileen, hand in hand.

"Carl, I thought the place was yours again," Brad said.

"Not quite. But soon," Dallas answered for him.

"I'll go find the pastries, and start some coffee," Keri said. "And tea, if anyone would prefer."

Grunts that basically assured her coffee was fine went around.

"Hey, you prepared that fantastic dinner," Carl said. "You should sit and relax, and let someone else get the pastries."

"You made a great dinner, and we weren't invited?" Brad teased.

"Every now and then." Keri turned to Carl. "I know where everything is. I'll only be a minute."

She fled toward the kitchen, and realized she was being followed. Serena was close on her heels, smiling and peppy as ever.

"You know where everything is but direct me. We didn't mean to put you out," she told Keri. "And you know me. Restless as ever. I'd love to be doing something."

"Okay, thanks. The catering company is good. They left all kinds of wonderful individual desserts—little pecan tarts, blueberry tarts, cherry tarts, little brownies," Keri said. "I'll start coffee. It will only take a few minutes, I imagine. Oh, and the flatware is in that drawer, plates up there in the cupboard."

"Got it," Serena said, blond hair swinging around her face as she reached into the cabinet. She set plates down on the counter and looked around. "I think I'm anxious to get back in here, with the cops or FBI or whatever." She paused and looked at Keri, and then whispered, "So…have you experienced anything? Footsteps, doors closing… This place is *soooo* haunted."

"Ah, well, I'm not a paranormal expert," Keri said.

"We should be allowed to come back to stay at the inn, too," Serena said. "That cop, Detective Billings, she was by today. As far as she knew, we could come. I don't know why that FBI guy is being so weird about us. We're the ones who should be in here."

"Well, I know Dallas plans on allowing you in soon," Keri said.

Serena shrugged. "I know how horrible and serious it all is, but hey, bad things happen in other places, and when it's a business, people have to get back at it. Carl should be fighting harder for us. I mean, we agreed to do this for him, so—"

"Carl is a good person. I'm sure he's doing his best."

"So, you haven't been seeing ghosts. What have you been doing?"

"A lot of reading," Keri said.

"Oh, of course, trying to solve the old murder, right?"

"Right," Keri said. "I'll just take the plates out."

She started toward the door and saw that Joe was just inside the kitchen. She didn't know how long he had been there, but she smiled. He and Dallas were great watchdogs. She really was never alone with anyone—including cute, little, energetic Serena.

"Thought I should see if I could help, too," he said. "Want me to grab something?"

"Cups—no, let's go with mugs," Keri said. "I'll grab the cream and sugar and a bunch of the mini desserts."

When they entered the tavern with their first delivery of food and utensils, Carl jumped up, insisting he could help. One more trip and everything was out of the kitchen and set on a table. The group stood and helped themselves, and then found chairs at tables close together.

Apparently, Brad had been as persistent with Dallas about getting back in as he had been with Keri. Dallas, however, was cool, smooth and unmovable.

"Brad, I swear, when I'm finished with everything I need to do here," Dallas said, "I will be clearing Carl to let you back in."

"And you'll be leaving?" Brad asked hopefully. "We work best alone. Ghosts don't show when there are skeptics in the house," he said, adding a smile to his words, as if to make them pleasant but true.

Dallas smiled, glancing over at Joe. "We'll be here as long as we need to be here," he said.

"Is there anything new at all?" Serena asked. "I feel like we're on pins and needles, waiting."

"You know that we can't tell you anything in an active investigation," Dallas said.

"Still following leads," Joe said. "So, what have you been doing? How do you like York County? Have you taken any trips around the countryside?"

Eileen, seated close to Pete and holding hands, laughed softly. "Well, I think we've tried out most of the chain restaurants off the highway."

"Hey, that was almost a joke from Miss I'm-so-serious," Serena said, reaching out to pat Eileen and Pete's joined hands. "Yes, we have tried them all," she said, beaming happily.

"Not so funny," Brad said. "Sorry, Eileen, I mean funny in a sad way. I've been fielding calls from people at other haunted locations who would appreciate us investigating for them. But, Carl, I'm waiting here. Unless, it reaches a point where I just can't anymore."

Mike wasn't paying attention to any of them. He was appreciating one of the desserts. "This chocolate thing is amazing," he informed them.

"We really can't stay, huh?" Eileen asked.

"Eileen," Pete muttered, uncomfortable.

"Hey, it's fine by me," she said.

"I'm not surprised," Joe said easily, "after what you witnessed. You did mention that you thought you might have been pushed down the stairs."

"It might have been my own lack of coordination. Or who knows, maybe one of the ghosts of Miller Inn and Tavern was trying to contact me, warn me, and knocked me down instead. Keri is right. It was so traumatic, we don't know what we really saw or felt. Thank goodness Keri was there and got us out," Eileen said. "Although the danger was gone by then. Poor Agent Castro. It was all over before she was down there. But I'll be ready to come back. You never know... If we get back in here, maybe Agent Castro will show herself somehow, help us find out exactly what happened."

"That's always a possibility, maybe something on an EVP," Serena said earnestly.

They went on talking about the many ways they just might hone in on Julie and perhaps prove what had happened years before.

Finally, Dallas rose. "Hey, guys, I'm on this, I promise. For now, we've all got to get some sleep. We'll see you out to your car. There are still cops out there, but at the moment, it makes me happy when we're all super safe."

Brad rose, and Mike and Pete did the same. Pete was still holding hands with Eileen and drew her up with him.

Serena bounced up, smiling. "Thanks, Dallas, Joe. Carl. Keri. It's good being back in here. Thank you for letting us stay. And good to know that the catering company makes such great desserts."

"We really, really do want to get back in as soon as possible," Brad told Dallas as they walked toward the door.

"I think," Joe said, "that Dallas really, really knows that." He inclined his head as he looked at Brad, partially joking and partially serious.

"Okay, okay," Brad said. "Not tonight, not tomorrow. How about the next day?"

"A true possibility," Dallas said.

Then, at last, they were gone.

"Okay, sleep," Dallas said, looking at Joe.

"First shift again," Joe said.

"Fine with me," Dallas said.

He walked to the front door, assuring himself that it was locked. Joe walked over to the basement door. There was no bolt on it, but there was a lock, and he checked it. Outside, the padlock remained on the hatch cellar door.

"Shall we?" Joe asked, looking at Carl and Keri.

Keri went ahead up the stairs, followed by Carl, then Joe and then Dallas. Dallas headed into his room and Joe set up the chair between Keri's and Carl's.

"Good night. And thanks, Dallas, Joe," Carl said.

Keri offered her thanks as well. Then, once again, she curled into bed in her jeans and the soft knit T she'd chosen to wear for the day.

She didn't think that she would sleep; she lay there, curled toward the connecting door, watching Joe as he sat in the chair, reading off his phone.

Eventually, she did sleep, and it was strange. She knew she had fallen asleep, but she was still aware, and in that awareness, she knew that she'd been afraid to sleep because of her dreams.

The woman in white was near her, whispering to her. "Please, it's all right, you must follow the path, and then you'll know."

The woman in white was gone.

Keri was in back of the tavern, and to her left, she could see the old abandoned church and the graveyard. To her right was the forest.

Soft mist was falling again. It was white and powdery, slightly damp and pleasant against her skin.

She heard chanting.

As the chanting began, the mist began to darken, and she felt the shadows come. She started to run, and the world seemed to have combined, different parts of the landscape colliding so that she raced through trees and through all the broken stones in the graveyard.

The chanting grew louder...

It looked almost as if she was in the basement of the Miller Inn and Tavern, but the walls were trees, and the ceiling was strange sky, but the mist was everywhere, growing darker and darker.

There was the altar, like the altar in the church, like the stone slab John Newby had kept in his basement.

Where Julie had been brought, dead and sliced to ribbons and doused in her own blood.

Keri struggled to awaken; there was something on the altar. Someone...

She didn't want to see. She was so afraid she'd face what was left of her own image.

She heard the whispering again, from the woman in white, Beatrice Bergen.

"You must see and remember, you must remember..."

She forced herself not to scream as she managed to waken at last.

She was safe and sound in the bed, and Dallas and

Joe were just changing positions. Joe started to walk through to his room.

"Please," she said softly.

He paused a long moment, and then he said, "Sure."

And he lay down beside her, far on his side of the bed. Not touching her.

And yet, it was as if she felt every inch of him. She hoped that she would sleep quickly again, because then, and only then, she could do as she wanted...

Inch closer and feel his warmth and strength.

11

"Eileen. She was the one on the basement stairs," Dallas said.

"Yes, so, I'm going to imagine that Pete is involved, too. They're attached to one another almost as if their skin has fused," Joe agreed.

He and Dallas were at the kitchen entry with the door wide open. They could see through the space behind the bar and into the museum where Keri and Carl were, Carl with his head buried in a screenplay, and Keri behind the desk, going through more and more of the many folders kept in the drawer there.

Joe and Dallas spoke quietly, throwing out theories.

"Brad. He's the great leader," Dallas said. "Anxious to get back in here. Is he afraid that he missed something and the forensic teams missed it as well?"

"Maybe. I don't know. Too obvious? Also, Brad seems to be too successful. Growing more successful all the time. He's the one who chooses what they do and don't do. The others go home when they're not on an 'investigation.'"

"Home is New York City for him," Dallas noted.

"Yes, four or five hours to get out here, depending on traffic and who's driving," Joe agreed. "Easy enough to be involved in something. I don't think that they dance with the devil nightly," he added dryly.

"I guess the devil likes to dance," Dallas mused. "Eileen and Pete are also from New York City—easy enough commute—unless it's a parade day in NYC. Then, it could take four or so hours just from one end of the island to the other."

"Okay, Mike's home is in Chicago, a longer commute, and Serena Nelson is from Charleston—a much longer commute."

"Angela is tracking their credit card records, searching for one of them who might not have had handy cash for regular Pennsylvania trips and never suspected that they'd be suspects. Back to Brad, internet ghost-guy superstar. He made the arrangements, he lives in New York, and he's driving everyone nuts about accessing the inn. You don't seem to think of him as guilty. Why is that?" Dallas asked.

"I could be way off. I believe Brad in a way I'm not sure I do the others. Hey, I did find someone I do trust a lot. Belinda—Officer Belinda Emory. And she's not local. She just married a man from Lancaster."

"I liked her and her partner," Dallas agreed. "They seem clean as whistles, and while there can always be a dirty cop, I'm hoping we don't have that situation here. If there is a dirty cop, I don't think it's one of them. However, I think there is one Truth Seeker not being truthful in the least. Serena Nelson—Miss Annoyingly Cheerful."

"Possibly, but not because she's annoyingly cheerful. I just can't find a real reason to suspect her. She was in the room with the others when Eileen went down the stairs and Keri went after her."

"However, with all the missing footage from the cameras, we don't know who was where when, except for those last few minutes. When Eileen stumbled down the stairs and Keri followed, the others all swear that they were together in room 207."

"Carl was with one of them or the other almost all the time, but he wasn't with *everyone* all the time. Say it is a group perpetrating this murder and possibly others— one of the group could have not physically committed the murder, and yet still be in on it," Joe said. "Anyway, I should get Keri, and we should get going. I'm hoping to hell that Dot Harrington and Jared Cabot might have found something in Philadelphia and that Ed Newel will be coherent now and might be able to tell us more. Of course, Harrington or Cabot should have reported anything to you, but there's still nothing like being there and doing the questioning yourself."

Dallas grinned, looking at him, and agreed.

"Sorry, I can stay here, and you can go, if you like."

Dallas shook his head. "No, I trust your instincts. That's why you're going to make a great Krewe agent. I keep thinking that maybe if I'm here, the ghosts that appear for Miss Wolf will make an appearance for me, and that they'll give us what we need."

"So far, our woman in white, Beatrice Bergen, seems

to want to clear her father's name. Her father has made one brief appearance. I didn't see him at all, I just know what Keri told me. Anyway, I figure three to four hours travel time and a few hours in the city." He glanced at his watch. "Nine a.m. We'll be back by dark."

"Take what time you need. I think if we do let the Truth Seekers back in tomorrow, I'll call for reinforcements from the head office—there are five of them, two of us, and even with cops outside, I'd like better odds. Hard to bodyguard two people and carry out an investigation."

"Good plan," Joe said. "I'll get Keri."

He walked behind the bar and across to the entry to the museum room.

Keri looked up at him, smiling. "I know we have to get to the hospital, but after, I'd really appreciate it if we could spare an hour. I have an old friend in the city who helped me years ago on my second book, when I was working on a Colonial murder case. Dr. Sam Jeffries. I didn't think of it before this morning, but when I was going through these files this morning, I found an article he wrote on the inn and the surrounding area. He might have some insight."

"Absolutely," Joe assured her. "Should we head out?"

"So," Carl said, "it's just me and Dallas hanging here?"

"And two cops outside," Dallas reminded him. "We'll be fine."

"You won't leave me, right?" Carl asked him.

"I won't leave you," Dallas promised.

"You know, I'm really not bad with a sword. I had a great cameo in a pirate movie, and we had to learn how to sword fight. Spent a lot of time with a master. Maybe I should find a sword to run around with. I'm not fond of guns. I'm always afraid that I'd shoot myself before I managed to use it for any kind of defense. Not that I mind you guys having guns, but you know what you're doing with them. Sorry, I'm babbling. I have reading, of course, but Dallas, if you want to explore…?"

"I think a check on the whole of the inn is always in order," Dallas told him. "We'll lock these guys out and get started."

Dallas and Carl followed them to the door. Carl hugged Keri. She smiled, hugging him back, and then Joe and Keri were finally out.

They waved to the new foursome of cops who were on duty. The cops waved back.

"Philadelphia is a really big city, you know," Keri told Carl as they drove.

"The sixth most populated in the United States," he said.

"How can you think that we'll find anything there? But I'm thrilled that I found the article by Dr. Sam Jeffries. He's an amazing man—taught at Yale and Harvard. And so nice. He was great with me, even though I didn't have much of a record when I asked for his help."

"I'll be looking forward to meeting him," Joe said. He glanced her way. "What was your take on the Truth Seekers when you met them?"

"My take," she repeated, staring at the new hotel as they rounded the curve onto the highway that would take them to Philadelphia. "Naturally, I looked up what Brad did. My publicist, Carmen Menendez, is brilliant and does all kinds of things I wouldn't begin to know how to do. Reading is subjective, so you have to hit the right audience." She stopped speaking, wincing as she glanced over at him.

"What?" he asked.

"This may seem off point, but it's the whole story and why I feel the way I do."

"Long drive," he assured her. "Talk away."

"Okay, so… Carl's people contacted Carmen and gave her all the information about the inn and about the Truth Seekers. I admit, I thought it was ridiculous. I will never claim to be a historian, but I do meticulous research on what I do write. I wasn't sure about people who turn every creak of a floorboard into a ghostly occurrence. I'm from Richmond, my house is over one hundred and fifty years old, and floorboards creak all the time.

"Anyway, Carmen was so excited she could have imploded. She thought that this would be fantastic— a chance to sell tens of thousands more books, in her mind. Personally, I think she has a crush on Carl, but I looked up the Truth Seekers and watched a number of their videos. Several of them proved that the noises were faulty pipes and that lights flickering had to do with bad wiring. I liked what I saw.

"And I have to admit, the story of the Miller Inn and Tavern is wonderful without any ghostly occurrences. Ghost stories have taken over, but… It's like Philadelphia, I guess. I love just standing where those men used words and the power of persuasion to create a country. I love walking into Independence Hall and imagining what it was like—fiery and fierce as they all put forth their ideas on what should be." She hesitated. "Just as there were such brilliant men in history—we can look back at this place and the roster of those who went through—brilliant men, willing to fight for right and justice. History has always given us heroes—and monsters. And right now I guess we're dealing with monsters."

"Whatever's been going on, it all started a long time ago," Joe said. "It's chilling to think that there might have been many, many victims throughout the years. It's certainly easier to believe that someone died quickly having their throat slit than it is to imagine them being slowly sliced up, but one way or the other, a life is stolen. If there is something that has been going on for years, many of the killers may have gotten away with it and lived out their natural lives."

"Do you really think that it could be so insidious and go so deep?" Keri asked him.

"I don't know. But I do think we're on to something. This is bugging me, though. If there have been murders committed by a strange sect of devil worshippers through the years, why practically invite in massive law enforcement by making such a show of Julie's body? Sometimes, I can't help but think that she was displayed as she was to put blame on others."

"Okay, that would mean that there are possibly two sets of people killing people? I think we're really grasping at straws there," Keri said. "We don't think it's possible for one person to have tricked Julie, sliced her throat, collected her blood, got her down to the basement and then displayed with the blood thrown all over her."

"Right," he agreed.

They eventually reached Philadelphia, and Joe was able to easily find the hospital. They gave their ID upon entering, and again on the floor where they encountered the guard watching over Agent Ed Newel.

Jared Cabot was in the room with Ed, and he came out to welcome them as Joe was pocketing his credentials. Joe looked around the room as they entered. Dot Harrington was not there.

"Dotty is out on the streets, watching the clothing store, seeing if anyone comes back in to use the phone," Jared explained. "And—" he turned to the bed where Newel lay connected to all kinds of wires and a pulley "—this is Special Agent Ed Newel. Ed, I'd like you to meet one of our new consultants, ready to head into the academy, and Miss Keri Wolf, historian and writer."

Ed Jewel was clearly doing better—he was conscious, and his bed was at an incline—but he still looked like hell. There were bandages on his nose, and his eyes still appeared to be blackened. He was in his midthirties with a full head of dark hair and large dark eyes, and he tried to smile when he lifted a hand. "Hey."

Jared indicated a chair; there was another across the bed. "Please, take the chairs. I've been sitting. A little stretch will be good."

"Thank you," Keri told him, sitting down.

Ed Newel studied her and tried another smile. "I've read a few of your books. I should read all of them."

"Thank you," she said. "I just deal with very old crimes. You put your life on the line every day."

"Desk duty for a good while now." There was a catch in his voice. "Which will be fine. I had the best partner in the world. Now, I don't." He sighed deeply. "And you're here hoping that I can tell you something that no one else has been able to get from me. Don't you think that I'd do anything—anything at all—to catch Julie's killer?"

"Absolutely," Joe said. "But you know as well as I do that tiny details remembered later can help. I know we're grasping at straws, and I know that Dot and Jared are your coworkers, and I'm so damned sorry to make you relive any of this. But will you go over it again?"

"Please," Keri said softly.

"Are you going to start writing about modern crime?" Ed asked.

"No," she said, a little shiver jolting through her visibly. She hesitated and then added, "I do believe, however, that the past may have something to do with what happened to Julie."

"Okay, so, one more time. Julie was with me but waiting," Ed said. "I was going in and out of consciousness, but I could swear, Julie got a phone call, and then rushed out. It must have been about Barbara Chrome. Searching for her was the reason we were in Philadelphia. We were following leads in New York when Julie got a call on her cell phone that brought us here."

"From someone claiming that they had seen Barbara Chrome, right?" Joe said.

"Yes. We'd traced the call to a clothing store. We

went there and had local police there, and we questioned the staff. The manager didn't believe that any of his people made the call. As you probably know, he believed that it had to be a regular, someone who knew right where the phone was. Identifying prints was almost impossible because there were prints on top of prints. We pulled credit card receipts for that day, looked into regular customers, but could find nothing more than parking tickets. Then…we were on the street, walking—oh, the original call came to Julie's cell phone, not the office. But she was convinced that the call was legitimate, and so was our assistant field director. With the reward money offered, we thought that someone in on the kidnapping might be ready to betray anyone else involved and give Barbara up. We weighted the possibility that Barbara left on her own. I'm sure you have thought about all these possibilities as well."

"Yes," Joe said simply. "How and when were you hit?"

"Right by Independence Hall. Julie thought that she saw Barbara and gave chase. I raced after her, and then…nothing."

"And the driver didn't stop. Julie didn't stop—there were no witnesses?"

"It was pretty late at night. The area wasn't busy. Some bars and restaurants were still open, but by the time the police and ambulance got there, everyone was gone. That's to the best of my knowledge. I don't know what happened after that one *wham*. Julie didn't see because she'd already rounded a corner. Go figure. All my training and I forget to look both ways before crossing a street and get slammed by some drunk asshole in a hurry to get home."

"We can all forget in the heat of pursuit," Joe assured him.

"But no one has any idea who hit you?" Keri asked.

Ed shook his head. "How dumb could I be?"

"Maybe not so dumb. Did it occur to you that someone might have hit you on purpose?"

"On purpose?" Ed asked.

"With you out of the way, it had to be much easier to get to Julie."

"You think Julie was targeted here?"

"I think it's more than possible. One agent is far easier to take by surprise than two agents. So, if you're out of commission, and things are happening so fast that she doesn't have backup right away, she would have been an easier mark. But let's go back. She thought that she saw Barbara Chrome here in Philadelphia?"

Ed nodded. "Dot and Jared have been following up on that, too. Barbara's picture is with the Philadelphia police, and it's been all over the media."

"Her appearance could be far different by now," Keri pointed out.

"Exactly," Joe said.

"But," Ed said, looking baffled, "they'd have to know that we'd send more agents."

"There might be a time factor in here," Joe said thoughtfully.

"But cops are crawling around everywhere, here and out in York County."

"I think it's a sound possibility that you were struck

on purpose," Joe said. "Barbara—or a lookalike—might have been bait to get you two out on the street, and the car might have been waiting." He paused. "Ed, I'm sorry, but is there anything that you can think of? I'm sure that someone else has told you by now that Julie's last meal was sushi. Do you know of any restaurants or even grocery stores she liked particularly?"

"I know she loved sushi. And I don't. I figured she was taking advantage of not having meals with me," Ed said. His eyes misted. "Julie was a good kid. She was a great agent. She worked all the overtime she could. Her parents died when she was young, and she was working really hard to keep the grandma who raised her in a decent assisted living facility. *Decent* is the key word. A lot of those places smell of urine and death and really suck."

"We're so sorry," Keri murmured.

"So sorry," Joe agreed, and then pressed, "Any place in particular. Especially between here and York County?"

"We never went out to York County," Ed said. "But…" He paused, his voice trailing, his bruised forehead wrinkling in concentration. "There is a place at the edge of the city. I mean, there was an Asian restaurant right by our hotel where we went a few times—they had sushi and Thai and Chinese entrees as well. But we had refrigerators in our rooms, and she liked this particular grocery store and I like it because they carry their own brand of soft drinks that are really good. The place is called Greta's. I'm trying to think of the address, but—"

"We can find an address," Joe assured him. He stood, looking over at Jared. "I guess we're going to head on over to Greta's, check on a few more things. Maybe walk the Independence Hall area and stop in on a historian. If anything—"

"Not to worry. I have your number on speed dial, yours and Dallas's," Jared said.

Keri was up as well, thanking Ed, telling him to get rest and to get better.

"Bring me a book. As soon as the headaches stop, I'm going to start reading," Ed told her.

"My pleasure and privilege," Keri told him.

Joe, too, paused by the bed and thanked Ed.

"I can't see how I helped. Except that, yeah, maybe I was hit on purpose. But there's no way you could catch that driver now. Anyway, not sure what that will do for you, but if I did help, God knows I'm grateful. I'd like to meet this person. Maybe not. I'd want to skin them alive, whoever did this."

They took their leave. Keri looked at him anxiously as they headed to the car. "If Ed was struck on purpose, and Julie was just ahead of him, chasing Barbara or someone who looked like her, Julie was a target, and this whole thing was more insidious than we even imagined."

"Right now, we need proof of something," Joe said, "or a confession from someone. I don't see anyone involved in this just breaking down and coming clean. I'd like to check out Greta's, and then we can see your historian friend."

"Don't you think that the police would have been out to the store by now, if they're checking local sushi places?"

"Maybe, maybe not. Greta's is a grocery store that sells prepared foods. It's not a restaurant, per se."

"Maybe it's a wild-goose chase. Well, at least we could have some sushi ourselves. I don't even know if you like sushi."

"I like almost any kind of food, anywhere," he assured her. "Black coffee and food. Was I a well-trained cop or what?"

She shook her head.

"What?"

"You don't like donuts," she reminded him.

"True, but in a pinch donuts will do."

He stopped, glancing at the clock in the dashboard. "I'd like to stay late and try the streets at night, though I don't know that we're going to get anything. I'll tell Dallas that we're okay with him bringing the Truth Seekers back in tomorrow, although I don't want them in the museum. I still think you might find something there." He glanced her way. "Sorry, we're already into the afternoon, and I want to make sure we see your professor."

"You still think that the past can help the present?"

"I do. I'm going to call Dallas and get us a couple of rooms booked here for the night, if that's okay with you."

"Yes, sure, but we don't need two rooms," she told him. "I've actually gotten some sleep—lots of disjointed dreams, but I have slept, because I haven't been afraid of someone sneaking in. You're a great watchdog."

"Well, thanks," he told, wondering if his tone was as dry as it tasted on his lips. Joe was glad that she'd had some sleep. He was low on sleep himself. Lying next to her, feeling her curl against him… It had made it hard to get real rest.

But he had to maintain control. That was a major lesson he'd learned in the police academy from a great instructor. Control and a poker face were essential for letting due process of law bring drug peddlers, child molesters and murderers to justice.

But, well, he'd had a few waking dreams himself, all about the way she felt against him, and the way she might feel against him…

"Sure, we can do one room," he said.

Control? It was one thing he had in abundance.

12

Philadelphia was truly one of the nation's great cities. Keri couldn't help but love it, from the contemporary energy exuding from the people on the streets to the reminders that it was here that the American forefathers had squabbled, given impassioned speeches, and somehow managed to come together and create a new nation.

She enjoyed the sights as they drove, from historic landmarks to new buildings and houses. An array of architecture spanning centuries. Finally, they reached their destination, a shining example of the new.

The parking lot for the grocery store was very large and busy, and on entering the store, she quickly saw why it was worth driving out to the edges of the city. Greta's was an amazing place.

Big. Eclectic. There were the usual groceries, dairy, meat, produce and so on, as well as many ethnic foods, including Mexican, Japanese, German and more.

"I wish this place was near me," Keri said.

"It is nice. Clean, organized," Joe said. "Let's take a loop around it, see the layout. Then, we'll find people and see what they might know, if anything."

One little booth in the center of the store specialized in teas. Another was a deli. And one was a little sushi kiosk.

"I see why Julie liked the place," Keri said. "I'll bet the sushi is as fresh as it gets."

"But alas, we're not shopping," Joe told her. "Let's get to it. Back to the office area up front."

Joe inquired about the store manager, and he and Keri were led to an office where Mr. Briggs—a stout little man, balding, but with a pleasant smile and courteous manner—was working on a computer. Briggs was surprised by the inquiry. No, as far as he knew, the police had not been out with photos of the federal agent who had been killed, though he'd seen her picture in the news.

He was polite to both of them, accepting Joe's credentials, but looking at him and Keri curiously, as if they made an odd pair for law enforcement.

"You're an agent—or a cop?" he asked Keri.

She started to answer; Joe did it for her. "She's a consultant, working with me."

A consultant.

Did it matter what she was called if they could find answers?

"We all heard about what happened," Briggs said. "Tragic. I'd have thought if one of my people saw Special Agent Castro they would have mentioned it. But let's see. I know I didn't see her, but I don't work the sushi kiosk," he told them. "I'll bring you out to Myrna. She's there most days, at least from 11:00 in the morning, when we open the sushi bar, to 9:00 at night, when we close. We can also check with the cashiers." He frowned, looking at Joe. "You have the pictures?"

"On my phone," he assured him.

He walked them from the front office to the sushi bar in the middle of the store. A pretty young woman of mixed Asian and European heritage was there, chatting with a man as she handed him the rolls he requested.

When her customer moved on, Briggs called out to her. "Myrna, these people are with law enforcement, trying to find out if the agent who was murdered out in York might have been in here."

"Oh!" Myrna looked at them with wide, concerned eyes. "I saw her picture on the news, and no, I'm so sorry. I didn't see her. Not in here. And I would know. The story about her death just seems so terrible. I hope you find whoever did it."

"So do we," Joe said. "Agent Castro's partner said that she loved this place, that they came here often."

"Well, we have package sushi in the refrigerator cases that people can just pick up, too. If I was busy and she was by, I might not have noticed."

"Thank you," Joe said. "I appreciate your help."

"We can go to the cashiers," Mr. Briggs said.

"Just one second," Joe asked, smiling politely. "And really, thank you for your time." He paused, flipping through his phone, producing another picture. It was of the kidnapping victim, Barbara Chrome.

"Did you ever see this young lady in here?" Joe asked.

"She's…familiar," Myrna said. "Oh, of course—I've seen her picture on the news, too. She's the girl who was kidnapped in New York." She studied the picture and frowned suddenly. "You know... I might have seen her in here. Not like this. The woman who was in here did look like this girl, but she had dark hair. Short, feathery, dark hair—it just framed her face. And she was wearing big glasses and a hat. Maybe I'm crazy, but looking at this picture again... I think that yes, she might have been in here."

"Thank you," Joe told her, and he turned back to Briggs. "May we speak with the cashiers?"

"Of course!"

Luckily, it wasn't a busy time, and they were able to go from cashier to cashier. They'd spoken with three women and one man before they came upon an older gentleman with big, wire-rimmed glasses. He nodded as soon as they asked him about seeing Julie Castro, before they even showed him a picture.

"I was so sad when I saw the news. Yes, I saw her... three times, I think. Twice with a nice-looking young man, and once I think she was alone. She loved the sushi here. I was always ringing up those to-go packs. We do a wonderful job with sushi here, but that Myrna, she could work anywhere she wanted, I daresay."

"It's a beautiful sushi bar," Keri assured him.

He smiled, then grew grave again, shaking his head. His spectacles fell down his nose a bit and he righted them. "So sad. She was always polite and kind. Once there was someone in line behind her with just two items and she insisted they go before her. Right kind of woman. Someone taught her manners, sadly lacking these days, it seems. Did you know her?"

"I didn't know her," Joe said, "but from everything

I've heard, she was lovely, just as you're saying. A bright and well-trained agent. We're determined to solve her murder and bring the killer to justice."

"Good," the man said. He offered his hand. "I'm George Colin," he said. "Wish I could give you more."

Joe and Keri each shook his hand, and then Keri waited quietly as Joe brought up the photos of Barbara Chrome on his phone.

"What about this woman?"

George peered at the screen. He shook his head but kept frowning. "No, no…haven't seen her, but…" He looked, then paused, shrugging. "Odd, she looks familiar, but no."

"Imagine her with short dark hair, big glasses and a droopy hat," Keri said.

"Hmm," George said thoughtfully, taking the phone from Dallas and eyeing it carefully through his bifocals. "Yeah, yeah. She bought sushi, too." He looked up at them. "It was the day before the news that the agent had been killed hit the media. But I tell you, I wouldn't have put her together with the blonde in the picture if you hadn't said what you did, miss," he told Keri. "I do remember her, because she wanted to buy cigarettes, but I wouldn't sell them to her. She said she forgot her ID, but I wasn't born yesterday. She might have been eighteen—you know how quickly girls mature these days—but I go by the rules. I'm retiring soon, beautiful pension from this place, and I'm not messing up a great record by selling smokes or alcohol to any minors. I said that was the way it was. I needed ID, I told her, or no sale."

"What did she do?" Joe asked.

"She paid and left, cursing at me," George said.

"What time, approximately?" Keri asked him.

"Well, I get off about four, and it was a bit before I got off, so… I think it must have been about three or three thirty in the afternoon."

They thanked George and the manager, Mr. Briggs, and headed outside to call Dallas and report on what had transpired through the day.

When he finished the call, he turned back to Keri and said, "I'm an idiot. We need to go back into the store."

"What did we forget to ask?"

"Nothing that I know of, but you like sushi, right? And it's well after lunchtime."

She smiled. "Why do I think that you don't really like sushi?"

"I like it fine. And if I didn't, I could choose a deli sandwich or something else. Might as well eat while we're here. And you might want to call your professor friend and see if it's all right if we get there within the next hour or so."

She pulled out her phone and texted the professor. He wrote right back, telling her he was just plugging away at a speech and any time that she arrived would be a welcome break. He was pleased to be of any assistance he could, especially as it referred to the recent atrocity that had taken place at the Miller Inn and Tavern.

"Okay, on to sushi, and then the professor," Joe said.

They headed to the sushi bar and stood in the queue. Myrna was very efficient and could create any roll within seconds, slice up sashimi, and prepare nigiri.

Keri ordered tuna and salmon with lots of avocado, freshly scooped, and Joe just asked Myrna to do a double for him of whatever Keri wanted.

They sat on the little stools in front of the kiosk and Keri quickly discovered why Joe had decided on sushi. She heard his phone as it vibrated, and he quickly showed her a new picture. It had been created by a computer artist at headquarters—Krewe headquarters, she presumed—and showed what Barbara Chrome would look like with short dark hair, sunglasses and a big, drooping hat.

He called to Myrna who came over to them. "Yes, yes, that's her. That's the missing girl from New York… with dark hair?"

"Computer manipulation," Joe explained. "And thank you."

"Oh, you're so welcome. Can I do anything else?" she asked.

Joe produced a card. "If you think of anything, call me."

"I will, of course," Myrna assured him. Keri lowered her head; Myrna seemed to have a little crush on him.

"Why are you smiling?" he whispered to her.

"She liked you."

"Some people do."

"I'm sure. I think I said that you were okay. Not the total jerk you were on first impression."

"Well, two people like you better than me."

"Oh?"

"George and Mr. Briggs."

"There you go. I'm likable, too."

"When you're not lying."

She inhaled and looked at him. "Not fair. You know why I lied."

"I do," he said, and he added gently, "And it's okay." He put his phone to his ear and she knew that he was calling Dallas. As he waited, he said, "Great sushi, huh?"

"It really is." She listened as he told Dallas that they should go with the picture and she knew that law enforcement and the media would be given the new image of Barbara Chrome, along with a message saying that there was a reward out for her safe return to her parents.

When he ended the call, he asked, "You ready to move on?"

"Yes, Almost-Special Agent Dunhill. And thank you for the sushi."

"Nice and reasonable here, good for the budget," he said. As she stood and they said goodbye and thank you again to Myrna, he set his hand on the small of her back, leading her out. She lowered her head; it was a courteous touch. It still did so much to her.

She hurried ahead of him as they walked to the car, quickly opening the door herself. She pulled up Dr. Sam Jeffries's address and Joe set it into the navigator. They found their way to Dr. Jeffries's apartment building, where Keri hit a button to announce that they were there. They were quickly buzzed up.

She hadn't seen Dr. Jeffries in a few years, but they kept up with one another through social media and the occasional email. Dr. Jeffries was a widower; he and his childhood sweetheart had been married almost fifty years. His home was filled with pictures of his children and grandchildren. Though he was in his early seventies, he still lectured and kept busy. He was slim—he watched his diet—and had a headful of white hair that went in every direction, powder-blue eyes and a deeply lined face. He was quick to greet them with pleasure.

"I ask the kids and grandkids to leave me alone a few days to work, and then I work, but I go a little crazy because the kids and grandkids aren't calling me," he said, greeting Keri with a hug and shaking Joe's hand. He looked Joe up and down, surveying with a judgmental eye. "Strapping fellow, eh? Good for you. Though I have seen some truly fine detectives who are tiny." He paused and tapped his head. "The brain is always our greatest weapon."

"He has a brain, I promise," Keri told Dr. Jeffries, trying to hide her smile.

"Brains and brawn. Good combo," he said. "So, come in and talk to me. The Miller Inn and Tavern... Let's head into the study."

He turned and started through the apartment. Joe looked at Keri, lifting an amused eye, and indicated that she should go first.

Dr. Jeffries's study was awash with books, folders, papers everywhere, and a computer and printer on his desk. There was one big plush chair and a love seat across from the desk. Keri chose the chair, leaving the love seat for Joe.

"I watched what there was of the videos put out by those Truth Seekers when they started up with this project," Dr. Jeffries said, "and then...nothing. And then, the news about the murder of the FBI agent came out. I figured you might be calling me, Keri, since I saw you on the introduction video. But just the same, I know that you did your homework on the case. So, what do you know, and what do you think I can help you with?"

She leaned forward, "Sam, I don't believe that Hank Bergen committed the infamous ax murders. He was a good church-going fellow, and it seemed that his daughter, Beatrice, was just as decent a human being. We've come to believe through old notes and newspapers and local rumor that a cult was operating at the time—not benign, old healing witchcraft, but something different. Something that smacked more of a Hellfire Club gone homicidal than anything else. The murders at the inn weren't discovered until the next day when a delivery was being made. After the coroner called in his little jury to view the scene, Hank Bergen was set upon by his neighbors, dragged out to a tree and hanged."

Dr. Jeffries picked up a file on his desk and read his notes.

Keri went on, "After Bergen was lynched, everyone denied being part of the mob, but the community wasn't that big. Everyone knew who had done what. They just weren't telling, either because they were involved, or because they were afraid of those who had been involved."

"I agree," Dr. Jeffries said. "Now, of course, I always assumed that those men who saw what had been done to the guests at the inn had to be part of the lynch mob."

"Okay," Keri said carefully, "here's what I started thinking—Hank Bergen didn't do it. John Newby almost assuredly killed Beatrice Bergen, but no one knew for sure. Maybe someone knew about his little torture chamber." She shrugged. "And who knows—they might have actually believed that Satan did have a part-time home in the woods and that they were worshipping him with human sacrifice."

"Your theory is that Newby wasn't alone in his depravity," Dr. Jeffries said.

Joe spoke up. "One of the very men brought in for the inquest might have been the killer. Whatever their little congregation was, it formed for purely evil purposes from the beginning. And someone else was in on it, obviously," he said. "But why kill Newby then?"

"Maybe they were afraid that Newby had become a danger to them. Perhaps they worried that someone was going to find his torture chamber because it was becoming so out of control? Before Beatrice, he might not have preyed upon anyone local. They killed Newby because they could blame it on Hank Bergen. Everyone knew that he was frantic over his daughter, and he had been saying that he had thought she'd gone to the tavern, looking for work that was off of her father's farm," Dr. Jeffries said. "Is there a reason you don't believe that Hank Bergen was the killer?" he asked Keri.

"A farmer not known for a bad deed in his life doesn't usually go off the deep end and kill one guilty man and six innocent people," Keri said.

"I agree with you," Dr. Jeffries said. "I've looked into the men who were asked to view the scene for the inquest. Three were farmers, one of whom was trying to buy some of Bergen's land. Bergen didn't want to sell. Another of the men, Frank Gold, was a butcher. Not that the killings took any anatomical skill. But all of them might have been accustomed to killing animals, and if they were worshipping the devil, either for real or for playing at a rite, they might have been long accustomed to making animal sacrifices. It might have been little more than a small jump for men like that to kill their fellow man—and woman." He paused and looked up. "Tea?"

"Pardon?" Keri asked.

"My most wonderful housekeeper, Ellie, heard I was having guests. She left all kinds of little sandwiches and said I just needed to turn on the pot for tea."

"We don't want to put you out in any way," Joe told him.

"I'm delighted to have you. We'll wander into the kitchen," Dr. Jeffries said, rising.

It was a delightfully big kitchen for an apartment in a large city. Joe stood by Keri as Dr. Jeffries turned on the little pot to boil water. "This is great," Joe said. "It's getting late, and we won't have to worry about dinner. We can just wander downtown a bit after. We're right by the National Historic Park."

Keri laughed. "We just had sushi."

"And now we'll have little sandwiches."

She smiled and set tea bags in cups. Dr. Jeffries indicated that they should sit at the big table in the center of the room.

"Keri, your instincts are always good with historic crimes, but I'm assuming this also has to do with the current situation."

"If there's a cult of devil worshippers in the area, and has been for ages, then, yes, I think it might have trickled down to the present," Keri said.

"Do you think that the murdered agent might have been part of the cult?" Dr. Jeffries asked.

Keri looked at Joe, letting him take that one.

"I don't think so," Joe said. "Julie had been with the FBI well over a decade and based in New York City. Now, I think that somehow, Barbara Chrome, the kidnapping victim, might be involved. But Barbara is just seventeen. I don't know how she could have been a member of anything in rural Pennsylvania."

"Why do you think she's involved? Can you say without divulging government secrets?" Dr. Jeffries asked.

"She's been seen in Philadelphia. Her appearance has been completely changed, but she was seen in a grocery store, and apparently was just shopping and not under any kind of duress," Joe said.

"Hmm. Well, there is such a thing as Stockholm syndrome," Dr. Jeffries said. "Like Patty Hearst—I was never sure that girl deserved the sentence she received. Kid was locked in a closet, beaten, raped… I'd probably have danced naked on the water if my captors had asked me to after everything she went through. Hers was an interesting trial—she was accused of freely joining in with the Symbionese Liberation folk. She was something like eighty pounds when she was found—and in prison, she suffered a collapsed lung. People said that the rich get away with more. That may be true, but I think Patty was punished for being rich—she wasn't pardoned until Bill Clinton was president. Anyway, her case is one for debate, but my point here is that we're talking about a very rich little girl who may or may not have been kidnapped. If she was kidnapped, she might be terrified. Threaten enough, torture enough, and people will do just about anything you want."

"I agree," Joe said.

Keri asked, "Sam, do you go out to that area often?"

"Not so much," he said. "My wife used to love to go to Lancaster and York Counties. She adored Amish quilts and the farmer's markets. Now, when I head out, I like going over to Gettysburg. Can never get enough of the history there." Dr. Jeffries waved a hand impatiently in the air. "Oh, I forgot what just may help you," he said, rising suddenly. He headed back to his office.

He returned in just a minute with an old, leather-bound volume and flipped through it carefully, telling them, "This is an old journal. I found it at a barn sale in Lancaster. This is how some of them used to come, beautifully bound in leather like this. I couldn't resist the craftsmanship. I don't know where it came from— neither did the guy I bought it from, he'd found it with other items in a trunk in his attic. But it seems to be the diary of a young Amish man who had just returned from Rumspringa. He talks about his trip to the city, and how he has determined that he will be baptized into his faith. But here… This borders on what you're talking about. See?" He brought the book to Keri, and Joe stood to come and stare over her shoulder.

Keri read aloud. "'The world is not safe. Only in our faith can we find strength, life, health and the safety of our company. Some temptations did not seem evil, merely self-serving. But when I met the fellow from York, it was like vast doors to hell itself opened. Darkness spread around his very person. He showed me an insignia and said that if I wanted the true freedom to be found in life, I would come with him. I have drawn it here to the best of my memory. I want it known to my children and their children. At any time that they see this sign, they must turn quickly, find peace and safety in the bosom of our people, and never be led so astray.'"

"It looks like a hawk with flared wings," Joe observed. "Flying over some kind of…ram or horned god. A devil sign, at least, like many I've seen depicted." He looked up at Dr. Jeffries. "Does this suggest to you a cult of Satanists?"

"At any rate, it suggests some kind of demon or devil worship. But I wish the young author would have kept going in his description. Most richly forested, out-of-the-way places do wind up with rumors of devils or demons or the like. People grab hold of hexes and witchcraft and all that, and you do have the famous murders from the 1920s," Dr. Jeffries said.

Keri was thoughtful.

"What are you thinking?" Joe asked her.

"Okay, let's say that back in 1926 it was one or more of the upstanding men brought in for the inquest who carried out the murders. They murdered Newby because he was getting out of control, and they could blame it on Bergen, who everyone knew was sick over his daughter. Then, lest Bergen have an alibi and be exonerated, they stirred up a lynch mob. No one was ever prosecuted for his death, and at the time, the assumption was that he had been the murderer and therefore, the murderer had been taken care of, case closed. If that's the case…"

"We're back to a conspiracy, then and now," Joe said. "We don't know just who might be involved, whether they had a personal agenda, or if it was all part of being in their cult," Joe said. "In my mind, people are being manipulated. Someone with an agenda is pulling the strings."

"Like a giant squid with many arms," Dr. Jeffries said. "Lop off the head, and the rest of them are useless."

"Find the head…or a weak arm. One willing to talk," Joe said.

"I wish I could give you a connection of some kind," Dr. Jeffries said. "Do I think that something may be going on in York County? Has it been going on forever? Could be. That's a pretty creepy insignia."

"While you have it there," Joe said, "I'll just shoot a picture of that insignia."

"Have you seen it before?" Dr. Jeffries asked as Joe used his cell phone to snap pictures.

"No, I haven't," Joe said. "Keri?"

"No, but I haven't gotten through all the drawers in the desk in the museum, much less everything that has been displayed there. Message the pictures to me, please?"

"Of course," Joe told her.

"Conspiracy and cultists," Dr. Jeffries said, nodding. "But I have a feeling you were figuring most of this already," he added, looking at Joe.

"Forming an equation," Joe said. "But until today,

I couldn't figure out who had killed everyone back in the twenties, and it would make sense if the same person or people who committed the mass murder in the Miller Inn and Tavern were the same ones who saw to it that Hank Bergen was lynched before he could defend himself. Something which might have bearing on the present." He looked over at Keri. "We should probably pick up here and get going."

"Pick up what? Paper plates and three teacups—get out of here. Go solve crimes," he told him.

Keri hugged him goodbye; Dr. Jeffries and Joe shook hands. "Nice to know we can call on you, sir," Joe told him.

"Any time," Dr. Jeffries said. "And any crime, young man. I need to challenge my mind these days. Keeps me from getting maudlin."

Downstairs, Keri headed for the car. Joe stopped her. "I think we should leave it parked where it is. Let's walk a bit, okay?"

Keri pointed to the acreage that made up National Historic Park. "We could walk around that way."

"You enter on Chestnut and go through security screening," Joe said. He smiled at her. "I know you wanted to stand where Washington and Jefferson stood, see the Independence Hall, Congress Hall and the exhibition center, but they're closed. If we go that way…"

"We reach the street where Ed was struck down. Where Julie thought she saw Barbara."

"Yeah," he admitted.

"Sounds good," she said.

They came around the corner and Joe said, "Hey,

there—one neon light is out, but it looks like the Liberty for All Wet Your Whistle Tavern is open. What's not to like about a bar with a name like that? Feel like a drink?"

"I guess I'm having one," Keri said, smiling.

They hurried down the street to the tavern; Joe stopped dead and Keri nearly crashed into him.

"From what I understand about the accident," Joe said, "Barbara was running through the building there, and Julie started after her. Then Ed was struck. The bar is right across the street, and while no one saw the car that struck Ed…"

"You're thinking that they may have seen Barbara in her disguise?"

"We can ask, but I was thinking someone might have seen a car drive around several times or notice one standing."

"Cops would have been called on something like that."

"Usually. But it was late at night. Cars can get away with more at night than they can during the day."

"Okay. So, a nightcap."

They walked into the bar. It was quiet this late. Despite the long name, it was really charming, with wooden booths, gold-colored bald eagles here and there, and framed copies of the Declaration of Independence, the Constitution and important speeches dotting the walls.

The bar stretched along one wall and offered dozens of different taps.

"Bar?" Joe said.

"I'm pretty sure that's where you get to chat with the bartender."

He gave her a glare, but then grinned and led her up to the bar where they chose two of the old-fashioned wooden stools. There was an older man down from them to the right, and a young couple to their left. The bartender was a grizzled-looking fellow with a long, full beard and a headful of salt-and-pepper hair. He had been talking to the younger man at the end of the bar but came to them quickly to ask what they'd like.

"Keri?" Joe asked.

She opted for Kahlua and cream.

"Impressive taps," Joe told the bartender. "You have a recommendation? I like a good ale."

The man suggested a local microbrew. "I'm an ale man myself. I'd rather have one good ale than three or four of those lite things they come up with. This is a good one."

The bartender served them, and Joe and Keri thanked him. "I'm Rich. If you want me, just holler. We're not much on ceremony here."

"It's a wonderful place," Joe told him.

"It is. We get tourist trade, being so close to Independence Hall and all. But we get a lot of locals, like old Tom down there. The name of the bar has changed, but it's been here a long, long time."

"And someone bright kept up the charm of it," Keri said.

Rich beamed. "That would be me."

"Well, kudos. It is warm, comfortable. All the right things," Keri said.

"I heard you had some excitement out here several nights ago. A man hospitalized after a hit-and-run," Joe said.

"A hit-and-run," Rich said with disgust. "You know, accidents happen. But just running away and leaving a man broken and bleeding on the road—no."

Tom, down at the end of the bar, heard him. "Saw the news. They said the guy is going to make it."

"He is," Joe said, and he looked levelly at Rich. "I'm a consultant for the FBI. Down here about the murder of the man's partner."

"Ah, thought you might be in some kind of security or law enforcement," Rich said. He shook his head. "Cops were in here, of course. I tell you, if anyone would have seen the accident, we would have reported it. Despite the music playing in here, we heard the thump and the scream and we all went racing out. But the car was gone."

"I heard," Joe said. "But I thought maybe you or one of your customers might have seen a car hanging around or circling the block."

"A white van," Tom said. He stood, bringing his beer with him, and walked over, taking the seat next to Keri's. "Didn't think nothing of it, not until you spoke up now. There's all kinds of delivery trucks around here, ride shares, other drivers looking for people. But now that you ask, yeah, I saw a white van. It kind of hovered around here, swooped a few times. That's my stool," he said, indicating the seat where he'd been before. "Sometimes, I just look out the window and watch the world go by. People-watch, I guess you'd say. There were a few FedEx trucks going around, a liquor delivery for a place down the road, a bunch of cars I didn't pay much heed—and that white van. I just figured he was looking for somebody, a pickup for a tourist who wandered out this way."

"A white van," Joe repeated, glancing over at Keri.

"Yes, sir."

"By any wild stretch of the imagination, did you get a license number?" Joe asked.

"That is a stretch of the imagination. No, sir, I did not get a license number."

"Well, thank you, I appreciate it very much," Joe said.

"I did notice that it was American made, and old. Looked almost like a hippie car, though it wasn't a Volkswagen."

"Any markings on it, like advertisements for a business?"

"No, sir. It was just white. Old. Not nice and shiny, and not too beat-up."

"Thank you," Joe told him.

"Now, I didn't see it do anything wrong, but…it did hover around this area. Don't know how that might help, but I hope it does."

"It does help," Joe said, pulling out his phone. He flipped to the computer rendition of Barbara Chrome with short, dark hair. "Have you seen this girl around here, by any chance?" he asked.

Tom looked at the picture. "Maybe. She's a kid, though. Did she come in for supper, maybe with her folks or something?"

Rich leaned over to look at the picture on the phone. "Hell, I've seen her. Practically had to throw her out of here."

Joe stared at Rich.

"She came swishing her way in, sat at the bar and asked me for a whiskey neat. I said, oh no, little girl, I don't serve minors. Then, she tried to flirt with me—with me! Hell, I could be her great-grandfather!"

"She was alone?" Keri asked.

"All alone. And when she realized that I really wasn't going to serve her, she grabbed a glass of ice someone had left and tossed it in my face. I told her to get out or I'd call the police. Then, she ran right out. Why? Who is she?" Rich asked.

"A girl who was kidnapped in New York City."

"Kidnapped, my ass," Rich said. "Sorry, miss."

"It's okay. I've heard the word before," Keri said.

"I think she's used it—on me." Joe glanced her way with a dry grin. "Anyway, you're certain about this, and certain that she was alone."

"I may be old, but my eyes are that of a young man," Rich said. "Yes, she was in here. Four or five, maybe six days ago, I'm not sure." He reached under the counter and produced a card. "This is me. Rich Tomlin. My cell phone is there, and the bar number is there. If you need anything you think we can help with, just give me a call. Sorry, I'm being a lousy bartender, and I'm usually the best. Want another beer?" Rich asked Joe.

"No, thank you. We haven't even checked into our hotel yet. But this place is wonderful, Rich. We'll be back, and I really appreciate the help from both of you. Tom, if you don't mind—"

"Tom O'Grady, sir, and I'll scratch my number on a napkin here," Tom said. "Rich, you got a pen?"

"Of course I've got a pen," Rich said, handing one to Tom. "I'm a bartender. And I'm falling apart at that job. Asked the gentleman, but not the lady. Miss, you okay—did you want another drink?"

"No, but thank you," Keri said.

"You can usually get Old Tom here, too," Rich said. "Barfly. One beer for hours and hours. He's the best, tends to the place sometimes when I'm not around."

Joe thanked him again and paid for their drinks and Tom's next one; they waved goodbye as they left.

Out on the street, Keri said excitedly, "You think that Ed was hit by the same van that scooped up Barbara? I don't know how it could have happened, but somehow, she was in league with these people. I don't know how she found them or even who they are. And of course, she is only seventeen, but—"

"It sure sounds like she's not so much the victim," Joe said. He paused, looking at her in the empty street. "A good day, Miss Wolf. I'd say we had a very good day."

"Yes, we found out all kinds of things, but..."

"But?"

"We still don't know who killed Julie."

He started for the car again. "Steps along a path, Keri. We're moving along all right now. And believe me, we *will* find out who murdered her, and he or she or they will be brought to justice. I swear it."

It was late when they finally checked into the hotel. Joe looked at Keri as the front desk clerk looked up their reservation and whispered, "Are you sure? I can see if they have connecting rooms. I can sit in a chair in the door like I did in the inn."

"I'm sure. You can't sit in a chair all night."

"Okay," he said, turning to the counter. The clerk, a middle-aged woman, was pretending to look off into the distance as she waited. She looked at Joe then, and he almost smiled—she seemed certain they were carrying on some kind of illicit affair.

The disapproval in her eyes deepened as he asked for toiletries for them both, toothbrushes and toothpaste.

Checked in, they headed for the elevator.

"Hotels are strange," Keri observed.

"How's that?"

"Rooms usually have soap, shampoo, conditioner, sometimes body lotion and mouthwash, but what's the one thing you really need? A toothbrush. You always have to ask for one if you've forgotten your toothbrush."

"Ah," Joe said, "but there are so many kinds of toothbrushes."

"That may be said of shampoo and conditioner, as well."

He smiled. "You got me. If I ever own a hotel, I promise I'll make sure we keep cheap toothbrushes in every room."

The room itself was basic but nice. He told Keri he was going to call Dallas and tell him about the bar and what he had learned from Rich and Tom. By the time he finished with his call, Keri was out of the bathroom. She'd showered—and made use of her new toothbrush. She'd opted to don one of the hotel's bathrobes, probably sick of her same clothing when she was so freshly clean. And sweet smelling.

"Be out in a minute," Joe said. "Guess I'll shower and dress in dirty clothes."

"They're not that dirty," Keri said, "we didn't roll in the mud or anything. They're not fresh, but a shower will still feel good. And there's a second robe if you want."

Joe checked the door to the room; it was closed and bolted, but he still told her that he'd leave the bathroom door ajar and be quick. He wished he had a clean shirt and shorts, but the shower was better than nothing.

When he came out of the bathroom, she was in bed. He walked over and sat down beside her, keeping to his edge, as he had back at the inn.

Except here he was in just a robe, and with her smelling so good.

She'd been watching the television while lying there; she flicked it off. The room was almost in darkness; he'd left the light on in the bathroom, and it streamed out, allowing for a soft golden glow.

"Good night," he told Keri as he tried to get comfortable. "And thank you. I think that your Dr. Sam Jeffries is a very smart man, and it was great to meet him."

"He is very smart, and a sweetheart."

There was silence between them for a few minutes. He felt her movement and quickly turned to look at her. She had risen up on an elbow and was surveying him with amusement.

"What?" he asked.

"We're here, alone—really alone—in a hotel room. We're in a lovely bed together, and you're next to me, and that's all you're going to do? Sleep?"

"I beg your pardon?"

"Oh, I do about give up," she told him. "Seriously? You haven't felt the slightest twinge? You haven't been tempted at any single moment to do more than...well, watch over me?"

The last was said so softly.

He hiked up on an elbow himself, close to her, not touching her, but their faces were just a breath away. "You do know that the nicest thing I think you've said about me is that I'm not a total jerk," he told her.

"Oh, seriously, I've said better than that, I'm sure."

"I really don't think so."

"You called me a liar."

"You were lying. We've established that. And I understand. I've forgiven you."

"I don't need to be forgiven. I—"

"I'm really trying not be a jerk," he told her. "But have I felt a twinge? Hell yes. You said you were able to sleep. Well, Miss Wolf, I've lain at your side while you've touched me, draped yourself over me—"

"Draped myself?" she asked.

"Draped. And I didn't get a wink of sleep. Twinge? I lay awake imagining you naked. I pictured so much, I had these amazing fantasies..." He touched her then, stroked her face, drawing his fingers in a gentle brush along her jawline.

"They don't have to be fantasies," she told him.

"You don't have to—"

"Oh, my God, and I told Dr. Sam that you had a brain," Keri said, and there was no mistaking her smile or her words or the way she moved into him.

He didn't hesitate a minute longer. He leaned just that little bit closer, and he kissed her lips. From that first touch, he drew her into his arms, fingers threading through her hair as their lips came together and the kiss deepened with their tongues clashing and mouths parting, zero to sixty in half a second. He held her in his arms, and then released her, fingers teasing at the neckline of the soft terry robe for just a few seconds before he kissed her throat, parted the robe farther and kissed her chest down to the rise of her breasts.

She rose against him, crawling over him, shrugging out of the robe herself and letting it fall around her. He pulled her against him, rolling with her, kissing her deeply once more, then rose to tug off his own robe. The shoulders caught, and he strained against them.

She laughed softly, reaching up to help, her fingers a feathery brush against his flesh. "Well, at least I have your attention now," she teased.

"You do," he assured her.

She arched up into his arms; they fumbled together in the tangle of terry robes they had then created, but soon they were cast onto the floor.

There was silence as they indulged again in kissing and caressing the flesh they had bared to one another, rolling to this side, then that, twisting and turning in their efforts to kiss and caress more and more, she half atop him, and then he atop her.

The sheets were cool beneath him, but it seemed that his body was burning with the heat of a fire long denied such an arousing fuel.

He was with her.

It didn't have to be fantasy. Not anymore.

Erotic, compelling, and more than he had ever imagined, her whispers, the softness of her skin, the way she moved against him... Something he'd imagined through long hours was now real, and he wanted to savor every minute, wanted to touch, kiss and caress every inch of her and feel in return every touch she dealt upon him.

Fingertips like feathers, her touch so light when it should be, then grew more firm... Her kiss, a breath, and then filled with passion, moved upon him and over him. They shifted and clung, as if afraid that such a thing might not come again, desperate to make every sensation last.

Then real desperation, and he was moving within her, feeling the incredible way she moved in return, each arch of her body. Each writhing movement escalated the pleasure to a point that was nearly unbearable.

The sensation that ripped through him with shattering force was excruciating, like lightning tearing into him, heat like he had never known.

She cried out softly beneath him; he smothered the sound with a deep, long-lasting kiss, and then he rolled to the side and they lay side by side, just breathing, looking at one another.

She jerked up, worried suddenly. "Oh no."

"I'm sorry," he began, "I thought—"

"No, no. I wanted this. But you're working, you're on duty. Did I...? This was wrong of me. I didn't mean to...well, cause problems. Not that I'll say anything."

He pressed his finger to her lips, smiling. "I hadn't actually planned to discuss the evening with anyone else, but you needn't worry. I haven't gone through the academy yet." He hesitated. "There's nothing against couples in the FBI, although they don't usually work together. Except in the Krewe… Of those I've met, many of the team members are couples. Well, I think the very nature of what being in the Krewe means creates a situation where you're drawn to people with an understanding of the differences in us."

She relaxed against him, drawing his arms around her. "I'm so glad. I didn't want to cause trouble."

"You won't cause trouble, although…"

"Although?"

He smiled down at her, glad just to have her there, damp and naked in his arms. He was still a bit amazed that they were there, as they were. "Although?" she repeated when he continued to simply stare at her.

"It's going to be damned hard to sit in a chair or just lie beside you again when we return to Miller Inn," he told her.

"It will be damned hard to sleep and know that you're there, close, and I could just roll over to you—"

"You've done that already. Nearly killed me," he told her.

"Really?"

"Really. I always found you tempting."

She flushed slightly, edging even closer to him. "We'd better appreciate the night then. Make use of it."

He rolled slightly, coming up on an elbow. "I'm game if you are." He took her into his arms again.

Neither one of them had very much sleep that night, but when they did drift off, they both slept very deeply.

And he didn't think that Keri was plagued by dreams, not at all.

When he finally woke and told himself that they had to get up and get going, she was still asleep, with a sweet, peaceful smile on her face.

He was loath to wake her. He watched her sleep for a minute, that lovely smile curved into her lips.

"Where have you been all my life?" he whispered softly. *And will you still be in it tomorrow?*

"Keri?" he said, shaking her lightly. It was time to head back to the Miller Inn and Tavern. It was well into the day, and puzzle pieces were falling together.

Her eyes opened. Her smile deepened. The light in her eyes was beautiful…and ever so slightly wicked.

Yes, they had to return. They had many more pieces to the puzzle to discover. They had to move quickly, because if the truth was as dark and deadly as he feared, another victim might soon be found.

She stretched out her arms to him, eyes so brilliant, smile so seductive…

They would get back.

Just a bit later than he had intended.

13

Keri sat behind the desk in the museum.

Things were a bit different on their return—Dallas had decided that he would bring the Truth Seekers back in, but only half of them.

That day, Brad Holden was moving into room 208. Serena had been allowed to accompany him, and she was settling into room 209. Brad had tried to change with Dallas, but Dallas wasn't budging.

If everything went well, Pete and Eileen and Mike could come back in a day. While Brad was deeply disappointed that he didn't have his entire crew, Dallas had explained that he wasn't prepared to watch over more people. He was hopeful that he'd have more members of the Krewe down the next day, but until they arrived, he didn't want more people in the inn.

Brad reminded him that police were still watching the house.

And that was a very good thing, Dallas agreed.

Brad had talked to Carl for a long time; Carl, being Carl, naturally wanted to make him happy. But things had to wait.

As Brad and Serena set up in their rooms, Carl escaped to join Keri in the museum, once again reading scripts as she sifted through the folders, books and other offerings in the museum room.

She'd been at it a long time when she found a single sheet of old paper, frayed at the edges, stuffed in with some accounting information from the early days of the last century. It obviously didn't belong there, its contents so different from the rest of the file, but when dealing with tons of paper, things often wound up in the wrong place. Was that what had happened here?

She didn't know, but what she saw on the paper made her leap up.

Carl startled, staring at her. "What?"

"Sorry, may be nothing. I just have to talk to Dallas. Be right back."

"No," Carl protested, setting his script down. "You're not leaving me alone—I'm coming with you."

"Okay." She raced behind the bar to the kitchen where Dallas and Joe were deep in conversation. "Look!" she cried, producing the paper. "Look!"

Joe took the paper from her, stared at it and showed it to Dallas.

"Where was this?" Joe asked.

"In with a bunch of accounting papers—not as old as this. It looked as if maybe the papers had fallen and were all just scooped up together," Keri said.

"What is it?" Carl asked, looking over Dallas's shoulder. "That looks like something out of…"

"Dante's *Inferno*," Dallas said.

Carl looked around. "This is, like, a sign? Some kind of devil symbol?"

"It's an insignia for a club. Have you found anything like this in any records from today or recent years?" Joe asked Keri.

"I never saw it before Dr. Jeffries showed it to us in that journal yesterday," she said. "After that, I was consciously looking for it."

There was a hard pounding at the front door to the tavern. Keri and Carl jumped; Joe and Dallas looked at one another. Dallas went to the door while Joe went to one of the tavern windows to look out.

"Detective Billings," Joe said.

Dallas nodded and opened the door.

Detective Billings stepped in, slowly closed the door behind her, and stared at Dallas and then over at Joe.

"Detective Billings, what can we do for you?" Dallas asked.

"Change your appalling behavior," she said, and then glared at Joe. "Control your lackey and get back into this investigation as if you actually mean to run a joint task force."

Keri was impressed that both Dallas and Joe managed to control their tempers.

"We've informed your department every step of the way," Dallas said.

"I informed Special Agent Wicker—acting lead in this case—of everything we've discovered or suspected, Detective," Joe said. "Frankly, I'm stunned."

"You're trying to make it appear as if the police are

lacking in their abilities and incompetent," Billings said, glaring from one of them to the other.

Next to Keri, Carl whispered, "What's she talking about?"

"Detective," Dallas began, "in the first place, there was no slur on any department. Philadelphia police questioned everyone regarding the accident that put Special Agent Ed Newel in the hospital. At the time, it was presumed to be a random accident. I'm shocked you're not pleased that there has been another step taken forward on solving this crime," Dallas said.

Detective Billings didn't answer Dallas. She turned to glare at Joe. "And this picture of Barbara Chrome. You don't know if this is real in any way, but you're running all over Philadelphia with it. You might well have created a nightmare for any girl out there with short dark hair," she told him.

"Detective, I stand by my work," Joe said quietly. "I was a cop for a very long time. I know what I'm doing, and I know how to work with other agencies. Frankly, I find it frightening that you're upset by this. All of us work to solve crimes, and any step taken by anyone in law enforcement should be appreciated and used by all."

Brad came running down the stairs, with Serena, blond hair bouncing, behind him.

"Hey, what's going on?" he asked, and then, seeing Detective Billings, he came to a dead stop. Behind him, Serena plowed into his back. Brad stepped forward enough to allow her to step off the last stair.

"Detective," he said.

Billings glared at him, then turned back to Dallas

again. "I've gone out of my way. I've given you round-the-clock protection here, four officers, *round-the-clock*. And you neglect to keep me in the loop. I don't go back on my word—you have them for the next few days. But don't you go around my back again," she told Dallas.

"No one went behind your back. I sent every bit of information, including the computer rendering of Barbara Chrome, to your headquarters immediately. You were also sent a picture of the insignia and the information regarding a white van that was given to Joe Dunhill yesterday," Dallas said.

"You're working with me—I want info sent to me, do you understand?" Billings said. "I'm lead on this for the police here. Information comes *directly* to me." She shook a finger at Dallas and went out, slamming the door behind her.

"Weren't you tempted to break that finger of hers?" Serena asked Joe. He was still stunned by the attitude Billings had shown.

"She's trying to mark her turf," Brad said. "Wow. I mean, she was a hard-ass every time she talked to us, but wow. She really is a monster. She's been calling and warning us not to leave town. She's not allowed to do that—I checked with our lawyer. Okay, so he's an entertainment attorney, but he went to law school. She can't make us stay. It's a good thing we want to."

"She just feels threatened," Dallas said. "It happens sometimes, when the federal government steps in. We try to be there to help, but—"

"I think maybe she has some kind of authority complex. Because she's a woman," Serena suggested.

"Who knows why another person is or isn't threatened," Joe said. "The good thing is she's leaving officers on the case for a few more days."

"We can pull from federal offices if we have to, from Philadelphia or New York," Dallas said. "That might be best. So—you're here," he said to Brad and Serena. "What are you planning to do?"

"Commune with the spirits, naturally. It would help if we had room 207," Brad said.

"You don't," Dallas said flatly.

"Well, with your blessing, we were going to take a walk out to the old church and the graveyard now. I think that it isn't a crime scene anymore?"

"Right. I think you're the first people who have wanted back into the church. Somehow, it didn't seem to be a particularly popular tourist attraction before all this," Dallas said. "I'll catch Detective Billings and see what she has to say."

He opened the door and didn't close it as he jogged down to the drive where the two patrol cars were parked alongside Detective Billings's unmarked car. She was still speaking with her officers.

"I know what it is," Serena said, watching Dallas approach Billings. "She knows something's been going on here. And she hasn't been able to stop it."

Joe glanced over at Keri. They all watched as Dallas indicated the church and the forest at the back of the property. Detective Billings waved a hand in the air.

"We can go," Brad said happily. He set his hands on

Serena's shoulders, spinning her around to face him. "We need to make sure we have EVPs. And while we're there, we're going to need extreme patience."

"Yes," Serena said, somber as she turned to look at Brad. "If we could reach that poor FBI lady, we might be able to solve her murder."

"I wasn't thinking so much that we'd reach her. I mean, she's the newly dead," he told Serena. "Come back upstairs for a minute and help me, we'll get our stuff and get out there while it's still daylight and we can see the cops. Hey, Carl, that's all right with you, yeah?"

"Sure," Carl said.

"You want to come with us, see how we work?" Brad asked.

"Ah, no. Thanks. Too much reading to do," Carl said.

They raced up the stairs. Joe looked at Carl. "What was that—*the newly dead*?"

"Joe," Keri said softly. "I think that Brad believes what he does is helpful, and who would any one of us be to question what we really don't understand?"

Joe stared at her, lowered his head and nodded slowly. "Right. Sorry. Anyway, maybe we should walk out there with them and see what we see."

Brad and Serena came back down the stairs.

"I'm going to take a look out there with you," Joe said to them.

"Guess we're all going," Carl said. "Except Dallas. I know him. He's not leaving the tavern alone, even with cops watching the place. He'll make sure no one slips in."

"Carl, you don't have to go. You can study your script," Keri told him.

He smiled at her and whispered for her alone, "Hell no, are you kidding me? I'm coming with you."

"You were here all day yesterday, alone with Dallas," she reminded him.

"And I followed him around so close I thought he was going to deck me," Carl said. "No, I'll be hanging with you. It will be great."

"All right now, please, Mr. Dunhill," Brad said, "if we're running our EVPs and trying to communicate, don't just start talking out of the blue. You'd be astonished what you can get off an EVP. And that graveyard has witnessed a lot. It must be just swarming with spirits caught between worlds, from all of our American wars, yellow fever, malaria…"

He headed out with Serena at his heels, Keri, Carl and Joe right behind her.

Joe waved to Dallas and the cops. "Heading to the graveyard," he called.

Keri looked back. Detective Billings leaned against one of the cars, watching them as if she was forced to watch bugs crawl away when she wasn't allowed to tromp on them. Dallas appeared to be fine, however, talking to the cops who were on daytime duty.

"She is…tough," Keri whispered to Joe as they walked around the tavern and toward the graveyard. "Strange. I've worked with so many female cops who are just great. No chips on their shoulders or any such thing. I mean, when I've done research on cold cases, that can be a touchy thing. Sometimes, police don't want to be bothered, but sometimes they're great."

"I don't think it's a sex thing with Billings," Joe said. "I think it's the fact that maybe we're closer to an answer to this thing than she'd like."

"You mean, she didn't solve it herself and someone from the FBI might solve it instead?"

They had reached the remnants of the stone wall. Joe helped her step over it. She liked the feel of his hand on hers, especially since she knew that was about all the affection they'd be able to show one another for a while.

She trembled slightly, still frightened by the depth of emotion she felt for him and frightened more that she already felt so comfortable with him, so certain that they shared so much. She remained surprised at how easily she'd initiated intimacy between them.

He wasn't answering her. She studied his face, noting Brad and Serena heading toward the church, with Carl following just behind them. "Joe?" she prompted.

"There's something about Detective Billings. I can't quite figure it yet."

Keri gasped. "You think she's in on this somehow?"

"I think she doesn't want us around here and wishes we'd go away," Joe said.

"Oh, Joe...you don't think that a local cop could have slit the throat of... I don't like her, particularly, but—"

"I don't know. There are a couple of things. She doesn't like the fact that we've circulated an image for what Barbara could look like now. Or that we have the educated guess that Ed was struck down on purpose by a white van. I don't have the answers yet. But I won't be leaving you alone around her, that's for certain."

"Do you think she might be covering up for someone else?" Keri asked.

"I don't know. I'm just going on some of her behavior, and…"

"And?"

"And maybe the fact that I don't particularly like her. So I have to be careful and thoughtful." He shrugged. "Let's catch up. Carl is waiting for us. Poor guy. He doesn't want to go into the church with them, but he doesn't like standing there alone. Let's save him."

Keri waved to Carl and they started for the church. On the way, she caught Joe's arm. "Joe, she's out here. The woman in white, Beatrice Bergen. Look over there, watching Carl standing in front of the church. Do you see her?" For a moment, she felt fear again—fear that she was seeing the dead and discovering that others saw them, as well.

"Yes, I see her. She's just watching them. She looks… worried."

"How do you just go up to a ghost and start talking to her?"

"Exactly like that. You walk up to her and start talking to her. If she wishes, she'll talk back, and if she doesn't wish, she'll just stand there or disappear." Joe raised his voice, calling out to Carl. "We're just going to look at a few headstones over here!"

Carl nodded, not moving, holding his ground.

Keri grasped Joe's hand as they started toward the

ghost. Beatrice Bergen wasn't looking as the two of them approached her; she was staring at the church.

"Beatrice," Joe said softly.

She still didn't look at them. "They are playing with what they must not," she said. Finally, she turned to them. "They must not play, it is too dangerous. It never goes away. It has never been rooted out. It dies down, and one would think that it is gone. But every time, it comes back, because the base remains. People are basically good. I will always believe that. But if there's a shred of evil, then there are those who will find it, and they will do with it what they will." She lifted a hand. "Please, stop it all… My father did not do this thing."

She started walking toward the church and faded away as she neared it.

Keri started after her and Joe followed. "I don't think she's going to allow them to get anything on their EVPs," Joe told her.

"I know, but… Joe, do you really think that Brad is involved in this?"

"He comes from New York and he's out here."

"Right, but until a month or so ago, no one knew that Carl was going to be buying the Miller Inn and Tavern. He couldn't have known that he'd be invited out here," Keri said. "And Serena is not from New York. I grant you, she can be annoyingly perky, but that doesn't make you guilty of being a murdering Satanist."

Joe stopped walking. "Eileen was on the ground when you went down to the basement the night you two stumbled upon Julie's body."

Keri sighed deeply. "No, she was on one of the bottom steps. She said that someone pushed her, if I re-member right, but she didn't seem to think that it was anyone living. We saw the body on the altar almost right away. And we got out."

"Eileen is from New York," he said.

Keri looked at him, shrugging. "Eileen and millions of other people."

"Brad started up the *Truth Seekers* a little less than two years ago," Joe said.

"That's right."

"I'm going to suggest that someone did know that the property was going to be sold," Joe said. "They knew Spencer Atkins couldn't hold on to the property and that it was going to go up for sale eventually. It didn't matter who bought the property. We should talk to Spencer Atkins."

"We should," Keri agreed.

"Let's go."

Carl was never happy when Keri was going to leave him, Joe noted. He wasn't sure if the man's attitude was irritating or endearing. He remembered thinking that they were a couple. Now, he knew that Keri did care for Carl, but not in any romantic way. That must have been something of a surprise for Carl, since most women, young and old, just about swooned when he walked in a room.

But he seemed to accept Keri's attitude toward him. Maybe he was just glad to have a real friend.

"I'll keep close watch on the household while you're gone," Dallas told Joe as they waited in the front entryway of the inn. "I've been wondering if Spencer Atkins would wind up paying us a visit. He hasn't yet." He eyed Joe. "I think you have to be right. Atkins knew he was going to have to sell the inn. If he is involved in whatever group is behind all this, then others in the group would know as well. But still, how could they know that Carl would call in the Truth Seekers?"

"I wonder if Atkins suggested that Carl call them," Joe said.

Years ago, John Newby had most probably headed his own sect of supposed devil worshippers, a hedonistic group ready to indulge in any vice, including brutal murder. He had probably been killed in a coup in the organization. He'd gone too far and was taken down, and a lot of innocent people had paid the price.

Was Spencer Atkins playing the same game?

"Easy enough to find out if it was Atkins's suggestion," Dallas said. "What does Carl say? We know that Atkins gave him the information about the caterers, but how could he explain that he knew about the Truth Seekers?"

"The internet. That's where Brad is famous," Joe said.

"What about Billings? Just a disgruntled cop? Or is there something about her being such a witch—no offense to the Pennsylvania Dutch intended there—that has to do with all this?"

"Hard to tell."

Keri, her bag slung over her shoulder, was heading toward them along with Carl.

"Hey, Dallas, they're going off again," Carl said. "I'm

going to be hanging with you again, I guess. I hope I'm not driving you crazy."

"Only a little," Dallas told him. He grinned. "All I have to say is that I'm getting married soon. If Kristin and I have little ones, and you continue being a rising star, you'd better give me plenty of signed autographs for my kids."

Carl laughed. "You got it." He grinned at Joe and Keri. "Dallas and I go way back."

"Yeah, just about three months," Joe said. "Like you and I go way back, right?"

Carl shrugged.

"Okay, we'll be back. Brad and Serena are crawling around the graveyard now," Joe said. "You can see them." He turned to Carl. "When you called in the Truth Seekers, was there a reason you called them specifically?"

"Yeah. I checked out all kinds of groups before I asked them to come," Carl said. "I didn't want anyone who just wanted sensationalism. I wanted them to really investigate."

"Spencer Atkins gave you the names of the caterers, right? Did he suggest the Truth Seekers, too?"

Carl frowned. "Well, he knew that I intended to bring in a group of paranormal investigators. He said he didn't believe in any of that rot, but when I mentioned them, he did say that they were better than others because they didn't scream every second the wind blew."

"He did know you were bringing them in, though."

"Of course. He was here that day when they came in."

Joe nodded. "Thanks. Dallas—"

"You'll be back. I have my eye on Brad and Serena. I will know where they are at all times," Dallas promised.

Joe waved, setting his hand on the small of Keri's back as he led her out to the car. He opened the passenger door for her and she looked back.

"Carl makes me feel like I'm locking my puppy in when I leave the house for a long day," Keri said.

"He likes you."

"I care about him, but like he said, he and Dallas go way back."

Joe slid into the driver's seat and switched on the ignition. He knew the way to the old house where Spencer Atkins was living, and it was a short drive.

"It's too bad," Keri said.

"What's too bad?"

She turned and smiled at him. He glanced her way, loving that light in her green-gold eyes and the way her dark hair fell around her face. Loving the curl of her lips...

"Too bad we can't just drive back to Philadelphia." She smiled wickedly. "Anyway. What does Dallas think of our theory?"

"I think we're all in line with believing that there is a group or a club—whatever you want to call their weird sect. I don't think it's any kind of worship that they're into, not even Satanism. Though they may carry out certain rites, and maybe one or two of the adherents do believe that honoring the devil is the only way to go. Let's see what Atkins has to say."

"Are you going to accuse him of murder?"

"I don't know. We'll see when we get there."

* * *

Atkins came to the door almost before Joe knocked, as if he'd been expecting company.

"Hello there, Joe Dunhill, right? And, Keri, a delight to see you again. How are you doing? And what can I do for you?" he asked. "Come in, come in. Coffee? A soft drink? Something stronger?"

"I'm fine," Joe said. "Keri?"

"No, nothing, thank you," Keri said.

"Come in and sit down. Welcome into my parlor," Atkins said and laughed softly.

"Said the spider to the fly," Keri mumbled, then followed into the parlor, where Atkins indicated they should sit.

"What can I do for you?" he asked. Before they could answer, he looked at Keri and added, "And how are you doing with all the material in the museum? Did Hank Bergen do it? Or are you now convinced that he was innocent?"

"I'm convinced that he was innocent. I believe that the real killer instigated the lynch mob."

"Wow! I wish I'd had the patience to go through the junk in that museum. I had years to do it, but I admit, sometimes, too much research bores me," Atkins said.

"We think that there's a sect or a cult here, near the Miller Inn and Tavern," Joe said flatly. "We believe that there's a conspiracy involved with the murder of Julie Castro."

"A conspiracy? Here? We're not that big. I mean, of course, there's more of a population these days, and people travel more easily, but…here?"

"If one existed in the 1920s, I'd say there is a damned good chance that one exists today," Joe said.

"You think there's a cult out here today?" Atkins asked. He sounded incredulous. Was he really?

"It's scary. Yes, lots of cults do exist. And I think that there might be one out here today."

"And that I know about it?" he still sounded incredulous.

"Perhaps you know something. Something you don't even know you know."

Atkins stared back at him. "Nope... I think you're just asking questions. I see where you're going with this. John Newby, proprietor, was head of your supposed conspiracy sect years ago. I was an innkeeper— that means I had to be the grand chief or high priest of some kind of an evil society—right?"

"Were you? Are you?" Joe asked.

"Oh, come on, please."

"Okay. But there's an aspect of Julie's murder that made it seem as though it was staged specifically for the Truth Seekers, and you suggested Brad Holden and his team to Carl Brentwood."

"I hate crap like that," Atkins said, snorting. "But hey, Carl came in, bought the place, and he intends to do the right thing with it. I believed in Carl—I do believe in Carl. When he told me that he was planning to hire the Truth Seekers, I said that from what I'd seen and heard from ghost-hunter types through the years, Brad Holden and his crew were probably the best of the lot. Please don't forget that I was in the city that day. I did not murder Special Agent Julie Castro, or anyone else for that matter, nor was I in on any conspiracy to do so."

Joe listened to his impassioned words. Was the man telling the truth?

"You're a local, Mr. Atkins," Keri said to him. "You did own the inn, and you knew all the stories, and you know this place. If something has been going on around here, you'd have heard rumors."

Atkins looked at her and sighed. "There have always been rumors. There is a major forest just behind the inn. For years, this place was remote and it's still basically isolated. Any time you have a deep, dark forest and nights that come in with a sweeping mist, you have stories."

"All well and good," Joe said. "And avoiding the issue. What specifically have you heard?"

Atkins waved a hand in the air dismissively. Then he sighed again, deeply this time. "I had a housekeeper once who said that she was waiting out back, smoking a cigarette, when she heard some kind of chanting from the graveyard. She was sure that ghosts were rising in the mist. I was more certain that it was teenagers, drinking, trying to pick up girls, whatever. But I owned that place for over twenty years, and I never had a body in the basement, and even at Halloween, I never had anything bad or ridiculous happen. Who knows, maybe Brad and his Truth Seekers did waken some kind of evil instead of ghosts, but…" He paused.

"What is it?" Joe asked.

"Nothing. I mean, people disappear all the time. And I didn't think…"

"What are you talking about?" Joe asked him.

Atkins looked as if he was being tortured. He grimaced. "Once, about three or four years ago, a man came out to the inn. He was looking for his wife. But I didn't know his wife, and I'd never seen her. I don't even know if he ever found her. She had headed to Philadelphia, but she had told him about the inn, and he thought that she might have come this way. I never thought anything of it. I figured that even though he appeared to be a good guy, he might have been a wife-beater, and she had just tried to escape him. Or, maybe he'd been okay, and she'd just run off with the deliveryman or something."

Joe pulled out his phone and brought up the photo of the insignia that Dr. Sam Jeffries had first shown him and that Keri had found among the papers in the museum desk.

"Have you ever seen this before?" he asked.

Atkins stared at the paper. "No," he said, but there was something husky in his voice, something tight in the way he was sitting.

"You're sure?"

"Positive," Atkins said.

Joe flicked through his phone and produced the photo of Barbara that had been created by computer artists. "This is Barbara Chrome, the kidnapped teenager Special Agent Castro was seeking when she was murdered here."

Atkins shook his head, frowning, studying the image intently. "No, I haven't see her. I'd know if I had. Pretty kid. The kind you remember."

He was telling the truth.

But he'd lied about the insignia.

"Thanks," Joe told him. "And thanks for talking with us." He looked at Keri and she stood, knowing he was ready to leave.

"You haven't any real leads?" Atkins asked, rising to walk them out.

"We have leads, and we're following them, and they will take us where we need to go," Joe told him.

"I hope so. That poor woman."

"Yes, that poor woman, who had family and friends and a life in service to others," Joe said. "Anyway, thanks again."

"Anytime," Atkins said.

Joe paused at the door. "We believe that someone involved in Barbara's kidnapping was ready to sell out. It was one hell of a big reward being offered for her. Maybe someone wanted to collect and get the hell out of Pennsylvania."

Atkins lowered his head. "Was that supposed to draw some kind of big confession out of me?"

"No. If I believed you were guilty, I'd have figured out enough of a charge to get you down to the police station. That was just in case you know anything, say, suspect that a friend might be involved. Whoever it is, they need to turn themselves in. They are in extreme danger," Joe told him.

"Noted. If I knew who to tell, I would."

"Okay, thanks."

Atkins bid them a chilly farewell and they left. When they were in the car, Keri said, "How strange. I believe that he hadn't seen Barbara before, but he was lying about the insignia. Why?"

"Because he does know something. He's seen that insignia somewhere," Joe told her. "If he isn't involved, he might have an idea of who is."

"Yes, I figured you were thinking that."

"Damn. I wish to hell we knew who was going to turn Barbara in. Barbara's out here somewhere."

"Okay. But where? I really don't believe that Atkins has her stashed in his house."

"We're getting close. There's an APB out on the van that mowed down Ed and possibly picked up Barbara, but I'm sure it's in a lake somewhere. Here's another question that bothers me. The cops were told to check out restaurants, not grocery stores. I still think that Detective Billings might have thought of Greta's. How could you live out here and not know about such a unique store not so far away?"

"You really think that a detective might be involved? That's so…"

"Bad. And I hate it." Joe took a deep breath. "Most cops are great. But with all this going on, it's possible."

"Well, she's not the person who was going to betray the group," Keri said.

"Why do you say that?"

"Because she's still alive," Keri said. "But we haven't found any other bodies, either, so maybe the group is still trying to figure out who betrayed them. Of course, once they do, whoever that person is, they're definitely dead."

14

When they returned to the Miller Inn and Tavern, the police on guard were changing shifts. Keri was delighted to see that Officer Belinda Emory and her partner, Jamie Hawkins, were back on, along with the officers they'd served with two nights before, Milo Roser and Henry Schultz.

Joe and Keri parked and walked over, greeting them.

"We'll get dinner going soon. I hope you'll come in, two by two," Keri told them.

"You don't have to cook for us, Keri," Belinda told her.

"She's not going to cook tonight. I am," Joe told them. He grinned at Belinda. "I'll do all the hard work, then I get to sit around for the cleanup."

Belinda laughed. "Share and share alike," she said.

"Have you seen Dallas and the others out here?" Joe asked.

"Earlier. He told me they were all going down in the basement. Brad wanted to investigate there, and apparently Dallas was willing to go along with it," Jamie said. He rolled his eyes, apparently not much of a believer in the occult.

"This has got to be hard on Dallas. He's looking for a flesh-and-blood murderer. Brad and his people want to raise the dead," Belinda said.

"Maybe they'll go hand in hand," Joe said lightly. "Okay, you know where to find us. And I'll give a holler as soon as we have dinner going."

He caught Keri's hand and they headed into the inn. He went straight for the basement stairs and then turned back to Keri, "Are you okay to go down there?"

She smiled. "Places aren't bad. It's what people do in them that can be cruel and evil."

He nodded, smiling, and they descended together.

Dallas was leaning against the wall by the hatch door, watching, his arms crossed over his chest. Carl was near Dallas, close enough to jump into his arms, if need be. Brad and Serena were at the head of the stone altar, their hands set upon it.

They heard Joe and Keri enter, and Brad turned to stare at them.

"We were just about to contact Julie Castro," he said.

"Don't mind us," Joe told him and took up a position against a basement wall.

They watched. Brad had his recorder on the altar, talking to the dead.

"Julie, we want to help you. You weren't killed here, but others were before you, and you were brought here, to be found doused in your own blood. We want to help you, and we think that you were good at your job. Really good. You don't have to be embarrassed that you were tricked. The best of us can be. We're all so sorry, and we want to help you move on. We want to find your killer and let you find eternal reward. You were a good person, Julie. I didn't know you, but I know people who did know you and love you. We want to help you."

Nothing moved; nothing stirred. Then the arrow on one of Brad's little gadgets bounced along its dial.

Brad gasped. "Julie, you're here."

Julie wasn't there at all. Keri squeezed Joe's hand and she knew that he saw what she saw. The woman in white was in the basement again. Beatrice Bergen. She was staring at Brad as if wondering if he could possibly be for real.

She looked over at Keri and Joe and almost smiled. Then, she was gone.

As she disappeared, Brad was going on and on with Serena about the reading they had taken. "If only we could get more. When the others are back in, we'll try again," Brad was saying. "Maybe we'll get recorders out everywhere and get something. That's happened before."

"I think I'll get dinner started," Joe said. "Keri, want to give me a hand?"

"Hell yes," Carl said.

Joe laughed. "I said *Keri*."

"But I'd just love to help," Carl said.

"Sure," Joe said, glancing over at Dallas.

Keri had to wonder if Dallas's patience was fading, but he just grinned and shrugged.

"Dallas," Brad began, "I know you're not changing rooms, but could we hang out in 207 for a while? You've said that nothing has happened there, but you're not receptive—we are."

"All right," Dallas said. "I have to make a few phone calls. I'll hang in the hallway. You have to keep the door open."

"Will do," Brad promised.

Keri headed up the stairs first and then straight for the kitchen. Joe and Carl were behind her.

"We're ready to serve, oh, great chef," she told Joe. "What are we creating?"

"Whatever we can throw in the oven," he told her, grinning and digging into one of the big refrigerators. "Hey, we've got sausages, sauerkraut, red cabbage... ah, wow, German potato salad. Looks great. Carl, see if you can find mustard up there in the cabinets. Oh, and paper plates. We'll keep the cleanup as easy as possible."

They set to work, Joe going through the sausages, choosing one to chop up finely for the sauerkraut and some to cook. Keri found plates and napkins and asked Carl to help her put together a salad; they were done soon, and Joe called Dallas to have him let the cops know to come in when they could.

They decided to eat in the kitchen. Milo Roser and Henry Schultz came in first, and Brad questioned them about ghosts. Milo, who was local, said that they would tell all kinds of wild stories about the place when they were in school.

Joe asked him about local beliefs.

"Well, the devil lives in the woods out back there, you know," Milo said, amused. "I wasn't allowed to play there or at the old church. My mother said that they were tainted—hexed."

"Have you ever seen anything like this?" Joe asked, showing them the insignia.

"Creepy," Milo said, frowning. "Maybe. I think I have, maybe when I was a kid. But I don't remember where, or what it is."

"If you do remember, tell me?" Joe asked.

"Sure," Milo said.

"Henry?"

"It's kind of cool and very creepy, but I've never seen it before. But hey, I'm from Jersey," Henry said. "We just had the old Jersey Devil, real or not, who the hell knows. He doesn't travel into Pennsylvania that I know about."

"Jersey Devil, pretty cool. Have you ever seen it?" Brad asked.

"No, I haven't," Henry told him.

"The pictures that I've seen look just as creepy as that devil's sign Joe keeps showing around. Ugh." Brad shuddered.

"And you look for ghosts," Milo said.

"Ghosts are just people. Not creepy at all," Brad explained.

Henry and Milo finished and went out, and Belinda and Jamie came in. Brad was anxious to get back to room 207, and Dallas agreed that he and Serena could have the room another hour or so. Then they'd have to get out. People were going to be getting tired, and they'd have to settle in for the night.

Keri enjoyed seeing Belinda again. Joe showed her the picture of the insignia, as well.

"I do think I've seen that somewhere," Belinda said, frowning as she studied it. She gasped suddenly and then stared around, looking guilty.

"What?" Joe asked.

She glanced over at Jamie, and he looked as sick as she did.

"What? Please, it's crucial," Joe said.

"I—we—I—"

"Belinda," Joe said quietly.

"We—we have to say something," Jamie told her.

Belinda inhaled deeply. "I saw it as a medallion. I thought it meant something like 'really tough cop.'" She hesitated again.

"We saw it once on Detective Billings's key chain," Jamie said. "She pushed her keys into the drawer really quickly, but—"

"I guess she took it off her key chain. I never saw it again," Belinda said.

Joe stood up and started to leave the kitchen, then came back. "Please, you two, don't leave here until I'm back down," he said. Then he was gone.

"Oh, man, we're in trouble," Belinda said.

"No, don't worry. Joe and Dallas won't let this fall on you," Keri assured them.

Carl reached across the table and took Belinda's hand. "Hey, if Detective Billings is involved, well, you don't want a bad rap for your whole station, right? You guys are good cops."

Belinda nodded. "I mean, she's a bitch. She's always

been a bitch. But this…" She winced. "She's given us explicit directions on guarding the inn, too. We were supposed to report to her any time you all came and went, where you went. All that."

Keri sat back, still not believing what she was hearing.

Joe was back in a minute. "Thank you," he told the two of them.

"What's going to happen?" Belinda asked.

"It won't come down on you—the federal government is just going to be asking her a few questions," Joe said. "There's an APB out on her now."

"I can call her," Belinda said, pulling out her phone. "I could tell her you took off somewhere, and I'm sure she'll come and check on you."

"Do it, please," Joe said.

She dialed.

Detective Billings didn't answer.

Joe really couldn't have slept that night, no matter what.

"We really don't have a damned thing on her," Dallas told him.

They were upstairs. Brad and Serena had gone to their rooms and locked their doors, as Dallas had instructed them. Serena decided she wasn't going to stay alone, and now, they were both locked in Brad's room. Joe was going to take the chair between Carl's and Keri's rooms for the first watch while Dallas was going to try to get some sleep.

No one as yet had heard from Detective Billings, and the ABP had not brought about any sightings, either.

"She must have known that we suspected her of something," Joe said.

"We still only suspect her," Dallas reminded him. "But suspicious behavior isn't evidence of any kind. If we could place her in New York, if we could place her out here the day that Julie was murdered, it would help. We have nothing but a possible sighting of an insignia that might have to do with a Satanic cult or a weird club. Thankfully, Jackson Crow pulled some government strings. We can call her in for questioning, and she might be held for a few hours, but that's it."

"She's been controlling the cops she's had in front of the inn," Joe protested. "They all answer to her beck and call."

"That could just be a concern for us. It's still not evidence."

"Oh, bull."

"It's certainly something she could argue. She's no fool."

"And where the hell is she?"

"Afraid, maybe. Running. Or hiding."

"Or worse. Setting up a plan to kill someone else," Joe said.

"Possibly. Now, I'm going to get some sleep. Take your post. Wake me when it's my turn."

Dallas headed for his bed. Joe headed for the chair. Carl was already asleep, curled up in his clothing on the bed—he'd either fallen asleep that way by accident, or he'd stayed dressed just in case—just in case he needed to be up quickly.

Joe walked through Carl's room and over to Keri's. She was lying there awake.

"Dreaming?" he asked her. "Afraid of nightmares?"

She laughed. "Fantasies. Go away. I won't sleep with you staring at me. I'll be imagining things."

He lingered a minute, smiling. "Things you liked, I hope?"

"Things that were decent," she said.

"Decent. Great. I didn't intend to be decent."

"Okay, well, I was imagining... Ugh, it's too frustrating. Go away, please?"

He grinned and went to his chair. It was going to be a long night.

He tried to get interested in reading again. Sitting in the chair, watching words blur in front of him, he realized that he was exhausted. The days were very long. He rose and grabbed a bottle of water from the dresser, thinking that they really needed a little coffeepot up here.

He sat again and began reading about the area, how hex signs and various artworks featuring them had gained popularity when tourism began flourishing. He read about the Mennonites and the Amish and the Anabaptists. He respected their religions, just as he respected all religions.

But what was going on here had nothing to do with any religion that held human life sacred.

He must have become more absorbed than he knew;

he heard Dallas come through Carl's room to where Joe sat.

"My watch," Dallas said.

"Thanks, yeah, I'll try to get some sleep," Joe said.

He left the chair to Dallas and crawled into bed next to Keri, keeping his distance, smiling when he remembered the night—and early morning—that they had shared.

He willed himself to close his eyes and rest. He couldn't be useful without rest.

He had finally fallen asleep when he felt Keri moving at his side. He quickly sat up, looking from Keri to Dallas, who was already standing from the chair.

Keri was beginning to rise, her eyes open but glazed, as if unseeing.

Joe started to reach for her, to wake her.

"No," Dallas said softly.

"But…"

"Let's see what she does. We'll be right with her. Grab your gun."

Joe leaped out of bed, making it shake, but Keri, seated, didn't seem to notice. She got out of bed and started walking to the door to the hall.

"Follow her," Dallas ordered. "I'm right behind you. I'm going to tell Brad and Serena to stay locked in and I'm going to get Carl. I'm not going to leave him alone here."

"Gotcha," Joe told him.

Keri was moving slowly, opening the door to the hallway, heedless when he fell into step right behind her.

She went down the stairs. He thought she was going

to the basement at first, but she didn't; she headed toward the front door. She opened it and walked out.

The officers at their posts were all out of their patrol cars the minute the door opened. Joe waved a hand to them.

"It's all right. I'm with her," he called.

"All right," Belinda called back to them. "If you want us—"

"Two of you stay here and keep watch and two follow Dallas and Carl when they come out," Joe said, thinking, what the hell, if there was nothing, they'd get a little exercise. And if there was something…

It never hurt to have backup he believed in.

Keri kept walking around the side of the tavern. She was heading to the graveyard and the little church, he realized. The remnants of the old stone wall didn't deter her. She crawled over it and started making her way through the overgrown weeds and broken stones.

Dallas and Carl were soon behind him, along with Belinda and Jamie.

Keri walked into the church. Joe drew out his penlight. It was nearly pitch-dark inside, only a bit of moonlight filtering in. She walked to the altar and he followed, keeping his distance. It seemed she was certain she was going to find something there.

The altar was empty. Keri just stood there, staring at it.

Dallas caught up with Joe. Carl lingered back with Belinda and Jamie.

"I think she's sleepwalking," Belinda whispered to

s worked strange cases where the past intrudes on e present before."

Dickey nodded. Then he stood.

"Well, hell, I'm going to say it. I'm glad as hell that the FBI has taken the lead on this case. This mess is yours. Solve it, and make sure you do."

He started to walk out, but swung around, staring at his officers. "You four. You're on here until I tell you that you're off, you understand? The FBI has the investigation, but we will be watching. You do understand that, Mr. Dunhill, right? You'll make sure that Special Agent Wicker knows that we're watching—and of course, ready to assist in any way, if and when you need us."

"Yes, Captain. Thank you."

Dickey hesitated, looking around the inn, shaking his head again. "No, thank you. But solve this. Quickly."

He walked out of the tavern, closing the door behind him.

"Well, hmm. He didn't seem terribly upset," Carl said.

"And he didn't drag us all down to the station," Brad agreed. "Hey, I don't know. Detective Billings wasn't so nice. Maybe none of them liked her."

"We didn't particularly like her," Belinda said. "But that doesn't mean she should have died the way she did."

"Unless she got just what she gave to Julie Castro," Milo said.

Dallas walked back into the tavern then, sliding into e chair that Captain Dickey had just vacated.

"The medical examiner has taken Detective Bil- s?" Keri asked.

Jamie. "Perhaps they should wake her up. She's going to cut up her feet out here."

Dallas lifted a hand.

Keri turned suddenly, still not seeing them, walking down the aisle towards the front of the church. Now, she walked around the side.

It was there, on top of an old tomb, that they found Detective Catrina Billings.

Or what remained of her.

Keri sat in the tavern along with the others.

Carl had spent the last hour being ill, and Brad and Serena had asked so many questions that Dallas had finally lost patience and snapped that they really needed to just shut up.

Keri wasn't quite sick herself, though she was shocked; the full impact of what had happened was just sinking in. Joe had whisked her away from the body before she was even fully conscious. Dallas had called for the medical examiner and Belinda had reported back to her headquarters, radioing in that they'd found a body.

Now, the medical examiner was out with the body, and a forensic team was combing the entire area of the graveyard.

This time, it was a local police captain who came out—Captain William Dickey, head of the whole department. He was decent enough, a tall, bald man of about fifty.

Dallas was out at the church with the forensic team, and Joe sat with Keri as she tried to explain to the captain what had happened.

"I wish I could tell you. I don't know. I was sleep-walking," Keri said.

"You sleepwalk often?" Dickey asked.

"Never before in my life, that I know of," Keri said.

"How the hell did you find her—unless you knew where to look?" he demanded.

"Sir," she said, leaning forward, her hands folded on the tavern table, "I haven't the faintest idea. But I can tell you I have been in front of someone every minute of the day. I have been with FBI Special Agent Dallas Wicker and an FBI consultant all day long. I was not in the graveyard today."

Dickey looked at Joe.

"She has not been out of our sight," Joe assured him.

Dickey sat back, shaking his head. "So, tonight I get a call from your field director, asking me to bring Detective Billings in. Then later, I get a call that she's found here, dead." He glared across the room. "Catrina is dead."

Even Brad was quiet now. Serena slunk at his side, obviously afraid.

At the next table, the four cops on duty sat in silence, wide-eyed as they looked at the captain, waiting for whatever came next.

"And you!" he barked. "You four. What the hell were you doing?"

"We weren't in the graveyard, sir. Detective Billings gave us strict instructions to watch the front of the inn, not to leave it. We were ordered to watch over the lives of the people in the inn, sir," Belinda said.

"She told you that you couldn't move?" Dickey asked.

"Sir, yes, sir," Milo said.

The four of them nodded in unison.

"What the hell is going on here?" Dickey aloud, his tone hard and irritated. "An FBI age of my own officers. What the hell?"

Keri sat silent; Joe pulled out his phone. "I this image was emailed to you, sir, and that it w plained to you that we do believe there's an active or deviant club."

He glanced over at the cops for a minute, but promised, he didn't give Belinda and Jamie away. "W have a witness who saw Catrina Billings with this image on her. A medallion, attached to her key chain. We believe that the same people who kidnapped Barbara Chrome from New York are the ones involved in the cult here. Because of the sizable reward offered, some-one called the FBI agent on the kidnapping case, Julie Castro. She and her partner, Ed Newel, came to Phil-adelphia where, we believe, Ed was purposely struck down so that Julie could be lured out here."

Joe paused. "We believe that Detective Billings murdered by the cult. She might have been the or murder Julie herself, but we also believe that her f cult members realized that she was the one w betrayed them and brought an FBI agent out h punishment for that betrayal was death."

Dickey stared back at him. "When this stood up and started sleepwalking, you j her?" he asked, gesturing at Keri.

"Yes, sir. That was Special Agent W

Dallas nodded.

"The same as…Julie Castro?" she asked.

"Not quite," Dallas said. "She looked quite a bit the same, except, in this case, the killers went into the stabbing frenzy *before* they slit her throat."

"Oh, God," Carl said. Leaping up, he hurried into the kitchen, clearly going to be sick again. Keri just felt empty.

They watched him go. They could see him from the tavern area, and so, no one jumped up to go with him.

Everyone was silent. Then Belinda spoke softly.

"This is…so bad. We worked with her almost every day," she said. "She was in on this, and we don't know who else…" She stood suddenly, her stance straight. "I know these guys—Jamie, Milo and Henry. We're good cops, I swear it. We should have been walking this whole area, watching the graveyard and the woods, probably. I mean, that's where the devil lives, isn't it—in the woods?

"Well, Captain Dickey ordered us to stay on patrol. So I'm going back out to my car, and I'm going to watch this place, and if I even think that anyone is out in the church, the graveyard or the forest, we're going to split duties and keep anything like this from happening again."

Jamie, Milo and Henry looked at one another; they, too, stood.

"We're on," Jamie told them all. "We're going to be good cops now, not just lackeys at anyone's command. We'll be watching."

"Thank you," Keri said, standing and looking at Joe.

"I'm going back in the museum. I know that there's more in there. I just have to find it."

Serena rose, still looking scared and stricken, and Brad followed suit.

"I can't solve anything," Serena whispered. "I'm— I'm so tired. I'm going back to sleep. Brad, please, come with me. I can't be up there alone."

Brad turned to Dallas. "Is it all right?"

"Yes," Dallas said. "Go ahead."

Keri started to head for the museum with Joe following behind her. Carl came rushing out of the kitchen. "Hey, hey! Where is everyone going? You all are leaving me?"

"We're right here, buddy," Dallas assured him.

"You can follow Dallas, or come to the museum with Keri and me," Joe said.

"Museum. Unless you need me, Dallas. Then, I'm with you. There's no way I can go back to bed."

"The museum is fine," Dallas said. "I've got some work to do, and I'll be right here at this table. I have to call Dot and Jared, and they'll come out here, I'm sure. And I'll get hold of headquarters. I'll be here."

Carl sighed with relief and followed Keri and Joe into the museum. They all set to work. They hadn't been there that long when Joe mentioned that they did need to eat. Carl protested, but when Joe made sandwiches and returned, he brought a box of crackers for Carl.

He managed to eat a few and told Joe he was grateful.

"It was a long night, turning into a long day, and it will be a long night again."

At first, Keri wasn't really sure how she was going

to manage to do anything. She didn't know exactly what went on at a crime scene, but she imagined that by then, the medical examiner had taken the body. Of course, crime scene investigators would comb the area for clues. Eventually, they would finish, too. She'd felt so numb, day had come and was on the way out once again, and she still felt as if she was numb or half frozen. She wasn't sick like Carl, fortunately. She might have somehow led them to Catrina's body, led in her sleep by some ghostly hand—but Joe had pulled her quickly away before she'd really taken in the sight. She wasn't a cop, and she wasn't a forensic expert, and she didn't mind that she hadn't seen anything. Carl had described the body for her.

She'd asked him to stop.

Now, he sat curled into a chair in a corner of the museum. Joe took down a volume on the history of Pennsylvania, and she started digging through everything in the desk again.

Hours passed. She found a newspaper article from 1930. It had been written by Creighton Mariner, the journalist who had described the scene in the Miller Inn and Tavern in 1926, after the massacre.

Our area recovers; a new buyer has purchased the old inn, which, so sadly, has lain dormant for years. Such history to be lost! And yet the inn is just the right size to survive. Farmers and friends come to the tavern for ale, and travelers come for a night and quickly leave the next morning. This goes well, I believe, for none should play in the woods by night; it is said that Satan keeps many a residence throughout the world, but I do swear that one lies deep there in the pines. This is my place in the world. I know.

She reflected on the piece, thinking that Creighton may well have been the man who murdered everyone in the tavern and led the lynch mob against Hank Bergen.

"Where are you?" she wondered aloud. "If I could just see you, if you just…"

She realized that Joe and Carl were staring at her.

"Sorry." She grimaced. "Talking to myself."

She kept leafing through the many newspaper articles that had been written about the Miller Inn and Tavern over the years. Many of them were by Creighton Mariner.

I am getting the impression that you were quite the deceiver, Mr. Mariner, cloaking the truth behind your written words, and yet such an egotist that you had to leave hints lying around.

He'd written another article, suggesting the Miller Inn and Tavern was a good highway stop for those traveling from the east and southeast if they were seeking to see the Amish country or going to Gettysburg or points in western Pennsylvania.

One can always find a good ale, and if the dogs bay by moonlight, know to hover by the great fires that burn, the company of friends—or even of strangers.

"He sure as hell knew something was going on, if he wasn't a major part of it."

She had spoken aloud again; Carl and Joe looked up at her. She smiled. "Sorry."

"Hey, I like the company," Carl said. "Even if you're not talking to me."

Digging again, she found another article—written after Creighton Mariner's death. At the age of seventy-eight, he had succumbed to heart disease in 1954. Another journalist had written a tribute to him, making use of an interview he'd had with Mariner right before his death.

Naturally, he'd asked him about the bad business in 1926.

"Mr. Mariner," the interviewer had asked, "I can only imagine the horror you and your fellows encountered when asked to witness the scene at the Miller Inn and Tavern after the brutal killings. Have you ever been dismayed that you were brought in, as it proved to be a futile endeavor, since Hank Bergen was dragged out of his home and lynched for the crime?"

"Nothing is futile," Mariner said. "At the time we entered the Miller Inn and Tavern, all that was known was that the guests and John Newby had been murdered. Since we would be called upon to describe the scene when it would have been time for charges to be brought, it was not a futile endeavor."

"And yet, there was never any proof discovered that Hank Bergen was the killer."

"The proof was in John Newby himself," Mariner said. "His excesses had grown to a terrible extent. He had taken a local girl, and one can only imagine her father's distress."

"Yes, but the torture chamber was not discovered until after the massacre took place. How could Hank Bergen have known that his daughter had been taken, tortured and killed by John Newby?"

"Rumor, sir. Rumors about the devil in the woods."

"I've heard that he proclaimed his innocence until he died," the interviewer said. And at that point, he interjected his own opinion, stating, *At this point, Mr. Creighton Mariner seemed distressed that I pursued this line of questioning. He was agitated and impatient with me.*

"This is all of no account," Mariner said. "Newby was a horrible man, filled with excesses and carelessness. He deserved very much to die."

"What of the innocents who died with him?"

I believe then, the interviewer wrote, that Mariner reverted to previous years—he had served in France during World War I—for he suddenly stated, "Collateral damage, sir, there is always collateral damage when a leader run amok must be taken down. That is the way with war!"

"That wasn't the war, Mr. Mariner. Innocent people died."

"We are none of us innocent!"

"Sir, were you part—"

"Hank Bergen did it. His daughter was dead, and then he was dead. As it should be. They were together in death. And Newby, the crazy rat-bastard, was gone. Case closed."

"Sir, this is a hard question. Were you involved with the lynch mob who killed Hank Bergen before he could have his day in court?"

"You're asking me to answer questions about events thirty years ago! I remember almost nothing. Nothing! This interview is over."

The interviewer went on to say that while Creighton Mariner had been a fine journalist in his day—and should be honored in death—he believed that the man, horrified by the scene at the Miller Inn and Tavern, had been involved with the lynch mob. It was disturbing to the interviewer that Mariner had seemed to far more appreciate the fact that Newby was dead than to rue the fact that so many innocent people had died.

"The lynch mob...and the murders," she said aloud.

"Did you find something?" Joe asked.

"I did. I seriously believe that Hank Bergen was innocent, and Creighton Mariner killed all those people back in 1926. You have to read this—the interviewer doesn't accuse Mariner of anything, but if you look at the subtext, you can see... I think the journalist might have suspected that Mariner committed the murders and, at the very least, instigated the lynch mob..."

They were both staring at her.

"And we have two women killed in the here and now," she whispered, carefully turning a page in the brittle old newspaper. "I still think that— Oh, my God!"

"What, what?" Carl demanded, jumping up.

Joe stood as well, staring at her with a fierce frown. She beckoned to him; Carl was already at her side.

"There's a picture of Mariner in his coffin," she said, handing the newspaper over to Joe as Carl peered over her.

Joe looked at it.

Creighton Mariner was wearing a medallion. It hung just above his hands, folded in prayer. The medallion had the same insignia that Dr. Sam Jeffries had shown Joe and Keri. The same one that Belinda and Jamie had seen on Detective Billings's key chain.

A hawk, flying above a seated man with a horned ram's head.

"He did it," Keri said flatly. "Creighton Mariner committed the murders. I don't believe that there's any way to prove it now, but I intend to write up everything that I've learned, and hopefully, at least as far as history goes, clear Hank Bergen's name."

Joe was looking at her thoughtfully.

Carl said, "Well, Keri, I know your work, and I'm sure you'll do an excellent job."

"It says something." Joe nodded. "It's important that you found what we now believe to be the truth about the old murders. It's another puzzle piece. We'll get it put together."

Dallas came striding into the room, knocking lightly at the open door so as not to startle them.

"Jackson Crow and Angela Hawkins will be down by tonight," he said. "Late, I guess, since it's already getting dark again. Belinda is going to remain on duty in the house, while Jamie watches outside. Tomorrow, Special Agent Cabot will come out while Special Agent Harrington will stay in the city and watch over Ed until he's out of the hospital.

"As of tomorrow, we'll have four Krewe members and an NYC agent with us. I've also asked Captain Dickey to leave us with the police we have and divide them into two twelve-hour shifts. Four people we trust. I went out and checked with the officers. They're good with the plan, and Captain Dickey is fine with it, too.

"I'm heading back out to the graveyard. One of the forensic team members has something to show me."

"Maybe you should have company," Joe said.

"I am armed, and members of the forensic team are still out there."

"Wait, Dallas, please. Could I go out there with you?" Keri asked.

"Okay."

"I am not going back out to that graveyard," Carl said.

"We won't be gone long," Keri said.

She showed Dallas the newspaper clipping she had found and said, "There's also this. They never did find Beatrice Bergen's body, but her father was buried out there, in the graveyard by the church. A memorial was set up for her there, too. Some neighbors decried what happened, saying they were certain that Hank Bergen hadn't committed the crime, and they saw to it that he was buried and that Beatrice was given a memorial stone as well. I think that maybe once I get all this out there, well, Hank and Beatrice can rest in peace. I'm not sure how it all works, but the burial ground is still hallowed, even if the church was deconsecrated. His grave is about twenty feet to the right of the church. If I can't find it right away, I'll give up." She looked from Dallas to Joe. "I need to see that grave. Please."

Joe nodded to Dallas, silently waiting for an objection.

"All right," Dallas said, "but stick close with me."

"Like glue," she promised.

Joe looked at Dallas and shrugged. "Carl and I will bond some more."

Dallas grinned. "Don't forget that Brad and Serena are upstairs. Belinda is in the tavern, ready to do whatever is necessary, and Jamie is in his car outside."

"We're covered," Joe said. He looked at Keri and added, "I'll be here."

Then he stood and walked over to her, taking her hands and standing close. "You're okay, you know. You're really okay."

"Well, of course, she's okay. She's the best," Carl said.

Joe smiled.

Keri knew what he meant. "I am."

Joe whispered, "Wish them the best for me."

"What are you people talking about?" Carl asked.

"The spirits, Carl. In the graveyard. She's going to tell them that she's found the truth." Joe took his chair again and leaned back, smiling.

"And you know," he said softly, "the truth will set you free."

15

Joe had wanted to be with Keri, especially if she was out to hunt for the ghosts who had plagued her, awake and asleep.

But he understood. Carl wasn't really a coward—he was smart. He didn't have training, and despite what he might have learned for movies, he wasn't in a position to defend himself against an unknown enemy intent to actually kill.

Joe couldn't blame Carl for being ill at what he had seen. Granted, Detective Billings hadn't awakened any love in any of them, and she might have deserved some justice, but she was a human being, and such horror visited on a woman was enough to shake the strongest constitution.

They wouldn't be long; Dallas was a big believer in power in numbers.

Joe sat back to read again, hoping that Carl wasn't feeling talkative. Thankfully, he was more tired than chatty. He sat in a chair with his head leaned against the wall, his eyes closed.

But before Joe could begin to concentrate on anything, his phone rang. He looked at the caller ID. "Hey," he said, surprised that Angela Hawkins from headquarters had called him instead of Dallas.

"Hey, just tried Dallas, but I didn't get him."

"Ah," Joe said.

"First, is everything all right? Well, other than Detective Billings being murdered last night."

"Dallas is meeting with one of the forensic experts," Joe explained. "We only have Brad and Serena here from the Truth Seekers in the inn, Carl is with me, and we have one officer in the tavern and one out in his car."

"We're already on the way," Angela promised. "Thought about flying, but really, even with Adam's plane, it's just as fast to drive. But I have some news. In a preliminary search on the dark web, I came across something potentially worth following. There's something called the Order of the Deep Woods, and we believe that it's run by someone from out there. The church's website is a mass of double-talk, offering an unknown place for those who seek escape. It's just the type of thing that would appeal to a rebellious teenager, promising drugs and sex and absolute freedom.

"The tech department is trying to find the source, but it's bounced off dozens of servers and hard to trace. But it seems likely that this Order of the Deep Woods could be a title for whatever is going on out in York County. There's a mention of a commonwealth, and there are only four in the United States—Kentucky, Virginia, Massachusetts and Pennsylvania. There's something about the birth of freedom and a mention of 'the bell that rings,' which could be the Liberty Bell. We're still going on supposition, but you need to know that this appears to be a well-orchestrated machine that probably has been operating for years."

"Thanks, Angela. Deep Woods, eh? There's a large, heavily forested area to the right of the backside of the tavern. We'll need to get a good group going to check it out."

"We can do that. We'll draw on the FBI offices for manpower."

"There are good cops here, too, despite what happened."

"I believe you, but Jackson can get what he wants from the FBI and I'm not so sure he wants to start ordering the local police around. Of course, we'll take what help we can."

"I'll tell Dallas as soon as I see him. He won't be long."

"Thanks. So how are you doing on this?"

Joe smiled. "Really well. Other than the corpses part of it, of course. It feels like I'm doing the work I'm meant to do. See you when you get here."

He ended the call and saw that Carl was awake, watching him. "Hey, if you ever hear that I'm about to buy a historic tavern again, do me a favor?"

"What's that?"

"Talk me out of it," Carl told him.

Joe chuckled and gave his attention back to his book. But he wasn't seeing the words.

Catrina Billings had managed to kill Julie Castro, but she'd had help. The organization—the Order of the

Deep Woods, if Angela was right—had helped her. But had condemned her as well.

Who else might be calling the shots?

He heard movement out in the tavern and stood, ready to draw, but it was just Belinda, walking toward them from her position.

"I'm starving. I'm going to hit the kitchen," she told him. "Want anything?"

"An energy bar of some kind," Carl said. "I think the catering company brought some they make themselves. I'd love one if you can find any."

"I'm fine, but thank you," Joe said.

She disappeared. A minute later, she called back, "It's me, bringing an energy bar for Carl. These are delicious. That company is really good. They catered a birthday party for a friend, and the food was out of sight."

She tossed Carl a bar, smiled at Joe, and said, "Back to my post." From her vantage point at a corner table in the tavern, she could see the back of the bar, the front door of the tavern and the door to the kitchen, and even the stairs up and the stairs to the basement.

Joe thought about Detective Billings again. She'd obviously risen to a position of power. She was local, and she'd grown up with all the truth and all the lies and the legends. Maybe she'd suffered at the hands of superior officers—things were growing easier for women today, but in many instances, there were men who still wanted to dominate in particular work venues. Maybe she'd even felt put upon at times, wanting to belong, and therefore, she'd become an easy target for a cult leader.

But who the hell was the leader? And what was the connection to New York City?

He glanced over at Carl, who appeared to be resting again after his snack, eyes closed and leaning comfortably back in his seat. Pulling out his phone, Joe hit Redial on Angela's number.

Eileen had been the one to first see Julie's body in the basement. She hailed from New York, and Joe's mind had been turning that way. Of course, she wouldn't be the only one involved—if it was a cult, that would mean a membership, except that this membership would be small and very particular.

"Joe, anything happen?" Angela asked.

"No, no, but can you get your tech wizards on the Truth Seekers again? Particularly the two who are not from New York—Mike Lerner and Serena Nelson. I'm trying to find out if they have ties to the city and might know about rich New Yorkers and private schools and—"

"Barbara Chrome's family?"

"Yes."

"They've done initial checks, but I'll have them dig deeper."

He thanked her and hung up and looked over at Carl. Now, his mouth was open. He hadn't heard the call. He was gently snoring.

Keri accepted Dallas's hand to help her crawl over a piece of the stone wall that still half surrounded the cemetery. They'd let Jamie, seated in his patrol car, know that they were walking around to the graveyard.

As they neared it, Keri could see in the gray dusk

light that two of the forensic team members remained behind by the church. One was putting a box in the back of their van. The other was waiting for Dallas.

Keri noticed that Dallas paused and looked around the graveyard, as if making sure that they were the only people in the area.

"I'll be right over there," Keri said. "I think that's Hank's grave with the small headstone and the brass plaque."

"All right. You get over to me if you see anyone at all coming toward you."

"Yes, sir," she told him.

She watched him head toward the forensic team. Then she walked over the tangled weeds and broken stone that brought her to the grave of Hank Bergen.

It was simple and rough-hewn with his name on a brass plaque: Hank Bergen. No middle name, and no indication that Hank had been short for Henry. It listed his date of birth as 1885 and his date of death as 1926.

Beside it was another plaque with a brass marker just like Hank's. This one had an angel etched into the metal and didn't list dates at all. It simply said, *In memory, an angel in life, may she rest with the angels, wherever her earthly remains may lie. Beatrice Marie Bergen, daughter of Hank. Loved by those graced by her kindness.*

Keri stood by the grave and closed her eyes, letting the breeze rustle through her hair. A part of her still wanted to insist that it was all too much. Talking to ghosts. How could it even be possible?

Another part of her knew that she had the power to help, that she could allow a good man to finally rest.

"I have enough. I'm not an attorney, nor have I any political power," she said. "But I can gather information and get it out there, using all the right sources. People will know that you were innocent. I sincerely believe, from all that I have read, that you were truly innocent, Hank. And I will do my best to write it all up and hand it out to the public. I believe that people will see what I have seen, and perhaps others may offer information, and the truths that I have found will be amplified. I hope that this helps you.

"Beatrice, I am so sorry. I know now that you were there, that you would have helped Julie if you could have and that you cried for her because she met your fate, and you knew what she suffered."

Keri opened her eyes.

They were both there, Hank with an arm around his daughter's shoulder, smiling at her.

"Thank you."

She wasn't sure if he said the words, or if she heard them on the breeze. Or, perhaps they were just whispers in her own mind, and it was all a trick of the light.

But she realized that Dallas had come up behind her. He stood very still, and she knew that he saw them, too.

"Sir," Dallas said softly, "Miss Bergen. If you could help us…"

When Hank Bergen spoke next, Keri knew that she was hearing him and not a fantasy she was making up in her mind.

"They wear hoods, ridiculous hoods," Hank said, his words bitter and biting. "They have an insignia on them, a bird over a human with a ram's head. They wore them when they attacked me, lest they be seen and recognized. They are despicable cowards. I would help you more… Yesterday, I saw Catrina Billings. She came from the woods and crossed in back of the tavern, sneaking around. She didn't want her own police officers to know she was here. She went into the church."

"We never heard her scream," Beatrice said.

"When they took you, what happened?" Keri asked her.

"My father told me not to go near the tavern," Beatrice said. She glanced his way sorrowfully. "But I heard that Newby was hiring housekeepers and… Well, we'd had troubled times with the harvest that year, and I wanted to help. I could have been a very good maid. Newby asked me down to the basement, and when we were there…he knocked me out. And…"

Hank set his arm around her shoulders, pulling her to him.

"Those 'fine gentlemen' brought in by the coroner," Hank said. "I believe at least two of them were in on it. They waited until it was late at night. The rumors about the tavern were getting out of hand. People were starting to wonder about Newby—travelers who started out from the east sometimes didn't make it to their destinations.

"Those men killed. They sacrificed to their demon god or their own depravity, but they found those who were tragically poor, who had nothing, who came through with no real destination. Who notices when a drifter drifts on? But then, Newby killed Beatrice, and I started asking questions, and they knew that I would not let it rest."

Hank seemed to take a breath, and he appeared to Keri just as clearly as if he stood there in the flesh. "I believe that the same thing happened here again. Catrina was furious. She killed the FBI agent. She killed her here, in the church, and I bore witness. She ordered one of her hooded helpers to get the body and the blood down to the cellar, and then…you know. Catrina and all of them knew that there hadn't been a padlock on the cellar door in years. They were wearing the same hoods. Not even I can tell you the rest of the members."

Beatrice still seemed to be sobbing softly, held in her father's arms.

"Maybe we can leave now," Hank said, smoothing down his daughter's hair.

"Maybe," she whispered.

They were still there, but not as solid as they had been. There was no ray of light. They did not soar up to the heavens.

"I'm all right, Papa," she told him. "I'm all right now." She turned to Keri just before she faded away, the same as she always had before.

"I will help you, anytime that I can."

The high-pitched, terrified scream from somewhere brought Joe leaping to his feet. He ran for the stairs.

"Wait!" Carl screamed.

"Follow me!" Joe ordered.

He meant to tell Belinda to follow, to be ready for trouble, but Belinda wasn't there. Had she run up already, beat him to the draw after the scream? Impossible. He had run out of the museum like a bat out of hell.

He took the stairs two at a time, bursting into room 208 where Brad and Serena were supposed to be staying.

There was no one there.

With Carl on his heels, he covered every room on the second floor.

They must have gone downstairs.

The scream sounded again, this time as if it was coming from underwater. Joe drew his gun and threw open the basement door.

Carl was at his heels, but gasping. "Can't move... I don't know..."

For the moment, Joe had to ignore Carl's problems. He took the stairs quickly, alert, ready for whatever, and near the bottom, he nearly tripped over a body.

Belinda.

The basement was dark; shadows were moving. He started to stoop down to check for a pulse.

"Oh, God!" Carl screamed.

Joe spun around quickly, ready to shoot.

He couldn't; a figure in a black robe and hood held Carl precariously in the middle of the staircase. There was a knife at his throat.

"He's so pretty, isn't he, Mr. Dunhill? The poor boy is passing out in my arms. He must have had one of those energy bars. I hope you appreciate the irony in that—energy bar?"

Joe knew the voice. "Let him go. Anything you do from this point forward will work against you. We know that Detective Billings killed Special Agent Julie Castro. Right now, you can stop this, tell us your side of the story, how you were coerced into this—and you could walk or do just a few easy years."

"Oh, Mr. Dunhill. Please. Do you really think that any of us would fall for that?"

"Well, you could take off that ridiculous hood."

"You know who I am?"

Carl was slumping. If Joe didn't do something quickly, Carl would wind up dying because the razor-sharp edge of the hooded figure's knife would slide through his flesh as he stood.

"What do you want from me?" Joe asked. "Why would you be doing this now? Law enforcement is going to come down on this place like a hammer soon."

"Ah, but it won't be soon enough. You, sir, have been a thorn in our sides. So, drop your weapon. Or Carl dies. I can draw a little blood, if you like…"

"More FBI agents are on their way."

"Yes, and they'll find me just coming to. Come on, no one will be out here until tomorrow, and by then… You're stalling. Put the gun down. Aren't you supposed to save lives? Seriously. You're not getting out of here now. You'll just make him die as well."

Joe wasn't getting out. That meant someone else was in the basement and surely had a gun trained on him as well.

Joe set his Glock down. They might shoot or kill him now—and God knew, Carl could die anyway—but he needed to play for time. And hope there would be a chance to use the knife strapped at his ankle.

Behind him, the shadows moved. In his peripheral

vision, he saw a giant candlestick coming down on his head. He tried to spin, to stop the blow…

He managed to shield himself from the brunt of the hit, but even as he crashed to his knees, pain tore through his head like a rocket. Through the haze, he saw Carl tumble down the stairs.

Then, as he cursed himself, the world began to fade. *Keri.*

He had promised her that he'd be there when she returned. And he had failed her.

As the world went black, he heard someone laughing. "He should have had an energy bar. Easier than a thump on the head."

"Is that how how it usually is?" Keri asked Dallas, walking back toward the inn. "You see the dead, sometimes in your dreams and sometimes the way we just saw them?"

"There really isn't much of a usual. I'd have imagined that those two remained behind to find someone who could prove the truth, but you told them that you would do that. So there's another reason they're still here, I think, because they want to move on." He smiled at her. "Three of our agents are brothers. The McFaddens first saw the dead when their parents, a pair of famous actors, were killed by a crashing chandelier on stage. Their spirits are still hanging around—talk about your in-law problems. But they're charming, too, and they stay because they're convinced that they help. And they weren't ready to leave their sons. I can only compare being a ghost to…going to the gym. The more you work at it, the better you become. But no one's experience is ever exactly the same. Somehow, Beatrice and Hank got into your mind as you slept and led you out here, where we found Detective Billings."

They came around the corner of the inn. Dallas paused for a minute, looking out at the patrol car.

"What the hell is Jamie doing?" he muttered.

"Probably getting very tired," Keri said. "I'm going to run in."

Dallas headed for the patrol car. "Great," he said. "I kept them because I trusted them, and he fell asleep."

Keri ran up the porch steps and into the tavern. "Belinda?"

She didn't see the officer in her seat at the far tavern table. Hurrying, Keri rushed through to the museum, but Joe wasn't there. She shouted his name, but there was no answer.

She hurried into the kitchen. "Belinda? Joe? Carl?"

Silence. She found herself looking at the cutting board on the counter. And the knife that lay on it. She reached for the knife, her sense of alarm growing, and slid it into the pocket of her jeans.

Then she heard a cry. "Please...help!"

Belinda?

Keri started to run to the basement. She froze. This had happened before. Wincing, she realized that she had to go. Someone could really be hurt and desperate for help.

She moved cautiously for the stairs. When she reached them, she felt a touch on her shoulder and turned quickly.

It was the ghost of Beatrice Bergen, and she was looking at Keri with huge, frightened eyes.

"No," she told Keri. "No."

Too late. She felt an arm come around her from behind, and the edge of a knife at her throat.

"Quiet. Not a word, or you'll watch your life's blood flow away right here, right now."

They must have Joe. If they didn't have him, he would have been there.

But Dallas was outside. He would come, and he would find her, and they would find Joe...

She was half led and half dragged down the stairs. At the bottom, she nearly tripped over a body.

Belinda!

As ridiculous as it might have been at the moment, she was glad that the officer she had liked so much was not among these homicidal maniacs.

Did it matter? She was going to die, and Belinda might well already be dead.

On the basement floor, she was surrounded by figures in cloaks and hoods, all bearing the strange insignia of the hawk flying above the ram's head demon. As she was hauled out through the cellar door, she heard Dallas calling to her. She was ready to scream, but the cellar door shut, and she knew... She could scream...

But he would not hear her, and then all hope would be lost.

16

Joe came to slowly, the burning pain in his head pulsing. For a moment, he couldn't see a thing. He closed his eyes, and then blinked, and at last, his vision came into focus.

He was in a clearing in the woods, and it was growing dark, but torches had been stuck into the ground and lit. There was an altar, like the one Spencer Atkins had set up in the basement, an imitation of the one used by John Newby in his original torture chamber.

Joe tried to move and realized that he was tied to a tree, seated with his arms bound tight to his sides, and his legs out in front of him. It was a giant oak, and the rope circled the entire trunk. He looked around the clearing and saw no one.

That meant that the members were busy elsewhere, taking down Dallas and... *Keri.*

A good thing he hadn't eaten their poisoned energy bar. He'd shielded himself from some of the blow that had felled him, and he was conscious again.

How long had he been out?

Not long, he thought. Darkness had already been coming on. And at the moment, he was unguarded.

He worked at the ropes that bound him. There was not enough time to rub them ragged against the trunk of the tree, but if he could twist around enough, he might be able to slip his knife from the little shield at his ankle. He could still feel it in his boot.

He began to work at the ties that bound him, not trying to break them, but loosen them enough so that he could bend forward.

He could tell himself that he had been on the right track at last, even if it had been a little too late. But then again, the cult members believed that no one was coming until the morning—and Jackson and Angela were on the way right now. By the time they got out here, they'd know that something was very wrong. They would be calling along the way, and when they received no answer... Or, if Dallas was able to sense the trap and escape it, extra law enforcement could already be on the way.

Joe worked and worked at the ties, and finally the rope stretched enough. He tilted his body far to one side, drawing his leg up toward his bound arm, and he was able to reach his knife. Once he grabbed it, he began to twist and turn it against the ties at his side.

The rope began to give.

He jerked free, rubbed his hands, and pushed himself up. For a moment, his head spun again. He stood still, waiting for the dizziness to ebb.

He heard a soft drumbeat.

He crept into the trees, and then he stopped and

crouched, watching. He didn't have his Glock. All he had was his knife. But they were coming now...

They had Keri, he was certain. She had been with Dallas, but her captors must have done something. They had tricked Dallas somehow and gotten to Keri...

He didn't know who else they had. Dallas, too?

The drumbeat kept sounding. Someone was coming through the forest.

A figure broke into the clearing, gliding quickly to the altar. She lifted her arms and in a single movement, shed the hooded cloak she had been wearing.

She was naked. Slim and pale and very young. Barbara Chrome, the seventeen-year-old Julie Castro had been so desperate to find and save. The girl for whom the agent had given her life.

There was a long, glittering knife on the altar. Barbara picked it up, raised it toward the night sky, and called out, "Dear Lord Satan, tonight, you will drink of beauty. Our sacrifice will be the finest we have found for you, and you will grant us, your willing servants, all the gifts due from that sweet blood sacrifice, and there will be more, dear Lord Satan, more... Tonight, you feast!"

Four more hooded figures had followed her into the clearing, with Keri between them. She was walking on her own, her expression disdainful, her head high. Two more figures followed, carrying a makeshift stretcher with Carl upon it, unconscious.

All six of them carried knives.

Joe winced, wondering at his own power to defeat so many. Most of the time, such people were cowards.

He didn't see Dallas among them. Did that mean

they didn't have him? If they had managed an escape into the woods quickly enough, Dallas wouldn't know where they were. Angela would guess, after what she had discovered and what Joe had asked, but...

Could they get here quickly enough?

At least one of the caterers was among the hooded figures—someone who had laced the energy bars. The caterers were all cult members, he was suddenly sure. And so was sweet, bubbly, annoyingly perky Serena Nelson. He'd recognized her voice the moment she'd spoken.

Who else was under the hoods?

Spencer Atkins?

Joe moved farther back into the trees, keeping his eyes on the hooded figures. His heel hit something, and he nearly tripped. He hunkered down for a closer look.

Spencer Atkins was not among the hooded figures. He was here, on the ground, his blood seeping into the dirt.

Something inside Keri fought the obvious with a fierce resolve.

She wasn't going to die.

Well, she most probably was. Unless there was a miracle very soon. But she refused to give up hope.

They had taken a dozen twists and turns through the trees. Even if Dallas had called in every trooper in Pennsylvania, she would be dead before they could find their way to this clearing. That, of course, was why no one had stumbled upon this, the real sacrifice place, throughout the years.

Had this awful thing been continuous? Or had these

people found their own lives so dreary and horrible that they had discovered a history of this cult and recreated it for the twenty-first century?

Did it matter?

Somehow she still had the knife she'd picked up. A knife from the cheese tray, while these people were carrying blades that would have done the frontiersman Jim Bowie proud.

One of the hooded figures touched her arm. "Faster."

She smiled. "Serena Nelson. Wow. I thought of you as an absolute airhead, but seriously, never quite this stupid."

"I'm stupid? You're the one who is going to die."

The figure who had run ahead stood naked before the altar. She turned, and Keri recognized Barbara Chrome.

"Stop speaking!" Barbara yelled. "The chant needs to begin. You dishonor our lord!"

Serena shoved Keri hard in the ribs, and they crossed the clearing to Barbara's side.

"Now!" Serena told her. "Lie down on the table."

"I don't see a table."

"The altar," someone else hissed.

"You guys really have a seventeen-year-old girl calling the shots?" Keri demanded.

She was pushed forward onto their makeshift altar. It had been made of gravestones, she realized. And it was surrounded by...

Skulls. Human skulls.

"She's not calling the shots," a male voice snapped. Keri fought hard to recognize the voice.

Barbara began singing and chanting, but the man interrupted again, heedless of ceremonial rites.

"Where the hell is the cop? Where is Joe Dunhill?"

"There, tied to the tree," someone else said.

"Like hell! There's no one tied to the tree! Dammit, he's out there. You assholes! You let him go, you said that he was secure and knocked out, damnation!"

Joe! They'd had Joe... But they didn't have him now.

"He's gone," someone else said. "We need to do this and get the hell out of here."

"We can't! He knows who I am!" Serena cried. "We have to find him."

"Find him?" someone else demanded. "In these trees, we never will. Oh no, Serena—you're going to have to pay the price."

"Like hell!" Serena said. "If I go down, you're all going down! Find him."

The tallest of them, the man who'd noticed Joe was missing, walked up to Serena.

"Find him!" she demanded, shoving at him.

Keri realized it was Pete Wright—which meant that Eileen must also be one of the figures. So, that was their cult. Serena, Pete and Eileen, and the damned caterers.

"We will not go down!" Pete roared at her.

He slammed his knife into Serena's chest, fast and with great force. She barely got out a whimper before she slipped to the ground.

Keri nearly screamed, stunned, forced to awareness that killing meant nothing to them. "Now!" Pete shouted. "Continue!"

Barbara laughed delightedly and began her sing-song chant once again.

"Get her on that altar," Pete demanded.

"I can get on it myself," Keri said. She crawled up, reaching in her pocket, thankful she was still clothed when Barbara, continuing the proceedings, was naked.

As were the others, she found out. The instant she was atop the altar, they shed their cloaks and hoods and stepped around the altar, their only accessory their knives.

Five of them now, with Serena lying dead, were ready to come at her...

And she would die of the dozens of vicious stab wounds that would soon descend upon her.

There was no choice—he had to act now or never.

It helped that they had killed Serena; Joe had been trained that the right thing to do was to bring a perpetrator to justice. He was not judge or jury.

But in this instance, he needed more of them completely incapacitated.

He picked up the massive rock he'd found by Spencer, the one that been used to bash in the man's skull. Had he been one of them? Had he gone against the group?

That didn't matter right now. What mattered was getting to Keri.

He slipped back through the trees as quietly as he could. He hefted the rock, weighing it mentally, praying that his aim would be true.

Barbara was dancing away, sing-chanting, ready to slice into Keri with the first cut.

Then, to Joe's amazement, Keri sat up, screaming

something like an enraged she-wolf cry. She had a knife—a little knife.

She slammed it into Barbara's breast, sending her back reeling and screaming. "No, no! I'm perfect, I'm beautiful…!"

"Asshole!" Pete shouted, reaching for Keri.

Joe threw his rock. Hard. He hit Pete dead center in the back of his skull; Pete went down without a whimper.

Keri leaped from the altar and grabbed up Pete's knife just as Joe burst into the clearing, running with pure fury. He slashed as he tore into the circle, easily causing a dozen wounds against naked flesh.

"Your back to mine!" he shouted to Keri, and she understood, and both of them faced out as the cultists came at them.

Eileen wasn't with them; she was sobbing on the ground, over Pete. Barbara was slumped against a tree, crying in pain and fury.

"Edge toward the path you came down," Joe said.

"Got it." Keri took a swipe at Rod, who was trying to rush her.

Facing Stan, Joe couldn't see her, but her thrust must have been true. He heard Rod's cry of pain.

"You're going to die!" Rod screamed, and he was rushing again.

Joe spun around just in time, skewering him as Rod flew at them. Screaming and clutching his gut, Rod fell to the ground.

Joe spun again, hearing the whisk of air as Milly flew at him, knife raised high above her head.

Her mistake.

This group really didn't know their knives. They could put a razor-sharp blade to a throat, and they could slice up a prone and dying victim. But they didn't know real knife fighting.

Joe feinted and thrust his own weapon, catching Milly in the middle of her rib cage, his knife going deep. She howled and fell on top of her husband.

Only Stan, bleeding profusely, was still standing. He started toward Joe and lifted his blade, ready for the fight.

But then Stan dropped his weapon, just staring at Joe. Accepting defeat.

They were down. Barbara, teen-murderer, was slumped by a tree. Pete had been felled by the rock, and Eileen was holding him in her arms, sobbing. Serena lay a few feet away, killed by Pete.

Rod and Milly were down as well, while Stan just stood there, naked and bleeding.

Still, one of them might rise, and Joe edged Keri behind him and began to back away.

Lights suddenly burst through the trees.

"FBI!" Dallas shouted. "Throw down your weapons."

Joe looked at Keri and shrugged, smiling slowly. "Dallas!" he called. "Keri and I are the only ones who have weapons now. We need some EMTs out here, pretty quickly."

Dallas came striding into the clearing, looking from Joe and Keri to the scene before him—naked people, strewn about and bleeding. He stared at Joe again with astonishment.

"You did this single-handed?" Dallas asked. "Re-mind me never to get into a knife fight with you."

"Not single-handed," Joe said. He turned and smiled at Keri. "I had amazing backup."

"Amazing," Keri said, but then she fell into his arms. Passed out.

He looked up at Dallas, shaking his head.

"Pete killed Serena," he said. "She disagreed with his plan of action once they saw that I'd escaped. Carl should be fine. He's back there on that stretcher. If Pete is alive, he's going to have a hell of a headache. Oh, and Spencer is back there in the trees. I don't know if he was one of them or just a victim. And I don't know if he's alive. Bad head wound, lots of blood."

Other law enforcement was sweeping into the clear-ing. Joe saw that Jackson and Angela had arrived, both of them quickly assessing their situation, shouting to other officers, and calling back for the EMTs to hurry out.

Keri was limp in his arms. Joe looked at Dallas. "I think I should get her back to the inn," he said softly. "How is Belinda? Jamie? Brad?"

"Alive," Dallas told him. "Fighting off the effects of tainted energy bars."

"Thank God. How did you find us?"

Dallas turned to Angela. The delicate blonde in her navy pantsuit looked bizarrely out of place in the woods. Jackson towered beside her, his striking features catch-ing the moving beams of the officers' flashlights.

"Angela led us here," Dallas said. "You two talked about the deep, dark woods today. Get out of here and get back to the inn. The others have come to. They'll be there to meet you. We'll discuss it all later."

"I'll go back with them," Angela said. "I know the way."

Joe carried Keri through the bodies on the ground. He didn't look down; he couldn't regret the violence.

Halfway along the path, Keri stirred and looked up into his eyes. She struggled against his hold, her eyes wide.

"Oh, my God, I passed out," she said with horror.

"It's all right," he said, holding her tightly lest she fall.

She gaped, clinging to him with fresh fear as she saw Angela.

"It's all right, it's all right," Angela said quickly. "Special Agent Angela Hawkins, Krewe of Hunters. You might have passed out, Miss Wolf, but you sure came to the fore when you were needed. You two survived a knife fight against pretty rough odds. I might have passed out after that, and I've been at this a long time now."

Keri eased back in his arms again, smiling with relief.

"We are alive," she whispered. And then she struggled in earnest. "I can walk," she assured him. As he eased her down, she turned to Angela. "I've heard about you. I'm so glad to meet you. And so grateful that you came so quickly."

"We should have been quicker," Angela said. "We all suspected members of the Truth Seekers. But go figure. The *caterers.*"

"It's a pity," Joe said. "Their food was really good. They should have stuck with cooking."

Puzzle pieces had come together—almost.

Back at the inn, Belinda and Jamie were seated in

the tavern with Brad, drinking coffee and fighting the effects of the energy bars. They'd been heavily laced with a sleeping medicine. Captain Dickey returned, along with other officers.

There was mass confusion as paperwork began; Keri and Joe did their best to fill in what had happened, but they didn't have all the answers.

Jackson headed to the hospital with the injured, and Serena, the only dead.

Stan, hurt the least, talked readily in order to plead himself the most innocent of the group.

Barbara had found the group on the dark web. Eileen and Pete had picked her up in New York City and brought her to Philadelphia while they'd waited for Carl to take over the inn and start his paranormal research. The tech department had ripped into her computer and discovered that she'd been communicating with them for months—giving them all the information they wanted, gaining their trust.

They had originally intended for Barbara to be their sacrifice, but she had quickly convinced them that she could float their entire enterprise with an account she'd set up under an assumed name—and because they'd quickly realized her homicidal potential. She was one of them.

The girl really belonged in a hospital. Her psychosis made her a danger to herself and, clearly, others. As she was taken away by the EMTs, she had screamed that she needed a plastic surgeon immediately.

While her involvement was new, the cult itself had been around for decades. Spencer Atkins had not been involved, but he had begun to suspect that something was going on near the inn. He'd hoped to find something to show Dallas and Joe and get them off his back as a potential suspect. Searching the woods, he'd come upon Pete—who had bashed him in the head.

Pete and Catrina had been the real murderers, Stan told them.

Julie Castro had been on the hunt for Barbara—and Barbara had not wanted to go back. So Catrina Billings had ordered Pete and Eileen to get rid of Julie's partner, Ed. With a begging phone call from Barbara, they'd lured Julie out to the abandoned church, where the group had taken her by surprise, killed her and planted her body to be found in the basement.

That hadn't set well with Pete, who considered himself the high priest of their group. Furious that Billings—who had been ready to hand Barbara over for the ransom money—had brought an FBI agent among them, he'd ordered the rest of them to take care of the detective.

From the beginning, they'd planned to kill Carl and Keri in a grand offering, truly dancing naked with the devil in the woods. They had believed that, by leaving Brad and the cops alive, they'd be able to slip back into their usual positions and watch with feigned dismay as the FBI and law enforcement searched and searched and found nothing.

Brad was horrified. He didn't think that he could ever do another paranormal investigation.

"All that's left is Mike and I," he said. "Three of them, slipping around... Eileen, pretending such horror when she had helped bring down Julie Castro's body... How could I have been so blind? They were with me on so many investigations, and when we were on breaks, they were driving out of New York to come here for their meetings...and whatever else they were doing while they were here." He shook his head. "I know now that they were communicating with the living— not the dead! What goes on in that dark web...it's terrifying. Still terrifying just to know!"

Carl was surprisingly calm. But then, he hadn't come to until he was back at the inn, where, seeing Brad, Jamie and Belinda, he had refused medical attention himself. He wasn't leaving people he considered to be his real friends.

"You'll just be more famous than ever," Brad told Carl.

"This isn't a time to plan the future," Carl replied. "We have to give ourselves time to think."

It was daylight again before they finished with the paperwork and heard everything Jackson had to say after he returned from the hospital.

Keri said that she couldn't stand feeling the way she did any longer. She and Joe were both covered in blood from the fight, and she wanted nothing more than to take a shower. Both Captain Dickey and Jackson apologized—yes, they would be allowed to shower right away.

Joe and Keri got into the shower together, but they were both so exhausted they wound up simply holding one another while the hot water washed over them, and after, they were asleep almost before they hit the bed.

That night, Joe slept deeply, peacefully, his arms wrapped around his Keri and for once, completely off guard duty. He'd never felt safer, now that Keri was safe.

When they awoke, it was no longer morning, but afternoon, and refreshed, they made love. And it felt perfect and easy, and the world seemed lighter and brighter. Every sensation seemed heightened even above the incredible way it had been before, each touch, each caress, ever more intimate. They were alive, and together.

Curled into one another and happy to let the others believe they were still asleep—or if not, they were welcome to believe whatever they chose—Joe and Keri talked about what was to come. There was never a suggestion that they wouldn't meet the future together.

"Do you need to be in Richmond?" he asked her.

"No, but I promised the ghosts of Beatrice and Hank Bergen that I would write the truth. She tried to warn me, Joe. She tried to keep me from the basement, but it was too late. And we might not have found Detective Billings for days without them. How do so many people become so…horrid?" she asked. "I don't need to be in Richmond, but I need access to things here."

"That's easy enough," Joe told her.

"It is?"

"Carl owns everything in the museum now. He'll pack it all up and get it to you. And you can do phone interviews, right?"

"Yes, I suppose. And…you'll be in the academy?"

"Right. I've been living in a long-stay hotel, but we can find a place together. I mean, if you're willing…"

"We will need a place."

"It'll be a good thing to find something we both love."

"Yes." She hesitated. "Salem."

"Pardon—Salem... Massachusetts?" he asked, confused.

She smiled and laughed. "My cat. Oh, lord, I hope you like cats!"

"I like all animals. I'll love your cat."

That brought a smile to her lips. And almost a tear to her eye. She turned into his arms again.

They indulged in a long kiss, and it deepened rather than ending. Her kisses and her fingertips traveled down the length of his body, and he pulled her to him, rolling with her, kissing her in return, feeling her fingers in his hair. He loved the rise of hunger that spun through them both, the exquisite intimacy, and then coming together until climax burst over them both.

Once again they lay in the sweet aftermath.

And then, a knock on the door.

Joe expected that Jackson or Dallas would be coming for them soon enough, but it was neither of them.

It was Carl.

"Um, sorry to bug you," he called from outside the door. "But a police crew is here with reps from the medical examiner's office. They're digging up the woods and the cellar, and they think they might have found Beatrice Bergen. Bones, of course, but there's a locket with a picture of a couple in it, and one of them is Hank Bergen, and we assume the other is her mother, and... Sorry, I just thought you'd like to know."

Joe and Keri rose and dressed quickly. Night would fall again and it would be theirs, and the night after that.

When they got downstairs, they found that the tavern was alive with all manner of experts—forensic anthropologists, medical examiners and more. The evidence revealed that killing had happened there, off and on, for a very long time.

"I will see to it that it never starts again," Carl assured them. "But they did find Beatrice. They've assured me we can bury her remains next to her father when all is done."

Dallas was still there, but with Jackson and Angela overseeing the wrap-up, he was free to walk out to the graveyard with Joe, Keri and Carl.

At the gravesite, Keri addressed Hank's tombstone. "It's really done now. You've stopped the cycle of killing. It will never come again. Carl will see to that, as will everyone around here. The police are on to it, and Carl will keep watch over the woods and this graveyard."

"Even the church," Carl said. "I'm going to see that it's restored, and that it's never used again for evil, for… murder."

"Thank you," Joe said softly.

They began to appear, father and daughter, Hank and Beatrice smiling at them. "I'm so glad…" Beatrice whispered. "So very glad you made it."

"Oh, my God," Carl gasped. "Oh, my God!"

"You see them?" Keri asked.

"I do."

"Thank you," Dallas said to the pair.

And then, there was the moment Joe had only ever heard about, only seen in movies. A light shone from the sky, creating a ray of dazzling colors over the ghosts. They faded into a shimmer of light, and they were gone.

Joe slipped an arm around Keri's shoulder and turned away. Keri slipped her free arm around Carl, who was still half-amazed…and already doubting what he'd seen.

"Was it…? Did I see that? I couldn't have seen that… I mean…"

"It's all right, Carl," Dallas assured him. He looped his arm around Carl's free side. Together, they all headed back to the Miller Inn and Tavern.

"Amazing," Carl said. "All this—all this…"

"A horrible case," Dallas said. "But I believe we might have saved many lives that could have been taken in the future."

"Not to mention our own." Carl nodded. "Yes, good. Solved. But… I didn't get to fall in love."

Joe grinned, looking down at Keri. "I did," he said.

She smiled. "Me, too."

"Okay, okay, moving on," Carl said. "Dallas and I don't need to watch that… Oh, you're already kissing and it's all…oh, way too much!"

Joe was indeed already kissing her. And she was kissing him.

And it would never, ever be too much.

* * * * *

Keep reading for an exclusive preview of the
next thrilling story in the Krewe of Hunters series
from New York Times bestselling author
Heather Graham.

A serial killer from her past haunts
Special Agent Cheyenne Donegal
and terrorizes the bayou in

The Stalking,

available September 24, 2019,
from MIRA Books.

Prologue

The jazz band played a mournful tune under great oaks that swayed in the breeze, dripping moss as if the trees themselves cried.

The priest moved forward, silent and somber, leading the funeral procession. Though it was the traditional funeral that should accompany the farewells for any member of Janine's family, it all seemed so very wrong to Cheyenne Donegal.

Step by step, they neared the cemetery, the Louisiana "city of the dead" where the body of Janine Dumas would soon lie in the family tomb of her ancestors, ashes to ashes in the fierce heat of the Louisiana sun, in a year and a day, as they said.

The special city of the dead began as a private, family cemetery, near an old mansion that was considered to be the most haunted for miles—perhaps in the state. It had a reputation for evil and death, and though that reputation had originated way back when, legends and myths never died. They just grew.

The procession had not had to come far; the funeral

parade had begun at the old Justine Plantation building, where Janine had lain for viewing for a night and a day after leaving the county morgue, and where, they said, the haunts of the old cemetery—begun by the Justine family in the early 1800s—came out to welcome the newly dead.

Still, this area had been Janine's home, where she had lived and loved and believed in a spectacular future for herself, adventure and excitement to come.

No more.

Janine had been just sixteen, a young and beautiful girl, full of energy and love and enthusiasm, a flirt, a tease perhaps, yet so full of life that her death still didn't seem possible, even though her family and loved ones had seen her lying in her coffin, had seen her mother scream and cry and try to pull her body out.

The coffin, drawn along in an old bier by two white mules, arrived at the cemetery. The jazz band, the pallbearers and the mourners entered the great ironwork gates of the cemetery and followed the row between the multitude of family crypts, coming at last to the one belonging to the family Dumas.

Cheyenne Donegal stood at her mother's side, along with their neighbors, teachers, friends and family as the rest of the procession entered the cemetery.

They took their positions at the Dumas family grave as the priest stepped out of the line of mourners.

Cheyenne heard her friends whispering to each other.

"You look so bereft… Janine wasn't perfect, you know," someone whispered at her side.

"She was so young," Cheyenne murmured, turning

to see the boy there—Christian Mayhew. He'd been in Janine's class, three years ahead of Cheyenne.

"She knew how to take me down a peg or two," Christian murmured. "She could be…cruel."

Cheyenne didn't reply; her mother was staring at her, frowning. At her mother's expression, she sensed something was wrong—and then she remembered what.

Christian Mayhew had died.

By his own hand almost a year ago. Cyber and otherwise bullied at school, he'd apparently been able to take no more. A slew of drugs had been found by his bedside. He'd lain there, rumor had it, as if he'd chosen a long nap—and taken it.

They had to have been wrong.

As the priest continued to drone on, Cheyenne heard another voice.

"Christian, I was never mean to you—yes, I might have teased you. But I was never mean to you on purpose."

It was a voice she knew well.

Her cousin Janine's!

Cheyenne managed not to scream, shout—or collapse.

Instead, she turned slightly. And there was Janine, next to Christian. Janine looked so beautiful, but then, she had always been a beauty, blessed with big dark eyes and sleek hair in the deepest brown, almost black.

The priest was still talking, his voice rich, his speech powerful, and still Cheyenne couldn't discern his words. How could Christian and Janine be there, standing slightly behind her, watching as she watched?

"Great funeral," Christian told her. "Mine was…not."

Janine didn't seem to hear him. She was staring across the crowd, across the neat rows of tombs, some a picture of "decaying elegance," lost to time, others meticulously maintained, kept up by those living but destined to join their family members within the mausoleums. Past angels and cherubs and Madonna statues, beautiful funerary art that could haunt the living and the dead. She was looking, Cheyenne thought, back toward the old plantation, now a mortuary chapel.

Cheyenne could have sworn that her cousin clutched her shoulder, that she felt her hand.

But of course, she did not. Her cousin was dead. Her earthly remains were being put into the family tomb, and there she would lie and decay, a year and a day in the blistering heat, down to bone and ash, scooped into the holding area, leaving room for the remains of family to come.

"That's him!" Janine cried. Her voice seemed to tremble. The hand that touched Cheyenne's shoulder was shaking. "That's him."

Him?

The police believed, Cheyenne knew, that Janine, her beautiful young cousin, had been killed by a man they called the Artiste.

His victims had been between the ages of sixteen and twenty-two, pretty, precocious and energetic. The first three had been working girls—vivacious, bright young women who had worked for an escort agency.

The fourth had gone missing after telling friends she was meeting with a drop-dead gorgeous man she had met through an online site.

The fifth had been a runaway, living in New Orleans.

And the sixth had been Janine.

Cheyenne looked at the man who was standing on the trail between the old plantation house and the tombs. And she knew who he was. Ryan Lassiter, a substitute teacher, sometime guitar player with various bands in New Orleans and all the way out to Lafayette, New Iberia and beyond. He was young, cool and hot. The kids loved him.

"Mr. Lassiter?" she said aloud.

"Cheyenne, dammit, don't you think I know what happened to me?" Janine asked, a catch in her ghostly voice. "I was so stupid! I thought I was so cool. Yes, I flirted with him. I had a ridiculous crush on him, and I thought he was... I thought I was so hot, and I was flattered, since for sure I had to be something...something for him to want to be with me."

Christian was looking at her. "Oh, Janine!" he said. "We saw it... So many nerds saw it. Jody Baylor said that you told him you were meeting with Lassiter— here, as a matter of fact, to do research on the old plantation house. Jody said that it was sick, gross. He's—older. You're still a kid, Janine... You *were* still a kid. And he took those pictures of you...in life and then he fixed you all up and took the pictures of you...in death."

Janine heard his words but didn't reply. She stared straight ahead at the man she claimed was her killer. "I was a fool...so ridiculously filled with myself and my infatuation. I thought he was going to wait for me to graduate, and then he'd marry me, and... You have to stop him, Cheyenne," Janine pleaded. "Tell them, tell them that he did it, that he killed me, that he stole my life, that he left me...there!"

Janine pointed to her casket and added, "I could be so careless of others… I could be self-centered, I know—selfish. But I would never want what happened to me to happen to anyone else, not my worst enemy. Cheyenne, don't let him get away with it—don't let him get away with what he did!"

She was looking at her cousin's killer—a man who acted so concerned, so kind, so giving with others. But he had done such cruel and horrible things to others; he had tortured women, mentally and physically.

How could she prove it? No one else could see Christian and Janine—her friend, the suicide, and her cousin, the murder victim. Would they just say that she was crazy?

"Do something, Cheyenne!" Janine begged.

The priest was still speaking; the members of the funerary jazz band were preparing to start up with another song. The cemetery workers were waiting for them all to leave so that Janine, in her coffin, might be sealed into the family tomb.

Ryan Lassiter was looking toward *her* then. Or was he? Here, just outside Fournier, the landscape curled and dipped. The old plantation house was up a very small rise, with a smokehouse, original kitchen, carriage house and other structures seeming to fall away just behind it; the cemetery sat down the hill and to the right of the sweeping entrance to the house.

Cheyenne looked around; her parents were there, Janine's parents, teachers, friends… Mr. Beaufort, the gym teacher; Mike Holiday, captain of the football team; Nelson Ridgeway and Katie Anson, seniors, a class ahead of Janine, but friends with whom she had studied and partied; Mr. Derringer, the organist from the church; Emil Justine, hereditary owner and operator here, tall and dignified, caring and capable; and many others who had come to pay their respects.

Who was Lassiter looking at? Was it someone who looked back at him, as if they shared a confidence, as if someone else knew?

"Cheyenne, it's up to you!" Christian whispered. "You have to do something."

"Please," Janine said softly, and then she turned to Christian, tears appearing to sting her eyes. "You could have been glad for what happened to me," she said. "I wasn't always so nice to you."

"You weren't my friend—but you didn't do this to me. It wasn't you, it was many things," Christian told her. "And I certainly forgive you. I hope that I am forgiven, too." Christian stared firmly at Cheyenne again. "Now, Cheyenne! You're the only one who can help right now."

"Please!" Janine said again.

Cheyenne thought about what had been done to her cousin—and the other young women. They had been kidnapped; they had been kept alive. Pictures had been taken of them and sent to the newspapers—he'd forced them to smile. And then he had killed them and dressed them up and set them in strange death poses, and sent those pictures to the papers, too.

And still, what could she do?

Something, anything!

She looked up for a moment at the massive winged angel kneeling above the family tomb. In a matter of minutes, the rite at the graveside would be over.

And Ryan Lassiter would have watched the spectacle, chuckling inwardly over every tear shed, and walked away, handsome and charming, never a suspect...

Free to kill again.

Cheyenne really didn't know what to do. And so she lifted her arm, pointing toward Lassiter, and she began to scream.

"That's him...that's the man who had Cheyenne!" she said. She didn't know how she would prove it, but more than one of their friends had seen Janine with him and they'd gossiped, that it was disgusting, the older man going for the teenaged girl. "Ryan Lassiter is the—the Artiste!"

The priest stopped speaking. Cheyenne heard discordant sounds as the musicians one by one stopped playing and turned to look at her.

"Cheyenne, Cheyenne," her mom said, turning to her and clutching her shoulders, eyes wide with surprise, worry and confusion. "Cheyenne, that's just Mr. Lassiter, the substitute teacher and musician, honey, he's not a—"

"He is—he's a monster. He seduced Janine—he had her meet up with him. She didn't want anyone to know. She had a thing for him, and you should have seen the way he looked at her! Mom, he killed her. Stop him, stop him!"

Lassiter, with his flashing dark eyes and a sexy brown lock of hair over his forehead, stared down the aisle between the tombs, gaze hard on Cheyenne. Then he pointed at her and mouthed the words, "You're dead!"

But he was seen, and the trombone player set down his instrument and went after Lassiter.

The musician, one Jimmy Mercury, was tall and handsome—and built like an ebony battleship. He shouted something to the guitar player next to him, another tall man, maybe eighteen or nineteen, blond and built like a brick house. Lassiter began to run, but he was no match for Jimmy, who had once played as a linebacker for Louisiana State—and now had him trapped with the sandy-haired young man already past him and doubling back to see that he didn't escape.

Lassiter went down hard. The musicians held him with knees on his back.

Soon the sound of sirens blared through the cemetery, all but shaking marble angels and cherubs.

Once the police were there, chaos reigned in the middle of funeral, as other young people who had been friends with Janine stepped forward, shouting accusations.

Ryan Lassiter protested all the while. There was no physical evidence—not there, not then. This was hysteria, he claimed. But for his own safety, the police assured him, they were taking him in. They would get to the bottom of it.

Cheyenne didn't really know the outcome that night; her parents called one of their friends—a fellow who had retired from the FBI just a year earlier—and he came over to keep an eye on her if Lassiter got out.

Her father had been a hunter in his younger days; he still had his shotgun.

Cheyenne didn't see her cousin or Christian again that day; they had disappeared in the melee.

It wasn't until the next morning—when she was

barely awake—that her mother came to sit by her, eyes filled concern once again.

"Cheyenne, they got a search warrant and a warrant for Lassiter's DNA and…you were right, he was a killer, he killed all those young women… He killed our beautiful Janine. The DNA isn't back yet, they told me, but they're sure they'll get matches. He confessed! He confessed! And…oh, my God, Cheyenne, he was holding another girl. They were able to get to her before…before he killed her. She was locked away, out in a storage shed. He—he would have killed her. He'd already sent her 'living' picture to the police. How—how did you just see him there, in the cemetery…and know it was him?"

Cheyenne carefully hid any expression from her mother. "I—I had heard kids talking. All the girls thought he was fine, cool…sexy. Janine wouldn't have gone with just anyone, but I know that she did think he was an amazing poet and…" She paused, smiling, yet with the sting of tears in her eyes. "It was almost as if Janine was there with me…right there, in the cemetery. And, Mom, I couldn't let him get away with it."

Her mother accepted her words.

Ryan Lassiter was tried for all six murders.

He received the death sentence, and began his long route for appeals.

The years went by. When Cheyenne was eighteen and about to leave New Iberia, Iberia Parish, Louisiana, for the big city of New Orleans and an education at Loyola, she went back for a final visit to the cemetery, and the family tomb.

The surname Dumas was chiseled into the arch at the top; it was Cheyenne's mother's maiden name. When Cheyenne's time came, she would have a place waiting for her here, too. Her dad was what they called English, even though he was a mix of Irish, British and more—all American. Her mom had been born in Cajun country and was Cajun to the bone.

Cheyenne loved her heritage, her hometown, but she was ready to move on. And while home would only be about two and half hours away, she felt that she was leaving. And she had to say goodbye to Janine.

She stood by the tomb, her hand upon it, and spoke softly. "I'm heading out this afternoon, moving into my dorm. The big city—well, however big a city NOLA might be. Janine, I'll never know how, but…you did it. You got that man into prison. The cops had DNA and fingerprints, but even though Lassiter was substitute teaching, he'd managed to submit other fingerprints than his own into the system, so he wasn't flagged that way. Because of you—and Christian—he was caught. I have a scholarship—I'm going to major in forensics and criminology. I want to help others—and stop others from dying." She hesitated. Her cousin had been gone for five years now; she still felt overwhelming sadness when she was in the graveyard. "Like you did!" she said softly.

She nearly jumped a mile high when she felt a touch on her shoulder.

Janine was there, still so beautiful, her eyes alive and dark and flashing. And Christian was at her side—

standing just slightly behind her, as Janine rather liked others to be.

"You're still here!" Cheyenne whispered.

Janine smiled, slipping one of her ethereal arms around Christian. "No, no, no—we're not *still* here. We don't hang around in the cemetery—there are many, many better places to be!"

"Especially at Halloween," Christian said. "So much fun to scare the bejesus out of people at the haunted houses."

"He's still such a child," Janine said, rolling her eyes in mock horror, but with deep affection in her voice. "We go all over."

"We're here today for you," Christian explained. "The living apparently think that the dead hang around in cemeteries and graveyards. I mean, seriously?"

"Am I really seeing you?" Cheyenne whispered.

Janine laughed softly. Cheyenne felt spectral arms around her, as gentle as a whisper of air. "Cousin, I am here, and I am somehow ridiculously free. I've got Christian and…the thing is, we don't know exactly why we're still here."

"We just want you to know that we're watching over you—when we're not at some big social event that Janine just has to attend!" Christian said.

Janine bopped him on the shoulder, and then her face became sad and serious as she said, "I'll be there if you need me, Cheyenne. Oh, Cheyenne—remember Maw-Maw?"

Janine was referring to their grandmother, gone now for a good decade.

"Of course," Cheyenne said.

"She always said someone would have the *clairsentience* in the family. It's you—and it's strong in you. You gave me justice. I will be there for you!"

"We'll be there," Christian corrected.

They faded away, and Cheyenne stood alone in the old cemetery, amid the rows of tombs and marble angels, St. Michaels and weeping Madonna statues.

Night was beginning to fall. In the distance, she could see the old plantation house, high up on its hill, well maintained but still haunting in the looming dark with its columns, cupola and Victorian gingerbread balconies. To an unfamiliar observer, the very house could seem dark and evil.

But the house was not frightening to Cheyenne, nor were the darkness or rising mist—or the rows upon rows of tombs that graced the cemetery.

It was not the dead who threatened the innocent.

It was the evil in certain human beings who were very much alive.

The Stalking
by Heather Graham

Available September 24, 2019, from MIRA Books

It's been years since Brock McGovern was last in his hometown—the place where he was once accused of a crime he did not commit. Now, with the help of his high school sweetheart, Maura Antrim, he's investigating another murder... But can they find a criminal who has always remained in the shadows?

Read on for a sneak preview of
Tangled Threat,
by New York Times *bestselling author Heather Graham.*

"I've been assigned to go back to Florida. To stay at the Frampton Ranch and Resort—and investigate what we believe to be three kidnappings and a murder. And the kidnappings may have nothing to do with the resort, nor may the murder?" Brock McGovern asked, a small note of incredulity slipping into his voice, which was surprising to him—he was always careful to keep an even tone.

FBI assistant director Richard Egan had brought him into his office, and Brock had known he was going on assignment—he just hadn't expected this.

"Yes, not what you'd want, but, hey, maybe it'll be good for you—and perhaps necessary now, when time is of the essence and there is no one out there who could know the place or the circumstances with the same scope and experience you have," Egan told him. "Three young women have disappeared from the area. Two of them were guests of the Frampton Ranch and Resort shortly before their disappearances—the third had left St. Augustine and was on her way there. The Florida Department of Law Enforcement has naturally been there already. They asked for federal help on this. Shades of the past haunt them—they don't want any more unsolved murders—and everyone is hoping against hope that Lily Sylvester, Amy Bonham and Lydia Merkel might be found."

"These are Florida missing-person cases," Brock said. "And it's sad but true that young people go to Florida and get caught up in the beach life and the club scene. And regrettable but true once again—there's a drug and alcohol culture that does exist and people get caught up in it. Not just in Florida, of course, but everywhere." He smiled grimly. "I go where I'm told, but I'm curious— how is this an FBI affair? And forgive me, but—FBI out of New York?"

"Not out of New York. FDLE asked for you. Specifically."